SMUGGLERS

THE KING & SLATER SERIES BOOK FOURTEEN

MATT ROGERS

Join the Reader's Group and get a free 200-page book by Matt Rogers!

Sign up for a free copy of '**BLOOD MONEY**'.

Meet Ruby Nazarian, a government operative for a clandestine initiative known only as Lynx. She's in Monaco to infiltrate the entourage of Aaron Wayne, a real estate tycoon on the precipice of dipping his hands into blood money. She charms her way aboard the magnate's superyacht, but everyone seems suspicious of her, and as the party ebbs onward she prepares for war...

Maybe she's paranoid.

Maybe not.

Just click here.

Follow me on Facebook!
https://www.facebook.com/mattrogersbooks

Expect regular updates, cover reveals, giveaways, and more. I love interacting with fans. Feel free to send me a private message with any questions or comments. Looking forward to having you!

BOOKS BY MATT ROGERS

THE JASON KING SERIES

Isolated (Book 1)

Imprisoned (Book 2)

Reloaded (Book 3)

Betrayed (Book 4)

Corrupted (Book 5)

Hunted (Book 6)

THE JASON KING FILES

Cartel (Book 1)

Warrior (Book 2)

Savages (Book 3)

THE WILL SLATER SERIES

Wolf (Book 1)

Lion (Book 2)

Bear (Book 3)

Lynx (Book 4)

Bull (Book 5)

Hawk (Book 6)

THE KING & SLATER SERIES

Weapons (Book 1)

Contracts (Book 2)

LYNX SHORTS

BLACK FORCE SHORTS

PART I

1

Hours before the maiden voyage, the captain quit on the spot.

He was a tall, lean man with a long frame. Although his fingers resembled spiders' legs, nothing about him was frail. The way his tattered shirt hung off his bony shoulders implied deceptive core strength, developed from a lifetime of exchanging physical labour for enough cents to survive another day. A tight abdomen kept his back straight, and what little muscle laced his frame was dense, sinewy, like granite. If you spoke to him, you'd soon realise his soul was as hard as his body, the soft edges sharpened out of necessity. He grew up tender, known in his childhood shanty town for wearing his heart on his sleeve. No trace of that boy existed now. Above all else, humans endure, and if that means stripping away most of what makes you human in the first place, so be it.

Alain Da Silva was banking on the captain's toughness to help him overcome any trepidation, but the man took one look at the inside of the vessel and turned around on the ladder with a visible lump in his throat.

Da Silva said, '*Que?*'

Most spoke French here in this obscure and chokingly humid parcel of South America.

The captain's frame glistened with sweat. A salty bead ran from the tip of his deltoid down to the crook of his elbow as he reached his arm up to wipe his forehead.

Da Silva looked pointedly at his watch. Again, he said, 'What?'

The captain looked like he might pass out, and he clambered down the side of the vessel unprompted, clammy hands shaking on each rung. He dropped into a puddle of fetid water on the warehouse floor beside Da Silva. Really, it was less a warehouse and more a wooden skeleton frame in the middle of the jungle with a few huge sheets of corrugated metal thrown on top. Tropical rainforest pressed in on them, all four sides of the building exposed to the plants and the wildlife and the insidious weather, the humidity that rotted everything it touched.

The captain straightened up. He was a bad liar before he even opened his mouth. 'I've just remembered...'

Da Silva ran a hand through his hair, curly, thick, and greasy. 'What have you remembered?' He would have called the captain by name, but he hadn't bothered to learn it.

The captain swallowed. 'Family ... obligations...'

Da Silva raised an eyebrow. 'Oh?'

'I'm so sorry. Maybe we can ... find a different time. Reschedule...'

The captain didn't even know what he was saying; terror controlled his mind and his mouth. He was paralytic at the thought of what was to come, considering the claustrophobia and the isolation and the prospect of a deep, dark grave.

Da Silva shook his head. 'It's okay. Don't worry. I'll just replace you.'

The captain looked befuddled. 'But all my training...?'

Da Silva shrugged. 'We dragged it out for a month but we could have condensed it to days. I'll get someone ready quicker than you'd think.'

The captain understood the implication. Terror gave way to survival instinct. 'This job is insanity. Not even my kind are this desperate for money.'

'Your crew members' — Da Silva tilted his hand side to side — 'are a little harder to replace. People aren't lining up to put their life on the line for six thousand euros. But what you're getting paid? *Twenty-five* fucking thousand? You take all the same risks. The only difference is you navigate, which means steering. You're making four times more than your crew to hold the wheel. I could throw a rock through the nearest village and hit ten people who'd take your place.'

Da Silva wagered the figures would roll off the uneducated captain, the spiel intimidating him into submission, but instead of slumping his shoulders, the man looked back at the vessel with a scowl. 'That thing carries ten tons. The street value in America has to be, what, two hundred and fifty million?'

Street value? America? Da Silva hesitated. He hadn't put as much research as he thought into the prospects. He needed them illiterate and stupid, or they'd figure out they were getting fleeced, like this captain evidently had.

The man's scowl morphed in two different directions as his brow furrowed and his lip started quivering. He was angry, but unsure how to proceed. Unsure how he *could*. 'If I'm going in there,' he said, jerking his thumb over his shoulder, 'I want more money.'

Da Silva didn't blink. 'No.'

The quivering lip hardened. The corners of the captain's mouth tilted up in an expression that came close to mischievous. 'This is ... negotiation?'

Da Silva smiled back at him, which wiped any hint of a smirk off the captain's face. In all their interactions over the past month, not once had Alain Da Silva showed anything resembling a smile.

Da Silva shook his head as he reached for the back of his waistband. 'You thought I was bluffing.'

The captain's hands came up as Da Silva pulled his Taurus PT145 pistol, chambered in .45 ACP.

Why, Da Silva thought, *do they always realise too late?*

The captain dropped to his knees in the puddle. The wet *smack* reverberated through the warehouse, its atmosphere something physical, so oppressively humid it was like fighting through quicksand just moving around. He was already crying. Da Silva hid his admiration; it was no small feat. Most couldn't get the tears out before the bullet entered their skull.

'If-if-if-if—' the captain stammered uncontrollably. He sucked damp air through gritted teeth. 'If I could get word to my family, it would be okay. I'm not scared of death. I'm scared to leave them with nothing until I'm back. We barely get enough calories for the day. My wife and I go without. My baby girl ... she needs more food. She's so sick. Her bones ... tiny. Let me return to my village, tell them how long I'll be away, leave them with ... I don't know ... an advance?'

The hope in his eyes was all he had left.

Da Silva pressed the pistol barrel to his forehead.

The captain squeezed his eyes shut and wept.

Da Silva sighed and returned the Taurus to its holster. 'Go.'

The captain kept his eyes shut, not believing what he was hearing.

'Go,' Da Silva repeated.

The man stumbled to his feet, tears streaking down his face, and brought his palms together in a prayer gesture. Barely able to look at Da Silva, he sobbed in gratitude and turned to leave the warehouse.

Da Silva, shorter, well-fed, and heavily muscled, seized him from behind in a rear-naked choke. The captain only managed a splutter before the sound died in his throat, the pressure tearing his oesophagus, crushing his larynx, both cutting off the blood to his brain and rendering him incapable of taking another breath. Da Silva kept squeezing as the man slapped at his forearms, like fly swatters against a concrete pipe.

'You would run or you would talk,' he whispered in the man's ear, lower lip brushing the lobe. 'One or the other. I'm not wasting three million euros on this fucking project to helm it with a man like you.'

The captain's gargle was final. He went slack in Da Silva's arms, who kept squeezing until he could no longer feel his own fingers. Only then did he drop the body into the brown puddle.

There wasn't time to waste.

He went to find a new captain.

2

They moved like a procession from the bitter cold into the tavern's warmth.

At the apex of winter, Maine was ferocious. Inland, away from the coast, the snow piled on with no reprieve, dozens and dozens of inches falling without mercy. A blizzard swirled now, complicating the walk from their vehicles to the tavern door, but it made it all the more sweeter when the heat hit them like a physical wall. Flames licked a large fireplace across the room, separated from them by three pool tables and a broad expanse of tables for occasional dining and regular drinking. Ochre wooden beams ran up to a white roof adorned with a large skylight, but the conditions outside meant only a muted grey hue came down through the glass. The tavern was lit mostly by the fire and the medieval-style lanterns along the walls, and brought to life by the Mainers littered across chairs and barstools.

It was Saturday afternoon, and that was enough to justify overindulging.

Jason King didn't disagree.

In different circumstances, he would be back at home in front of the fire, feet up, resting the body before Sunday morning's long run, a staple of his training regime. This weekend he allowed himself a little slack. He hadn't expected to be a free man, let alone still here in Millinocket, his surroundings and routine unchanged. Through a combination of bold decisions and undeniable luck, the world he'd resided in for most of his career was done with both him and Slater. They had one of the most powerful men involved in U.S. covert ops on their side, and Grey would ensure they were left alone for the rest of their lives. That's what the old man had told them, and they believed him. If they caught a whiff of anything different, there'd be hell to pay.

So, peace.

He wasn't ordinarily one for celebrating, but certain achievements can't be denied.

He held the door open with his shoulder to usher Violetta inside, who swayed as she balanced Jason King Jr. in a mesh baby carrier strapped over her shoulders. His arms and legs swung with her natural motion, the back of his head bumping her chest with each step, and he smiled like he was on a rollercoaster. Will Slater followed, one arm draped over Alexis Diaz's shoulder, who let the side of her head fall to his deltoid. Behind them, thirteen-year-old Tyrell took up the rear, now as tall and broad as a man at five-ten and one-sixty. It seemed every time King saw the boy he had new insertions, stronger musculature, wider shoulders. There was plenty more growing and broadening to be done before puberty was over.

Tyrell eyed the craft beers on tap — Bissell Brothers Swish, Allagash White, Lone Pine Tessellation — and tapped Slater on the shoulder. 'Can I have a—?'

'No.'

King let the door swing shut behind him as he hid his smirk.

Tyrell jerked a thumb over his shoulder. 'He'd let me—'

King said, 'No.'

Tyrell turned and scowled, only half-mockingly. 'I know Will won't, but you'll have a few.'

'I think I'm *just* over twenty-one.' King held two fingers millimetres apart. 'Cutting it close, but I made it. You'll be there one day.'

Tyrell looked around. 'Yeah, and I won't be drinking here.'

Alexis smacked a palm gently off the back of his head. 'Don't be rude.'

They had to pass the pool tables to get to the bar, and for a little too long Tyrell eyed a big-bearded trio who looked like lumberjacks. One guy wearing a flannel shirt looked up from the green felt and stared at Tyrell. King bristled. He couldn't help anticipating confrontation everywhere he turned.

The big man said, 'You want in?'

Tyrell stopped. 'Hell yeah, I want in.'

A second man handed him a cue.

On the way past, Slater said, 'No matter how bad he gets beat, don't offer him beer as commiseration.'

It got a laugh from all three of them. One of them turned to Tyrell. 'You ain't so good, huh?'

'Rack 'em up,' Tyrell said, nodding to the black triangle. 'Dad doesn't know shit.'

King was following close behind Slater, Alexis, and Violetta as they drifted past to a big table near the bar, and he was afforded a good look at Slater's face. Perhaps Tyrell had only referred to him as "Dad," to save the trouble of a long-winded explanation, but King could still tell what it meant to Slater. The pride in his eyes was unmistakable, and for some reason King felt his own emotions stirring as they pulled out chairs and sat. They were all family, in some strange, interconnected way. No blood between any of them, of course, but something immaterial existed between him and Slater, and therefore, by extension, between him and Tyrell. It was a single chain that he was grateful to be a part of. He wouldn't want it any other way.

Alexis reclined, stretching against the seat back, and shook her head.

Violetta said, 'What?'

Alexis smirked. 'I can't help but think one of us should be out there in the cold, playing sentry.'

Violetta bounced Junior softly in her lap, his legs dangling from the harness as she began unfastening the straps. 'Maybe we still should be.'

Alexis shrugged. 'We weren't in the car during their talk with Grey. Hard for us to know what we should be doing.'

As one, they turned to King and Slater.

Slater said, 'It's fine. Trust us.'

Alexis said, 'How are we supposed to—?'

King rose abruptly, the chair legs scraping the tiles, audible above the tavern's murmur. It froze her mid-sentence. Without saying a word, he turned and walked away from the table.

A couple of minutes later he was back with two pints of Bissell Brothers Swish for him and Alexis, and zero-alcohol beer he put down in front of Slater and Violetta. Slater's sobriety was permanent, Violetta's temporary on account of breastfeeding.

He said, 'It's fine.'

'Jesus,' Alexis said. 'I thought I said something unforgivable.'

King winked at her.

Violetta said, 'So Grey's out there somewhere, vouching for us? Is that right?'

King sipped the froth off the top of the pint. He swore he could taste the tranquility. 'He'd better be.'

3

Washington D.C.

The get-together would usually suggest a national security crisis.

Grey stood before the Director of National Intelligence and the Director of the Central Intelligence Agency. He was aware how valuable their time was, how each second that passed in silence was a monumental waste, but his own presence also commanded that sort of weight. Here, though, he felt like a child in the principal's office, preparing to defend himself against shameful accusations.

Jack Raynor, the current D/CIA, leant forward. 'What, Jerry?'

Grey blinked. It seemed everyone was calling him by his real name these days, the mystique shattered. The truth was everyone beneath the pair in front of him still considered him a god, a deity, and, frankly, the DNI and D/CIA probably did, too. Ego is tricky, though. You might be the only person in the world who knows, and it can still ruin you.

Grey cleared his throat. 'I'm sure you're both aware I made an unsuccessful trip to Maine.'

Barbara Baker, the no-nonsense, razor-witted DNI, rolled her eyes. 'Do we need the preamble? Jack's down eight men from his Special Operations Group. We're all very aware that you monumentally botched *something*.'

'That's what I'm here to tell you. I was carrying out a coordinated strike on two high-value targets.'

'Jason King,' Raynor said. 'Will Slater.'

Grey hesitated.

The Director leant forward. 'Perry Briggs reached out.'

'Oh.'

Briggs, the Director of the FBI, had been present at the Chelsea Field Office when rogue fugitive Jason King walked in and asked to speak to someone in authority. Briggs had almost stormed into King's cell himself when Grey was on the plane over, only standing down after Grey directly ordered him to stay out of it. As King was leaving later that night, he and Briggs had a tense interaction, which, judging by the way Briggs spent the next couple of days sulking, hadn't gone the Director's way. This new information was surprising given the tricky communicative quagmire that existed between the CIA and the feds.

Grey said, 'What did Briggs tell you?'

Raynor didn't look away. 'That you were out of line. That the leeway you're granted is predicated on the fact you're a consummate professional, but he thinks you're losing touch and shouldn't be allowed to strut across the country, taking whichever troops you please and answering to no one.'

'And what did you tell him?'

'That you've always had those permissions and you always will.'

Grey stood still.

Jack said, 'I left it at that.'

'How should I interpret that?'

'However you wish.'

Grey didn't restrain his stare.

Barbara interjected. 'I used to love the dick-swinging contests, but I'm bored. Can we cut to the chase?'

Jack said, 'Did you get them, at least?'

Grey shook his head.

Jack threw his hands up, jacket sleeves bunching to reveal silver cufflinks.

Barbara said, 'So this is a call to arms?'

'No,' Grey said. 'The opposite.'

She stared pointedly at him, then shook her head. 'You're wasting my fucking time.'

'If I hear,' Grey said, raising his voice to freeze her, 'that *anyone* is taking action against them...'

'You'll do *what*?!' Barbara exploded.

It froze Grey in turn; he scanned his memory and couldn't find one time she'd raised her voice at him. He kept his face slack, his expression almost bored, but alarm bells rang in the pit of his stomach.

She sighed. It was the closest she'd get to an apology. 'I don't think you're talking to us, Jerry. I think you're talking to yourself.'

'Is that so?'

'King and Slater come from your side of this world. The deniable side. And every hostile action taken against them, by you or any of the men who came before you, was initiated from *your* side. You might have used CIA forces from the Special Activities Center, taken them from Jack here or the Directors that came before him, but the orders were always *yours* to hand down. The moratorium placed on King and Slater? Your side. The reneging of that moratorium?

Your side. And now you bring us together to tell us the moratorium's back in place, that we aren't to go near these men, aren't to even think about *looking* at them the wrong way. You tell us this like we've had any say in what's happened so far.'

Grey didn't know what to say.

She said, 'You should be talking to a mirror.'

She collected a sleek laptop and a cream-coloured dossier on the table before her and swept out of the room, gone before he could muster a response.

Jack said, 'Shit.'

It was him and Grey, alone in the windowless room.

Grey maintained composure as best he could. 'Make sure she doesn't do anything foolish.'

'Did you not hear a word she said?'

Silence.

Grey said, 'Sounds like she's fed up with how I'm treating the King and Slater situation. Sounds like she might do something about it.'

'She doesn't give two shits about King and Slater,' Jack said, rising in turn. 'Frankly, neither do I.'

Grey did all he could not to rock back.

The Director of the CIA said, 'She's fed up with you.'

Jack made for the door. Before he stepped out, he looked back. 'You have ultimate power in this world, and you know it. It's the nature of covert ops. Always will be. But stop coming to us about these two guys for the sole purpose of keeping us in the loop. We don't care. Do what you want with them. But don't think about taking anyone from SAC ever again. You've set my ops back months by whittling down my roster with your trip to Maine.'

Grey had spent more than half his life in the business of black operations. He'd never felt this foolish.

Jack said, 'Do you hear me, Jerry?'

'I hear you.'

The Director hesitated. 'You spoke with King at the Chelsea Field Office.'

'You have the audio transcription.'

'I know. I've listened to it.' A pause. 'Did you speak with him or Slater in Maine?'

'No.'

Jack gave him a knowing look. 'You keep pretending they don't have you by the balls and I'll pretend we had a productive conversation today.'

Silence.

Jack said, 'See you round,' and cleared out, leaving Grey alone in the room.

4

Two pints and a pleasant buzz later, King watched Tyrell saunter over from the pool tables.

As the teenager crossed the tavern, one of the flannel-shirted men called something out after him, followed by a hearty chuckle. Tyrell smiled, looked over his shoulder, and shouted something back. All three men laughed uproariously. King hadn't a clue what they were bantering about, but it put a smile on his face all the same. He wondered if it was the beer, but when he looked across the table, Slater was smiling too.

Tyrell came up behind Slater and put his hands on the man's giant shoulders. 'It's two against two and my team's up 2-0.'

'Wow,' Slater said, turning around in his seat, but he deliberately looked past Tyrell. 'Who's your teammate? He must be world-class.'

Tyrell murmured, 'Asshole.'

Slater smiled as he reached up and swatted a backhand at Tyrell's chest. 'Only playing. I've been keeping an eye on your shots. They look good.'

'You got some old life as a pool shark I don't know about?'

'You bet.'

'Nah,' Tyrell said, 'I know what it is.'

'Do you?'

'You have to be good at pool if you've played before.'

'Why?'

''Cause you couldn't bear giving anything a half-effort.'

One of the bearded men called across the room, and Tyrell ventured back to the pool tables.

Slater shook his head in bemusement, which made Alexis say, 'What?'

'For a kid from the hood,' Slater said, 'he can sure make friends anywhere.'

She said, 'He's a good kid.'

He nodded.

She said, 'He takes after you.'

King had been listening closely, proud of how far Slater had come since he'd first known him as a degenerate womaniser, but something snagged his attention across the room. In his peripheral vision he eyed a bush of steel-grey hair at the bar, and inadvertently his gaze drifted over. The elderly woman was seated on a barstool, hunched over a nearly empty pint of cider, atypical alongside the row of hard-looking outdoorsmen who constituted the tavern's regular heavy drinkers. She stood out, and it made King pay closer attention. When she finally glanced over her shoulder to survey the space, he recognised her. She didn't see him, turning back to her drink after a quick scan of the room. He thought he'd seen her flinch when she eyed the men by the pool tables.

King rose and collected the empty glasses. 'Another round?'

Slater mimed inebriation. 'Shit, why not?'

Similarly sarcastically, Violetta said, 'Gotta let the hair down every now and then.'

Alexis smiled and nodded.

King made a beeline for the bar.

As he eased between two stools, he caught a whiff of dried beer off its polished wooden surface, a painted canvas of spilled droplets, hours and hours worth. The woman didn't register his presence, transfixed by her reflection between smudged fingerprints. The contours of the glass warped her features.

King looked directly at her. He was close enough to be unavoidable. She had to address him if she intended on enjoying the rest of her time in the tavern. So she glanced sideways.

Her face changed.

'Oh,' she said. 'I remember you. From outside the grocer's.'

She was the first Mainer he spoke to when they arrived in Millinocket, only a couple of weeks ago. On a morning run through the town to acquaint himself with its idiosyncrasies, King had finished his route at the grocery store and held a short conversation with the elderly woman before Alonzo called, throwing everything into turmoil. He didn't have the chance to get her name.

King said, 'I thought it was you. How are you?'

Stubby fingers tapped him on the shoulder from behind, and a rugged male voice said, 'All yours, buddy. I'll let y'all catch up.'

He turned. A heavyset man in a flannel shirt levered off the neighbouring stool, gesturing for King to take his place. With a nod, King eased himself onto the stool and slid the pint glasses in his hands across the bar. He and the woman were now a comfortable distance apart.

She hadn't answered his question, and it didn't seem she would. She was facing her glass already, as if embarrassed to let anyone she mildly knew see her veil slipping. For her generation, wearing your heart on your sleeve didn't exactly embody virtue, and allowing your private issues into the public sphere was a sin often graver than the issues themselves.

He didn't mind making things uncomfortable.

Not if it was for the best.

He looked at her glass and said, 'I remember you telling me something about staying away from the bottle.'

'My dear,' she said softly, without taking her eyes off her own fingerprints, 'it doesn't say anywhere that you have to follow your own advice.'

He tried to see through the words, to who she really was beneath the pigeon hole that old-fashioned values had hammered her into. 'Bad day?'

'It sure is. They happen.'

'You were friendlier outside the grocer's.'

'That,' she said, taking a sip of cider, 'is true.'

Any sane person in his place would be across the room by now. She couldn't be any clearer about not wanting to talk. In King's experience, that was often when people most needed to talk — and why he and Slater seemed to run into trouble everywhere they went, finding a new problem with each step they took, the direction inconsequential.

Because they prodded the sore spots.

Diagnosed the issues.

He said, 'Not in the mood to chat?'

She closed her eyes and rattled her head side to side, lips trembling. Not politely, she said, 'I'm glad you see that.'

A.k.a. *Fuck off.*

'Maybe it'd be nice to talk about what happened,' he said. 'If something did. It might be ... cathartic.'

She bowed her head. 'I watched my dog get run over yesterday morning.'

5

King said, 'I'm sorry.'

'He was a big golden retriever. His name was Louie. I'm drinking to him.'

'How old was he?'

'Ten. With me since he was eight weeks old. There were maybe two weeks a year I wouldn't spend with him by my side.' She sipped more cider with a wince, not at all enjoying the experience of drinking but desperate for the numbing effects. 'A bond like that, there's no way to see it for what it is until it's gone. Because it's the best thing in your life, and it's happening to you every day, and then ... it's not.'

'He ran out on the road?'

'Yes.' Something shifted in her posture as she fought to hide a shudder. 'But there was time...'

King shifted forward on the stool. The bartender floated over to take his order, but he shooed the man away without taking his eyes off her. 'Time?'

When the bartender was out of earshot she said, 'Oh.' Long gaps between her sentences. 'I'm being silly.'

'You thought there was time for...?'

'For the car...'

She could only make progress a couple of words at a time, like she had a physical allergic reaction to voicing what she really thought. King paid attention to every word, held onto each morsel of information. 'To stop?'

'I thought so.'

'You think they ran Louie over on purpose?'

The notion seemed to both disgust and terrify her. 'No. Really, I mean it: I don't. There wasn't time for any ... I think the old boy's fate was sealed regardless. It wouldn't have made a difference either way. But I thought — I still think — there was time for them to *try*. They didn't even ... like the inconvenience of braking was worse than giving poor Louie a chance...'

King didn't respond.

The woman sighed and gestured haplessly at the glass, now nearly empty. 'That's why I'm drinking.'

'Did they stop afterwards?'

'No. They drove off. Sped up afterwards, in fact.'

'Did they realise what happened?'

She side-eyed him. 'He's a golden retriever. Not a chihuahua.' A scoff. 'What am I saying? You'd feel a chihuahua under your tyres, too.' She signalled to the bartender for another cider, then held up another finger on King's behalf. 'You drink cider?'

'Sure,' King said. 'Did you get a look at the driver?'

'Not really.'

'You saw *something*.'

'How do you figure that?'

'Because "*not really*" isn't "*no*."'

She pursed her lips as she drew inward. It was like her presence constricted over the empty glass, seconds before the bartender whisked it away and replaced it with a fresh pint, this one full to the brim. Foam sloshed around the rim. He handed the second pint directly to King.

King said, 'Appreciated,' and took a sip.

Seeing him drink appeared to calm the woman. She took a breath. 'I've lived a pretty good life minding my own business.'

'I've done the opposite and I'm still here.'

'Do you think you've lived a good life?'

'I like to think so.'

They drank from their pints in unison. Her sip must have been the straw that broke the camel's back, because as soon as she swivelled on her stool he could tell her lips had loosened. Everything that convention told her not to ask, she was about to.

'Tell me,' she said, 'what is it you did for a living? What made you your money?'

A fortnight ago, he hadn't said anything about the athletic-wear he'd worn on his run, but she'd been able to tell it was expensive.

He said, 'You're assuming I'm made of it?'

'You said you were here for peace. Made it sound like your career's over.'

'It is.'

'So?' she said. 'Let me hear it.'

He looked in her worn-down eyes. 'I'd just be lying.'

She blinked.

He said, 'What's your name?'

'Dawn.'

'Jason.'

'Jason...?'

'King.'

'Cates.'

He tilted his glass like doffing a cap. 'Pleased to meet you, Mrs. Cates.'

'Now that we're better acquainted,' she said, 'would you still have to lie?'

'Yes.'

He could see she desperately wanted to push it further, but she'd already pushed so hard against the walls of courtesy. All her life those walls had confined conversation, lined her potential responses up in neat little rows. Defying her conditioning didn't make her comfortable, but she was doing what she could, trying to read between the lines.

He cut through the bullshit. 'Just tell me what you saw.'

The alarm that flickered in her eyes asked, *Am I really doing this?* as she said, 'Just a logo on the side.'

'Was it a car? A truck?'

'Pickup.'

'Colour?'

'White.'

'Describe the logo.'

'Some godawful cartoon. A grinning jackal holding a wrench.'

'Do you have any idea...?'

All at once, she said, 'Lubec Body Works.'

Seized by an uncontrollable impulse, she picked up her glass and took a big gulp. Her hands shook as she returned it to the coaster. She hadn't asked follow-up questions about who he was, but through telling him what she knew she'd made it real, crossed a line she knew she couldn't step back over, *regardless* of who he was.

'Lubec?' he said. 'That's three hours east.'

She nodded, cheeks draining of colour.

'Your vision must be good to read that off the side of a speeding vehicle.'

She didn't answer.

'And with ... everything else going on.'

She just shook her head.

He watched her, but no explanation came forth, so he pushed it. 'You frequent an auto body shop on the other side of Maine?'

'No.'

'Then how did you know the logo?'

Another flicker in her eyes; not alarm. She was still a distinguished elderly lady, so she couldn't voice it, but this time her expression said, *Fuck it.*

She looked right at him. 'Because people talk.'

6

Slater could only see a sliver of King's bulk on the stool beside the old woman.

Violetta and Alexis tried to maintain an air of nonchalance as they talked, but he noticed the concerned glances between sentences, the understanding that King wouldn't dare talk to a stranger this long without a good reason.

Violetta was the first to break. She stopped herself midway through praising Junior's first time in the high chair, and turned to Slater. 'What's he doing?'

'I don't know.'

'Who's the woman?'

'Never seen her before.'

He felt her studying him, taking note of every micro-expression. Even if he knew something, she'd never be able to tell, but she was high on the list of people he'd never screw around.

'Really, Violetta,' he said, 'I don't know.'

Alexis threw a look over her shoulder, her first proper

assessment. From where she was seated, she had the best angle. She turned back. 'He's pressing.'

Slater said, 'Huh?'

'The old gal doesn't look thrilled.'

That's all it took. Each of them knew King deeply, enough to understand everything he did had a purpose. There wasn't a chance he'd be making her uncomfortable unless there was a damn good reason for it.

Violetta got to her feet.

Slater said, 'No.'

She shook her head. 'Don't worry. I'll go to the other end of the bar. But I need a real drink.' Before Slater could even glance at Junior wriggling in his high chair, Violetta said, 'I pumped enough for the evening. It's back in the fridge.'

'Why the drink?'

'Need to enjoy the downtime while it lasts.'

7

S poon-feeding Dawn questions had been necessary at first.

King figured it would only stifle the momentum now, so he kept quiet.

She waited for him to ask a follow-up, then elaborated of her own accord. 'Rumours spread fast through the small towns. It used to be important. We're not Portland. We need to look out for each other. Times are changing, and all this new technology's making things a little easier, but ... habits are hard to break. You run into someone you know from another town, you gossip about anything and everything.'

'You know somebody in Lubec?'

'Close enough. It was her nearest town.'

'A friend?'

'Used to be.'

He said nothing.

Dawn said, 'She passed away.'

He stiffened.

She read his body language and managed a soft chuckle. 'Oh, dear. I remember being your age. Something like that, it'd shock you.' She raised a bushy eyebrow. 'You suspect ... foul play?' Sarcastic.

'Not yet.'

She waved a hand. 'Well, Joyce was eighty-three years old. And this was a couple of months back. Heart attack. Her husband was there with her. Nothing to be done.'

Again, 'I'm sorry.'

She sighed. 'That's what happens. My friends are my age.'

'You don't look eighty.'

'Seventy-nine,' she said with a wink. 'Almost there.'

The cider had hit her bloodstream now, removing her inhibitions.

'But you gossiped,' he said, 'before she passed.'

'Back in summer. It'd have to be six months ago now. I hadn't much to report. If you and your friend had come to Millinocket before I saw Joyce, I'd have enough gossip to fill an hour. You know how it goes...' She sipped her cider. 'Anyway, Joyce had stuff on her mind. There were new arrivals in town. And rumblings of ... unsavoury behaviour.'

'Such as?'

She paused for a long time. In the interim, he took a drink. Finally she said, 'I don't quite know how to put this. Thing is, we never discussed specifics. About anything, really. It always seemed too personal. I don't know. She said things that I interpreted a certain way, but if I recited them to you, you wouldn't understand...'

'You just tell me what you think she was trying to say.'

She seemed grateful, like a weight had lifted from her shoulders. Like she needed reminding this wasn't a police interrogation.

'There was a lot of activity at Lubec Body Works,' she said, her cadence much slower. 'It'd been going on for some time already — weeks or months, hard to say — but Joyce thought they were trying not to draw attention to themselves. Like they didn't want people to know how busy they were. She said it was understandable, if the owner was wary of small-town jealousy. There's only a thousand or so people in Lubec. A town that small, someone starts doing well, they're the centre of attention. Some people don't want that spotlight. But new workers were turning up, faces she wasn't familiar with, and townsfolk she deeply respected were just letting these new guys get away with whatever they wanted.'

He opened his mouth, but she held up a finger.

'I know what you're going to say, and I don't know. Joyce was always vague. They were causing trouble, that's all I know. And the way she put it, it's like they had connections or something. These new guys who no one knew, but *they* sure knew someone, because they could do as they pleased without fearing the consequences. Never cared for those sorts. And what she hated most, she said, was they had this silly cartoon logo of a jackal, all happy and smiling, like they were a good-natured establishment. It rubbed her the wrong way.'

She fell quiet. He let her have the silence. Her head was down, processing.

When she looked up, she said, 'Six months go by and I forget all about the chat. Then the first time I see that logo in the flesh, it's on a pickup speeding out of Millinocket, with poor Louie's blood on the tyres.' A rattling breath. 'I loved that dog. I truly did.' She took a big sip, wiped her upper lip. 'Always will.'

'Have you told your husband?'

She blinked. 'Excuse me?'

'You said you were happily married. Outside the grocery store.'

'Oh.' She seemed to shake herself out of a momentary stupor. 'He knows Louie's dead, obviously. He's distraught. But I wouldn't burden him with a dead friend's unfounded gossip, y'know?'

King let the words hang there until they were swept away by the tavern's collective murmur. 'Is your husband a good man?'

'One of the best,' she said, a small smile on her face. 'I wasn't lying about "happily." But ... he's not who he thinks he is.'

'Oh?'

Her cheeks flushed, embarrassed. She waved both hands around, betraying inebriation. She overdid the gesture, her circles too large. 'Don't you worry about me. I ramble.'

'Not who he thinks he is, how?'

Dawn lowered her hands. She sensed the futility, now she'd let the cat out of the bag. 'You're nosy.'

'Yes I am.'

'His heart's in the right place,' she said. 'But he's harmless, and he doesn't know it. He's ... quixotic. If I told him, he'd head east and puff his chest up, all proud and righteous, but he'd only get himself in trouble. Get himself hurt. It's better this way. Better we just mourn and mind our own business. Better we drink.'

'So where is he?'

'Working.'

'On a Saturday?'

She gave him a pointed look. 'Not everyone does as well as you clearly have.'

He held up his hands. 'I didn't mean that the way it sounded.'

Her chin wobbled with a small smirk. 'I know.'

'Do you have anything else for me?'

'And what might you mean by that?'

'Anything else you might remember.'

'I don't see why it matters.'

He shrugged as he picked up his drink and placed a twenty on the coaster beneath it. 'Your choice.'

He could see it tearing at her as he rose off the stool. Beneath the pause in conversation, indecision rippled. He couldn't tell for sure, but she seemed to know it was going to happen, regardless. In that case, why hold back?

As he nodded a warm farewell, she said, 'I saw blond hair. Short blond hair.'

'Okay.'

'It was bleached. Almost white.'

He looked at her. 'I'm sorry for your loss.'

'I'm confused.'

'Don't be.' He placed a hand gently on her shoulder. 'I'll keep Louie in my thoughts.'

He walked back to his table.

8
_____

Slater had seen King in every stage of emotion.
There was nothing they hadn't experienced by each other's side.

So he watched King closely as the man returned from the bar and sat back down. Slater could only see determination. No hesitation, no discomfort. And nothing to hide.

Alexis said, 'You forgot the drinks.'

King raised his eyebrows, first at the Bissell Brothers pint in front of Violetta, then at Junior in the high chair.

'The high chair's at our discretion,' Violetta explained, motioning to Junior. 'They recommend six months, and he's just past that now. Look how well he's doing.'

King reached across the table and tickled Junior's chest. The baby beamed. 'Doing _so_ well.'

'There's milk at home. I allowed myself a drink.'

He smiled at her, shook his head. 'You don't need to justify it to me. You deserve it.'

She gave a small shrug. 'I figured you'd be going on a crusade.'

'Because I spoke to an old lady?'

'So you're not?'

'I met her outside the grocer's. Back when Alonzo called. She was the first to welcome us to Maine.'

'That's not an answer.'

King glanced over Slater's shoulder to check Tyrell was still over by the pool tables, out of earshot. The teenager was laser-focused on lining up a shot, but still able to exchange wisecracks with the workers as he did so. He'd go far in life with charisma like that.

King turned back to the table. 'Someone ran over her dog yesterday.'

Alexis grimaced. 'Oh, God...'

Slater sat expressionless, arms folded across his barrel chest.

Violetta seemed torn. Dejected by the news, but relieved that it might be something as simple as keeping an elderly woman company on a terrible day. 'How is she?'

'She's intimidated.'

Slater said, 'What?'

'It was a hit-and-run. She knows who did it. She won't do anything about it.'

'Because...?'

'The guy works for some auto body shop on the coast. Town's called Lubec. The business has a bad rep. They've got away with some shit before, sounds like.'

Violetta said, 'She should be telling this to the cops. Not to you.'

'She won't.'

'Persuade her.'

'She's got some information. It's her choice to do what she wants with it. She's scared, so she won't do a thing.'

Violetta said nothing.

King said, 'Now I've got some information...'

He glanced over at Slater, gave the man a look that said, *And remember what we promised.*

Slater interpreted it correctly. 'We owe Grey nothing.'

King said, 'You're right.'

They kept nothing from their partners, so no one at the table was out of the loop. Alexis said, 'We don't even know Grey's keeping true to his word. You owe him less than nothing.'

'You're right,' King said again. He eased back in his chair. 'I wrote off tomorrow's long run anyway by coming here. I figure I'll have a bit of a lazy morning, maybe take a solo drive out east, sniff around a bit. Anyone object?'

Slater and Alexis shook their heads, but King didn't lend their opinions the same weight. He watched Violetta closely.

She took a long drink from her beer, injecting herself with a little liquid courage. Then she shrugged. 'Sounds like a couple of warehouse workers with connections. What's the worst that could happen?'

9

Old habits die hard.

King had planned on skipping his weekly long run, but when he woke with a pounding head, the urge was all-encompassing.

Sunday morning came after a hearty evening of King and Alexis going drink for drink, cutting themselves off after five pints each and drunkenly declaring it a draw. They'd reached a similar state of inebriation, which King considered embarrassing. He was at least eighty pounds heavier than Alexis, carrying over a third more bodyweight, so it should have taken another couple of pints to reach her level. But a lack of conditioning reared its ugly head, and as they sauntered out to the cars, he'd conceded defeat.

'I'm rusty.'

She'd looked right at him. 'You seem dead sober.'

'I don't feel it.'

'You're like Will. You internalise it.'

'You've never seen him drink.'

'Not true. The night we met, he was wasted. The power went out in New York when he was in the club.'

'That's right.'

'I couldn't tell. Not until he told me. Just like you are now.'

He'd shaken his head. 'Whatever. You win anyway.'

Now, he rolled over in bed and found Violetta smirking at him, strands of hair draped over her face like blond silk. Usually they took it in turns to get up when Junior started crying, but King had slept straight through the night. She must have covered it.

He rubbed his eyes. 'What?'

'You should drink more often.'

'Should I?'

'If last night's activities were any indication, yeah.'

He nestled back against the pillow, thoughts drifting. Each morning, the house felt more like home, the events of a fortnight ago shrinking a little further in the rear-view mirror with every day that passed. He tried not to remember he and Slater replacing the windows, rolling the bodies up in rugs, washing the blood off the lawn.

She said, 'What are you thinking about?'

He stared up at the ceiling. 'I want it to be dark before I head to Lubec. That way, maybe I can catch them red-handed.'

'Red-handed doing *what*?'

'Not a clue,' he said. 'But that puts the run back on the table.'

She shook her head. 'You're insane. You don't actually care about it being dark, do you?'

He winked at her as he levered out of bed. 'I'm a sucker for endorphins.'

Twenty miles total took him east to the town of Medway and back.

The round trip was over before midday, and would have

finished much sooner if not for an extended stopover at the halfway point to fuel up on carbs, sugars, and sodium as he overlooked the Penobscot River. His breath steamed in front of his face as he chowed down on a lobster roll and a cheesesteak, one after the other. Running, he mused, is a brilliant excuse to justify gluttony. Your body needs to replenish glycogen, and often the greasier the fuel, the better. He felt no guilt as he consumed somewhere in the vicinity of a thousand calories before he set off for Millinocket, one brisk seven-minute mile at a time.

Thanks to an intricate understanding of his body and its energy requirements, he was no more tired when he arrived back home than when he left. Twenty miles at a seven-minute-per-mile pace in freezing temperatures would be enough to reduce even a seasoned athlete to tears, but King trained at a level of detail that would impress an Olympian. He had to. If he went too hard in a session and ended up rendered useless, overtrained, all the work would be for nothing. If someone was in need of urgent help and he was too exhausted to get out of bed, what use were his talents? He'd found it beneficial in the long run anyway. Go too hard too often and you stifle progress.

Small, slow, consistent steps over an inordinately long period of time.

That's the key; the Holy Grail.

For King, a seven-minute-mile carried the equivalent energy expenditure of an unfit man on a brisk walk. They would both be putting in the same effort, only King was much, much fitter. It had been his training (and life) philosophy for as long as he could remember: *slow is smooth, smooth is fast.*

He changed, showered, and spent all afternoon and early evening with Junior, without so much as a thought toward Lubec and its auto body shop. There was no guilt. He'd dedicated all of his twenties and most of his thirties to a vocation that broke him down physically, mentally, and emotionally, and they paid him handsomely for it. If he decided to spend time with his family instead of rushing into confrontation — especially in retirement — it was his hard-earned right.

And he wasn't missing these moments, not for anything.

Junior had recently discovered the ability to roll from his back to his stomach, fists balled up, legs kicking. Sometime after this revelation, he figured out he had feet. He could grab them, even put them in his mouth. This blew his little mind, and with the curiosity and determination of a King, he'd been working on the most efficient way to get his toes between his lips. He spent much of the afternoon wriggling around this way.

As he lay beside his child in front of the fireplace, in a place that felt like home, with a partner he loved with all his heart, King made sure to savour the gratitude he felt. It would do no good to let it slip away unrecognised, unacknowledged. It was everything he had worked for, and the moment could easily be missed.

He didn't want to one day find that he hadn't appreciated the good old days while he lived them.

As evening swelled and the snowy plains darkened, he finally let his mind turn to Dawn Cates. He pictured her in a rocking chair, overshadowed by the absence of a dog who'd spent the last decade of its life beside her. She had knowledge of who'd run Louie down, and no one to share it with other than a nosy stranger at the bar.

All the pickup had to do was stop.

Violetta drifted into the living room after dinner and studied the expression on his face. 'You're mad.'

'I like dogs.'

He got to his feet, looked down at her. 'Are *you* mad?'

She shook her head. She meant it. She stood up on her tiptoes and kissed him. 'I know who I chose to be with.'

'Do you wish it were different?'

'No,' she said, and even though she'd never spoken to Dawn, he could tell she was thinking of the old woman, too. 'I wish the world was different.'

'I should be back by morning.'

'Give 'em hell.'

He geared up and headed out to the Dodge RAM sitting in the driveway. He and Slater had retrieved their rides from Boston a few days earlier, the whole time anticipating an ambush. When no trouble came, they'd made the call to carry on with their lives when they got back to Maine. That's what the tavern trip had been: the turning over of a new leaf, an acknowledgement that Grey was doing his job.

King clambered up into the cabin for a night-time drive.

10

I n their garage, beside the Range Rover he thought he'd have to leave in Boston forever, Slater held pads for Alexis.

Halfway through a three-minute round, the door opened and Tyrell emerged. From the way he stood up a little straighter and paused a touch longer before he spoke, Slater knew he'd tried his hand at meditation. Slater had suggested it that morning.

Tyrell said, 'That was weird.'

'How long did you do?'

'Twenty minutes.'

Alexis fired a kick into the pads, using impressive flexibility to open her hips and twist into it. Her shinbone slammed the leather with a *crack*.

Slater shook his forearms out. 'Probably too long for your first go. Got distracted?'

'About a million times. Why can't I stop thinking?'

'Exactly.' To Alexis he said, 'One-two-one-two.'

She threw the four-punch combination with lethal

intentions. Slater had held pads thousands of times, so he didn't need to see the punches coming to meet them. He slapped the pads off her gloves in a blur, making that indescribably satisfying noise: *thwack-thwack-thwack-thwack.*

Like gunshots.

'Chill,' Tyrell joked. 'The neighbours will think I'm shooting again.'

Neither of them responded to that, their discomfort palpable.

Tyrell loitered, aware he'd aggravated a sore spot. Teenagers were prescient in that way. 'All that stuff is over, right?'

'Yes,' Slater said. 'We're safe here.'

'Cool.' Forgotten as soon as it was brought up, he hunched over his phone. Out the corner of his eye, Slater could see the familiar blue of the meditation app. 'I'm gonna go try this again.'

Slater said, 'Knock yourself out.'

Tyrell looked up and deliberately paused. 'Oh. Sorry. Thought you were being literal. Thought it might be one of your "exercises."'

The round finished after another couple of combinations, and Alexis stripped the gloves off, panting. 'Will used to practice knocking himself out all the time, you know. Explains a lot, really.'

Slater rolled his eyes. To change the topic, he asked Tyrell, 'Ready for Stearns?'

Tyrell shrugged. Tomorrow would be his first day at George W. Stearns High School, right here in Millinocket. 'It's whatever. I'll make the most of it.'

'Not thrilled?'

'Well, this place ain't exactly as *happening* as Boston. Had a good thing going at Lexington, y'know? I was settling in.'

It hit Slater in the chest. 'I'm sorry.'

Tyrell waved dismissively. 'Nah, I'm glad to get away from there. No one in Maine's tried to bundle me into a van.' He shrugged. 'Not yet, anyway.'

Slater thought of Danielle, a classmate whom Tyrell had a brief romance with. He thought of the opportunities he might be depriving the boy of, to find a circle, to fit in, to be part of something. 'If you want back into Lexington, you let me know. There must be some sort of boarding setup nearby. Whatever it takes, I'll get it done.'

Alexis raised her eyebrows.

Tyrell stared. 'You mean that?'

'Absolutely. You keep doing what you're doing and I'll set you up with whatever you want. Don't think all the work you're doing is going unnoticed. You deserve the life you earn.'

It stopped Tyrell in his tracks. He mulled for a moment, deep in thought. Then he shook his head. 'I haven't even given Stearns a shot. I can't be that stubborn. But I appreciate it, man. I really do. I'll let you know after I see how this school goes.'

Slater nodded. He had nothing more to say; it'd be extraneous. Tyrell knew the weight of his words.

The teenager nodded back and went inside.

When the door shut behind him, Alexis lowered her voice to guarantee discretion. 'I thought you'd be halfway to Lubec by now.'

Slater shook his head. 'King's on it.'

'I'm getting déjà vu.'

'This isn't Alonzo. It's an old woman and a dog.'

'Somehow it always starts that small. Somehow I always convince myself that's all it'll be.'

Slater shook the sweaty pads. 'You're hitting like a truck. You want to go help him out?'

'No,' she said. 'My head's still pounding. I want a bath.'

He smiled with her, and they followed Tyrell inside.

11

Y
ou could set a horror movie in rural Maine at the darkest of night.

Nothing could happen the whole runtime, and it would still incite terror. The desolation was immense; King's high beams barely cut into the never-ending darkness. He felt like he was traversing a frontier, barrelling through an unknown realm. Sleet fell intermittently, sluicing across the wipers. He blasted the heat, sometimes at full strength, but no matter how hard he tried, he couldn't seem to get the cold out of the cabin.

A drive like that gives you time to think.

The more glimpses he managed of regular civilian life as he settled into the idea of a future in Maine, the more he realised just how different he was from his neighbours, but not in the way he originally thought. Back when he could only wonder about re-integration, during downtime on some chaotic black op, he thought there'd be contrasts in major personality features. It wasn't the case. All humans, he now knew, were more or less the same in their broader opinions. We get caught up in politics and talking points and left and right, but what we fundamentally want is to matter, to show the world our place in it, and, eventually, to mean something to someone other than ourselves. In all these ways, he was no different to anyone he crossed paths with, even the worst of humanity.

A drug lord, a corrupt politician, a murderous gangster: they want nothing more than to *matter,* and they'll do anything to get there.

What separated King from the pack, he thought as he hurtled cross-country toward an unknown target, was the little details. An old woman he hardly knew mused on a travesty, and he thought nothing of making it his business. He could very well die trying to find out who ran over a dog, and although he was sure it wouldn't be so dire, it was possible. He didn't find that decision notable, because he'd lived that way too long to know any different.

The same went for making himself the type of person who *could* involve himself in the business of others. If he wasn't dangerously capable, his decision to help would mean nothing. Although it might not seem like it, making himself a human weapon was also a bunch of little details, tiny decisions to run, lift, shoot, bulletproof his mind. The big-picture view seemed daunting, but he'd never looked at it that way. Each day, he thought: *I could stay in bed, or lace up my shoes. I could sit on the sofa, or go pick up that barbell. I could relax, or take action.*

Small steps.

He'd taken those steps tens of thousands of times over the course of a life. That was all. So when Dawn Cates spoke of a warehouse she didn't want to mess with, he thought: *I'll do it.*

Another small step.

Nothing more.

Rural Route 1 dumped him in a tiny town named Whiting around eleven p.m., and from there it was a straight shot east to Lubec, less than a dozen miles. Maps told him he'd hit Lubec Body Works well before the town itself, only a mile or so south of the Cobscook Shores. Between Whiting and Lubec he passed manors converted into bed-and-breakfast motels, antiques shops and baptist churches dormant in the dark, surrounded by woods and sweeping fields of snow. He was familiar with places this isolated, parcels of the globe where you couldn't shake the sense that laws were open to interpretation, the emergency services so scattered across such a broad expanse that they may as well be out of reach.

He thrived in such places.

A sign read: PUMPING STATION ROAD.

He took it.

Turned onto the first deserted dirt track he spotted and let the big Dodge rumble to a halt. It was best to not even let regular pieces-of-shit know he was coming. If these were professional criminals he'd take a little more caution, but he couldn't imagine a serious amount of dirty money being made in a place as inaccessible as this. In all likelihood, it was small-timers with connections letting a bit of unscrupulous coin get to their heads, making them think they were better than everyone else. King had seen it too many times to count.

He killed the engine and slotted his pistol into its holster. He'd picked up the SIG Sauer P320 X-Series for its impressive recoil control after he figured the gun jerking in his hands was all that was keeping him from superhuman aim. He had the rest of the necessary skills in the bag already — a cool head under pressure, an unwaveringly steady hand, off-the-charts reaction speed, and thousands of hours of practice. It was a damn heavy weapon thanks to a tungsten poly blend on the grip, but he could handle weight, and the result was one of the softest recoils he'd experienced.

Not long after he stepped out of the cabin, the headlights faded, leaving him to fix the lightweight bulletproof vest to his torso in pitch black. He didn't mind. It helped knowing *he* was what criminals had to fear in the dark.

He trekked a mile through the woods.

He could have used his phone to navigate at its lowest brightness setting, but he used to do this sort of work for real, hunting guerrillas and warlords and terrorists, so figuring it out under faint moonlight was easy enough when the stakes were lower. This was nothing but a side project.

He came up on the auto body shop from the west, without a hint of noise to show for himself.

Lucky he took such care.

At the edge of the property, he almost walked directly into a guy taking a piss.

12

The stretch of land the warehouse sat on wasn't fenced, so all that separated King from the worker was a row of bushes.

Bushes the guy was in the process of urinating on.

Hard to make out much in the dark, but faint light spilled from the warehouse behind the man. The bulk of the building overshadowed his profile, silhouetting him, but the lights were on inside, and an aura emanated to the edge of the grass. Only a pale, barely visible halo, but enough to make out a full head of black hair.

Not King's man.

No matter.

The sound of urine splashing leaves wound down, and the guy shook out droplets, a universal epilogue to the process. King saw everything and the man saw nothing. King's eyes had adjusted to the dark, and it seemed the guy had come straight out of the warehouse. All he'd perceive was pissing into a solid wall of black.

When he zipped up and turned around, King reared forward and seized the back of his collar with both hands.

Then wrenched like he was trying to deadlift seven hundred pounds.

He yanked the guy all the way off his feet, choking him as he pulled. King slammed him down in the bushes he'd just pissed onto, hard enough to smash the breath from his lungs, then dragged his limp body through the branches, deeper into the woods. The worker wasn't unconscious, so in seconds he'd scream, as soon as he got his breath back.

King ripped out the SIG and jammed the barrel in the guy's mouth. '*Shhhh.*'

Wide, startled eyes.

Uncomprehending.

King said softly, 'Did that hurt?'

The guy mumbled something, and King jammed the barrel in harder. 'Nod or shake your head. I won't twitch.'

The guy nodded.

King said, 'You want to get hurt worse?'

The guy shook his head.

'Then don't make a sound when I do this.'

He eased the barrel out. It scraped gently between the man's teeth as he freed it.

The guy lay there, bewildered, panting, probably firing on all cylinders with adrenaline. Looking up from the earth, he wouldn't be able to make out much of King at all, which helped for anonymity's sake.

King pressed the barrel against his chest, leaning the full weight of the heavy pistol between the man's pectorals.

Just as quietly, he said, 'Look, I'll level with you. I'm not interested in you. So calm down.'

He waited, gave the worker all the time he needed to regulate his breathing. It wouldn't make for good television, not in a situation as tense as this, but piece by piece it stripped the chaotic energy out of the air. It was the same with exercise: sometimes you had to slow things down to get the results you were looking for.

Finally, almost a full minute later, King said, 'You work with a blond guy?'

The guy didn't nod or shake his head. Words were on his lips, desperate to be released.

King mouthed, '*Whisper.*'

'Two,' the guy whispered.

'Bleach job.'

'Oh. Yeah.'

'Is he inside?'

A nod.

King said, 'Take out your phone, call him, and get him out here.'

'What do I say?'

'Whatever you want. But you'd better make sure it's convincing.'

He pushed a little more weight through the barrel, enough to make the man grimace. The guy reached down, slipped his phone from his pocket, and hesitated. In that pause, King made out a distinct emotion in his eyes.

Fear.

But not of King.

So Dawn's concerns weren't unfounded.

Ultimately, the guy was human, and survival instinct is overpowering. He also didn't have that air of bellicosity that King saw in inexperienced men; they didn't know what a true fight was like, and they thought acting tough and angry would mask their ignorance, when really it only exposed it. This man wasn't a pretender, and he wanted to live.

So he made the call, and sold it like he was gunning for an Oscar. 'Bro, get the fuck out here. *Now.*'

King could make out every tinny word coming from the phone. *'Just come in, dumbass.'*

'Nah, nah ... it's about Ricky ... he won't pay out.'

The guy on the phone hissed, *'What?'* in response.

'I don't wanna talk in front of Jack, you fuckin' idiot. I didn't even need to piss. Get out here.'

He hung up, alarm flaring in his eyes as he did so. The gesture was final. Either the blond guy would come out, or he wouldn't. By hanging up, he'd made an ultimatum. He stared at the gun barrel pressing down on his chest, his hands shaking.

King said, 'Ricky?'

'A bookie a few towns over. We won big on the NHL a couple days back. We planned to pick up our profits tomorrow.'

'Jack's your boss?' King said, jerking a thumb at the warehouse. 'In there?'

A nod. 'Jack Michaud.'

'And you are?'

'Sam.'

'Blond guy — what's his name?'

'Ethan.'

'Very good,' King said, thinking it might be possible for this to go smoothly after all. Almost off-handedly, he asked, 'So what are you up to in there?'

A vein in Sam's neck throbbed and King's blood ran cold.

So much for the lack of bellicosity.

Sam snatched wildly for the gun.

 King wasn't in the business of shooting people who might not deserve it, but he came close.

To prevent something as catastrophic as an accidental discharge, he jerked the SIG away as Sam snatched for it. The worker's stubby fingers brushed the barrel, millimetres from closing to form a powerful grip. Although King was confident he'd win, the last thing he wanted was a tug-of-war with a heavyset mechanic.

It'd be loud as hell, and hard not to inadvertently shoot the man.

Sam used King's defensive motion to scramble to his feet. He got his legs underneath himself and reared up, sweating in the freezing air. King grabbed a handful of his shirt. Sam bucked like a mule, boots slipping in the dirt. The denim tore and King's fingers went numb from the burn.

Sam went to dive over the bushes, opening his mouth to shout for help at the same time.

King caught him from behind in a rear-naked choke and squeezed with all his might. All that came from Sam's lips was a helpless splutter, the foundation of a shout that

twisted grotesquely into a screech and then was cut off
before it could fully leave his lips. It still echoed in the night,
but the grounds of the auto body shop were still empty.

King choked him out in less than ten seconds as Sam
swatted at his forearm.

In the movies, that might be the solution, but real life is
never as straightforward. Sam would be awake in half a
minute, maybe less, and he'd proceed to make all sorts of
noise. He'd groan, cough, gasp as he resurfaced from
consciousness. King had nothing to gag him with, and if he
kept squeezing to the point where Sam *wouldn't* come to so
soon, there'd be irreversible brain damage or death. You
can't keep someone unconscious for as long as you want; the
brain isn't quite so pliable. Hold a choke too long, or keep
reapplying the same blood chokes, and you risk permanent
injury.

King didn't know the extent of Sam's guilt. All the guy
wanted to do was get away.

So King lowered his limp body to the forest floor and
waited.

Nothing else he could do, unless he threw away his
moral compass.

Which wasn't happening.

'Come on,' he whispered to himself, crouched over Sam.
The warehouse seemed to hum in the stillness. 'Come on,
where are you?'

There he was.

A silhouette appeared as a side door swung open, and
hesitated with what King interpreted as trepidation. King
could make out details quickly as he focused on the man —
most importantly, the short, close-cropped hair, bleached so
blond it looked white. Ethan wasn't as lucky after emerging
from artificial light. All he'd see was black, and he acted that

way as he stepped out, letting the door swing shut behind him. It took him longer than it should have to cross the field, to pad across the snow-dusted grass in his work boots and reach the tree line.

Right before he did, Sam groaned softly beneath King. The sound was guttural. '*Urrrgghhh...*'

The splutter came as he lifted his chin to his chest, resurfacing from the deep.

Ethan froze.

Like a deer hearing the snap of a stick.

King had to move, or all was lost.

He made it up on the fly. He stood up, kept his head down, hunched his shoulders, and groaned in identical fashion to Sam as he stomped through the bushes toward Ethan. He tried to mirror every detail, from tone to inflection to volume. He hoped he got away with it.

Ethan could make out the big shape coming slowly toward him, but not the horizontal Sam lying in the dirt, still coming to.

To King, he said, 'The fuck's wrong with you?'

King hacked a gob of phlegm and spat it in the dirt as he stepped out of the bushes. He was five or six paces from Ethan.

Key details emerged from the haze, becoming clearer. King could feel Ethan's brain connecting the dots. The figure was broader, taller, heavier than Sam. They probably walked differently. You pick up all sorts of subconscious behaviours from people you know, even if you're not consciously aware of it.

Ethan made a suspicious noise. 'Uh—'

King looked up finally, meeting his eyes. By now he was two paces away. Ethan tensed up at the unfamiliar face, immediately confrontational, but King brought the SIG up and jammed it against his ribs before things could escalate any further.

They were a pace apart, maybe less. Staring each other in the face, right up close in the dark.

King spoke like he was in church, sinisterly quiet. 'Make a sound any louder than how I'm talking now and you'll eat one in the liver.'

Behind him, Sam groaned again, this one laced with a little more terror. The guy was coming back to reality at night, in the freezing darkness. Trying to get his bearings, figure out where he was, what had happened. He was scared.

Ethan raised a perfectly shaped eyebrow, edges so straight it must have been waxed. King wondered how much shit his coworkers gave him for his appearance. As softly as King had spoken, he said, 'What did you do to him?'

'He'll be fine.'

'That crap about Ricky?'

'To get you out here.'

'And who are you?'

King patted him down with his spare hand. He worked his way along Ethan's belt and pulled free a worn pistol holster with no pistol in it. He waved it in the man's face. 'Not smart.'

Ethan bristled.

Satisfied he wouldn't catch a bullet for his troubles, King resorted to the trustworthiest of options: brute force. He circled round behind the man, who was tall and lean and strong. King had felt pronounced bones and hard muscle under Ethan's shirt while frisking him. He wasn't to be underestimated, so King shoved him hard. Ethan sprawled forward, taken off his feet. He hadn't expected such a hit. He careened through the bushes and came down on top of Sam, who spluttered uncontrollably.

King stomped through the bushes after them and clamped a hand down on Sam's mouth while Ethan collected himself after the fall.

To Sam, he said, 'You've been choked unconscious. I'm pointing a gun at you and I'll use it. Your focus is to keep quiet and do as I tell you.'

Eyes hazy, Sam still had the wherewithal to nod.

King pulled the pair to their feet, one by one, and forced them at gunpoint away from the warehouse.

Deeper into the dark.

14

When he was satisfied they were out of earshot, King said, 'Stop.'

They stopped trudging.

'Turn around.'

They turned around.

Sam looked like he'd seen a ghost. Maybe he'd never felt the effects of a blood choke before, and was harrowed by how easily he'd slipped away. His shoulders were slumped in submission, behaviour that came from flirting with death. King had seen that sort of fear many times before, and knew it intimately. Ethan was cocky. He'd been shoved off his feet, sure, but not stripped from consciousness, and he was scorned. He looked ready to pounce.

King aimed the SIG at Ethan's face. Sam didn't need a weapon trained on him; he wouldn't think of moving. King only had one, anyway. He hadn't brought his whole arsenal. He'd figured a dog-killer needed their head punched in, but Sam's reaction didn't exactly fill him with hope that this would go smoothly.

Ethan wore the faintest smirk.

King said, 'You got something to say?'

'I don't know what you think you're doing.'

'Talking to you. That was my plan. I'd say it's going swimmingly.'

'Uh-huh.' Ethan shoved his hands in his pockets and didn't so much as flinch when King slipped his finger impulsively inside the SIG's trigger guard, abandoning trigger discipline.

Sam, on the other hand, blanched, standing up ramrod straight with wide eyes. His cheeks paled in real-time.

King said to Ethan, 'Get those fucking hands up now. Show me your palms.'

'Oh, yeah? You gonna shoot me? *Here?*'

The air bristled.

Their breath clouded.

King hadn't expected a dynamic so odd. Ethan didn't seem well-versed in life-or-death situations — deep in his eyes, the gun appeared to genuinely frighten him — but above that was a total confidence, like he *knew* he wouldn't die tonight. King could only chalk it up to hubris. The young man — he looked late twenties — thought whatever was going on at Lubec Body Works made him untouchable, put him in the vicinity of people so feared that King wouldn't dare follow through with his threats.

Maybe Ethan was right.

King said, 'You ever been hit before?'

It struck the nerve he intended it to. Ethan's eyes flared with that masculine intensity, a natural testosterone-fuelled response to challenge. The gun didn't seem to matter anymore, so he *definitely* felt protected by the auto body shop's illicit operations. He took a slight step forward, almost walking into the barrel. He looked over the top of the SIG into King's eyes, barely visible under moonlight. 'Yeah, I been hit before. You think I'm some bitch?'

'You've been in fights, maybe. How'd they go?'

'Never lost one.'

'That's a fight, though. You ever been beaten? You ever taken *punishment*?'

A vein in Ethan's throat throbbed, adrenaline dumping in his system. 'You got some mouth on you.'

'What I mean,' King said, 'is have you ever been hit like this?'

Sam was still off to the side, motionless. A non-factor. King felt comfortable lowering the gun.

Ethan tensed up.

It didn't matter.

There's a "ten-thousand hours" rule for mastery: you want to perfect something, that's how long you practice. King figured he'd put nearly double that into physical training in all its facets — aerobic, strength, martial arts, firearms. Twenty thousand hours was three hours a day for eighteen years. If he wasn't there, he was damn close. So when he hit Ethan with a straight right to the centre of the stomach, digging into the soft flesh instead of the ribs so he didn't break his own knuckles, he knew with absolute certainty the guy had never been hit like that in his life.

Not even fucking close.

Breath exploded out the man's lips as he went totally slack, doubling over and falling forward like the punch had broken him in half. King's right fist went completely numb, but it didn't stop him switching hands with the SIG and snatching a handful of Ethan's bleached hair on the way down. He jerked Ethan up like the young man was a puppet, putting him back on his feet, so he could see the reaction in real-time.

There was a moment of complete shock before the pain hit.

Ethan's face contorted. He squeezed his eyes shut and pursed his lips before opening his mouth in a silent moan. He wouldn't have known a human being could feel sensations like that. He couldn't stay up; he sagged to his knees, despite his best efforts. Before long, tears were streaking down his cheeks as he devolved into total body shudders. He might be seriously hurt. King would get answers all the same.

He knelt in front of Ethan and jammed the gun under his chin, sealing his lips. 'Did you run over a dog?'

A good punch was truth serum. Between ragged breaths, Ethan cried, 'Yeah, man, yeah, I fuckin' did, I'm sorry. Was that your dog? Oh, God, shit...'

He pitched forward and retched.

King grabbed his hair again and wrenched him back upright, kept the gun where it was. 'No, Ethan. It wasn't my dog.'

'I saw some grandma. I didn't know it was you—'

'It wasn't me.'

A pause in which Ethan whimpered several times consecutively. A new wave of pain enveloped him, preventing him from speaking. King let him ride it out. Sam stood mortified beside them, dead silent.

King said, 'Why didn't you stop?'

Stuttering, spluttering, Ethan spewed forth his stream of consciousness. 'I just-I just-I just thought it'd take too long to deal with ... I know that's selfish as fuck but it's the truth and I don't wanna lie to you ... oh my God ... please don't hit me again ... I'll do anything, just ... *ohhh* ... and I knew...'

He snapped out of the trance all at once, eyes widening at what he'd almost revealed.

King crowded him, getting closer, giving him no space. 'You knew what?'

Above any fear of future danger, Ethan was terrified of getting punched again. Stooped like a hunchback on his knees, he said, 'I knew we had a bit of a rep. I knew even if she saw the logo and somehow tracked it down, it'd probably be okay.'

King scratched the barrel against the underside of his jaw. 'And why is that, Ethan?'

A crisis behind the man's eyes reached fever pitch.

The swell of emotion was so sudden, so decisive, that it caught King off-guard. He hesitated, when he should have reset the situation, cooled things down. Instead, he stayed right where he was, trying to figure out what had happened deep in Ethan's mind.

Ethan reached up with both hands, fast as a whip, and grabbed King's left hand holding the SIG.

There was no way he could have wrestled the gun away, but that's not what he wanted.

He closed down with his fingers as hard as he could, aided by adrenaline.

Depressed King's finger inside the trigger guard.

Blew his own head off.

15

To King, it was a freight train of motion and sensation.

A sudden, visceral experience.

Grip-pull-bang.

Ethan's body collapsed at his feet, pouring blood from the exit wound atop his skull. The gunshot reverberated through the forest, like a clap of thunder directly overhead. Considering the quiet that came before, it was akin to a nuclear blast. There wasn't a hope in hell they wouldn't hear it in the warehouse. No doubt a frantic and tension-fuelled emergency procedure would follow. Already they'd be torching evidence, anything incriminating destroyed according to predetermined plans.

Exactly what King hadn't wanted to happen had happened. He sighed, unable to help his fatalism, and turned wearily to Sam.

He said, 'That's that, then.'

Speaking more to himself than the no-doubt traumatised mechanic.

But the look in Sam's eyes made him do a double-take.

The man was no more scared than when King had first seized him. In fact, King thought he saw cold acceptance there, and Sam refused to look down at the body.

Like one way or another, Ethan had it coming, so what did it matter that it happened now instead of at some indeterminate future point.

Sam kept his eyes fixed on the SIG, laser-focused on tracking where the barrel drifted. 'That's what?'

King hesitated. He could handle seeing shocking, bone-chilling violence up close, but supposed civilians weren't usually as cool-headed. 'Your buddy just killed himself. I take it your employers are already in damage control.'

Sam shook his head. After a pause, he then added, 'He wasn't my buddy.'

King addressed the head-shake: 'No damage control?'

'It won't stop them. Too much at stake.'

King couldn't shake the notion that everything about this was off, that he must be totally off-base in his idea of the scale of the operation. Sam had just seen a coworker blow his own head off, right in front of his eyes, and it didn't seem like any sort of notable incident.

King said, 'You're doing something illegal and you hear a gunshot, you stop what you're doing.' There was silence before he added, 'Even if you know it's not the cops.'

Sam chuckled and lowered his head. '*Something illegal.* Cute.'

King didn't feel aiming the SIG was necessary. 'What are you doing here?'

'What I'm told.'

It was all King could do not to roll his eyes. 'And what are you—?'

'Hey, brother,' Sam interjected, now staring right at him. 'You need to wrap your head around the fuckin' situation.'

King adjusted his stance and his boot squelched under Ethan's lifeblood. 'Enlighten me.'

A shaky breath. 'You can say whatever you want, and do whatever you want, and stick that gun wherever you want. You can drag more guys out here and shoot them in front of me. What Ethan just did hasn't changed my mind, so nothing's gonna.' He sighed, bowed his head again, ran dirt-encrusted fingernails through his hair. When he looked back up, his eyes were hard with resolve. 'The bottom line is, I can't tell you shit. I just can't. You can be as theatrical as you want, man. It's easier this way, now that you know. So make up your mind. Do whatever you gotta do.'

King stared at him, and he stared right back, both their eyes adjusted to the moonlight. The ringing in their ears had passed, subtle sounds returning to earshot, and there was no audible commotion from the warehouse in the distance.

Ethan's blood steadily *drip-drip-drip*ped into the snow.

King said, 'You make some decent coin from this?'

'Enough.'

'You like what you do?'

'I don't have a choice. I have to do it.'

'Not what I asked.'

'I fucking hate it,' Sam said. 'But anyone standing where I am would say that. So I ain't gonna blame you if you don't believe me.'

The silence dragged.

King said, 'Have you hurt anyone, Sam?'

'Not directly.'

'Would you?'

'I haven't been asked to.'

'And if you were?'

'I always figured I'd cross that bridge when I came to it.'

The faint sound of an engine rumbling to life drifted between the trunks, tendrils of sound whispering into King's ears.

He sighed and slotted the SIG back in its holster. 'Okay.'

Sam stood motionless. 'Okay, what?'

King shooed him away.

Sam didn't move.

King said, 'Learn to take yes for an answer.'

'I don't understand...'

'Go.'

Sam shifted his weight foot to foot, and finally took a glance down at Ethan's body. He'd lowered his head multiple times, but had purposefully avoided putting the corpse in his line of sight. After a beat of quiet, he said, 'It's, uh ... it's probably better if you kill me.'

'You're that scared of your employers?'

Sam shrugged. 'More who *they* work for.'

'So you just give up?'

Sam made a sweeping, vague gesture, encompassing Ethan's grotesque corpse, King, the woods, the warehouse in the distance. 'This, uh ... this ain't me. I'm not built for this.'

'You haven't even tried,' King said. 'That's worse than paying the price. Take what you've made from this and start a new life somewhere. It's not so hard out here. Get a job on a boat. Doesn't matter if the pay's shit. Keep your head down and keep yourself alive.'

'It's not worth it. Always looking over my shoulder, being scared they'll track me down ... that's not any sort of life.'

'Then trust me.'

'Trust you with what?'

'That very soon there won't be anyone left to track you down.'

A pause. 'So you're like an undercover—?'

Sam looked down at the body and cut himself off. King saw him thinking, *No, not an undercover cop.*

King said, 'There's no point me trying to explain who I am.'

Sam met King's gaze, and the fear he'd been trying to hide was now there, unrestrained. 'Do me a favour and try to explain.'

King took a breath. 'You think whoever your employers work for are the worst people alive.'

'They are.'

'Well, I've seen worse.'

'You don't even know—'

'Exactly.'

Sam shook his head and said, 'You people are a different breed.'

But he walked away.

As the woods started to swallow him, King said, 'If you trust me, can you tell me who they are?'

Sam looked back and smiled sadly. 'No. Because they're gonna kill you, then they'll come for me. But if you're brave enough to be that stupid ... well, I guess I can try, like you said.'

He turned and kept walking, and only when he was a vague silhouette in the distance did he stop of his own accord. He glanced over his shoulder one final time. King could barely see his face, but could still make out the wince, the slightly gritted teeth, the doubt clawing at his features.

He took a breath that King heard from dozens of paces away, mustering courage before he said, 'Don't go for the warehouse. They've got alarms and sensors out the ass, and they're already moving out. Go to West Quoddy Head.'

It rang a bell. King recalled an article he'd scanned

absent-mindedly, sitting back in Boston trying to learn more about Maine. 'The state park? With the lighthouse?'

If he remembered correctly, it was the easternmost point of the continental United States.

Sam's silhouette nodded. 'Head for the lighthouse. On the way, you might see a dirt track. Might be on your left. You might find something interesting, if you follow it to the shore, if you look hard enough…' He trailed off and swore at himself as he turned around. 'Fuckin' idiot, Sam.'

He disappeared.

16

K ing let the night enclose his form, let the cold grip him, leaching through his multiple layers of clothing.

Deciding.

The distant sound of an engine had punctuated his conversation with Sam, right around the halfway point. A few minutes must have passed since then. He heard more commotion now: multiple engines, tyres on gravel, muffled and echoing shouts. If they weren't leaving the auto body shop unmanned, there should only be one or two men left behind to keep the warehouse secure and protected. King could probably stroll right in; if there was any resistance, it would be minimal.

And Sam's revelation was likely a lie.

It made sense to make something up. By the time King drove out to Quoddy Head, Sam could be back in touch with his coworkers and within minutes they'd be barrelling across Maine, fleeing the scene after scrounging up any incriminating evidence they could take with them. Yet despite it all, King couldn't shake the feeling Sam had told the truth. He had nothing concrete to go off, not even micro-expressions. It was usually easy for King to tell when someone was lying, but he needed a clear view of their face. He knew all the tell-tale signs to look for, but Sam could have exhibited all of them in the dark and King was none the wiser.

Ethan's skull continued dripping blood into the dirt.

King made his mind up. He left the body where it was and doubled back to where he'd parked the Dodge. He'd got this far trusting the right people, listening to hunches.

If it ain't broke, don't fix it.

He redoubled his focus as he trekked back, the new perspective sudden, enlightening. Each step he took, it sunk in a little deeper. This wasn't about a thug who thought he could get away with carelessly killing a dog. The situation had shifted, its scope expanding, but, in his core, King had always known it'd happen, knew it never would've been . straightforward. Although nothing Dawn said at the bar had registered as overly concerning, there'd been something underneath the conversation, an undercurrent that told King this would go the same way as everything else.

Because, really, had he ever got himself involved in something that resolved itself simply and linearly?

The opposite of the Midas touch: that's what he had.

Everything he touched turned to shit, but that wasn't exactly a bad thing. He had a knack for uncovering the worst of humanity, which was better than it never being brought to light. It complicated his life to no end, and he wouldn't have it any other way.

He found his truck undisturbed. It was chameleon-like, the way the big Dodge blended into the night, into the still-ness of the dirt track. He made sure to circle the vehicle twice in a concentric pattern, the first loop much wider than the last. He found nothing amiss. He was ready to kill at a moment's notice now; it was all different.

Back in the cabin, he consulted the GPS. Five miles to West Quoddy Head. A straight shot down South Lubec Road, parallel to the Canadian border, that invisible line resting out in the middle of the Quoddy Narrows. From the track Sam had mentioned, just before the lighthouse, he should have a northward view into Canada, of Campobello Island's coast.

Even from a top-down, digital satellite view, everything seemed desolate, untouched.

A breeding ground for crime.

He set off before he could think twice. No thought of Junior or Violetta or Slater. Just the toe of his boot to the accelerator and a twist of the wheel and he was in motion. It seemed almost no time passed before the road veered left, leaving the mainland behind for a narrow strip leading to West Quoddy Head. The state park sprawled out to his right under pale moonlight, broad and dense and unmoving. He felt intensely vulnerable, like even the slightest movement would betray his presence out here, let alone the growl of a truck engine.

He came to the mouth of a trail on the left.

Just as Sam said.

He slowed the Dodge to a crawl as he rumbled on past. Turning down the claustrophobic track, within which there'd be no easy way to turn a big vehicle around in the event of an ambush, was the equivalent of a death sentence. King knew he might be missing whatever it was that Sam had pointed him in the direction of, but he wasn't letting impatience seal his fate. He parked a few hundred feet further down South Lubec Road, close enough to the lighthouse to see the tip of its silhouette looming over the east coast like an obelisk guardian.

He killed the engine, got out, and exhaled a cloud of breath into the freezing dark. Then he turned and plunged into the woods, the trees enclosing him, their joined canopy draping overhead like a blanket. He chose the most difficult cross-country path possible, the type of trek through unknown terrain that you'd have to be clinically insane to take.

But he'd always favour discomfort over idiocy.

If there was a lesser chance of getting caught with his pants down, he'd put himself through unimaginable misery. This option, with branches scratching at him and the uneven ground threatening to twist an ankle at any moment, wasn't a big deal. Not compared to a bullet in the back.

He balanced the scales perfectly, moving silently across terrain that makes you loud. That way, not even the most seasoned sentries would see or hear him coming. They'd be looking elsewhere, having written off King's approach of choice under the assumption that no one could come that way without betraying their presence. He refused to make a sound, even if it meant slowing to a crawl.

As a result, he came to the edge of the trail in a cold sweat, heart straining from the exertion but lips sealed, taking controlled, measured breaths through his nose. He was near the end of the track, and could see the rocky shoreline of the Quoddy Narrows up ahead, soft waves lapping gently at the banks.

More importantly, he saw the fleet of huge vehicles lined up in a row on the shore. Two pickup trucks and two Sprinter vans. They'd all U-turned at the end of the trail and reversed down to the water. One of the pickups had deposited a thin, sleek cigarette boat into the water from an attached trailer. Its hull gleamed under moonlight as it bobbed on the surface.

King saw it all.

And they didn't see him.

It brought a smile to his face.

Just as a man walked by his left shoulder.

Close enough to touch.

17

Behind the wheel of the Sprinter, Jack Michaud packed his lower gums with dip.

He wished you could absorb nicotine faster. The burn at the roots of his teeth wasn't enough. The process took valuable seconds, seconds he didn't have.

He needed a cool head this instant.

Archie said, 'Chill, brother.'

The fat man's appearance was misleading, which is precisely what made Archie so good at his work. You wouldn't expect an oversized teddy bear with kind eyes to be the most ruthless person you've ever met. Archie was as dangerous as he was disarming. Jack couldn't hide his own envy. He'd always looked like a cold-blooded killer. He never surprised anyone.

Jack said, 'Tonight of all nights.'

'You knew what you were getting yourself into with those degenerates. We all did.'

'You said Nolan heard Ethan on the phone?'

'Yeah. Sam called him outside.'

Jack rolled his eyes. 'Dumbasses. Who you reckon did it?'

'Doesn't matter,' Archie said, without so much as the slightest change in tone. 'Whoever's left is dead as a fucking doornail.' It was near pitch-black in the cabin, but Jack still made out the excitement in Archie's eyes. A stranger might mistake the passion as innocent joy. It was fair enough; they were interchangeable. Archie felt the same attending the newest Marvel movie's midnight release as he did slitting a man's throat and watching arterial blood pour down the front of his chest.

Jack said, 'You think I'm paranoid?'

'I think one of 'em killed the other over that bookie shit. That's what I think. I think they're two of the biggest fuckin' morons walking the face of the earth and they didn't think twice about butting heads on the most important night of the month.'

'You think I'm paranoid.'

Archie shrugged. 'It don't matter. What does Brady do anyway? Let him play guard dog all you want. It's not like we're missing his talents.'

The nicotine hit and Jack stopped tapping his heel against the footwell. He thumbed the handheld radio and lifted the receiver to his lips. 'Brady.'

Nothing.

Jack peered out the windshield, looking up the trail to where Brady's faint silhouette sauntered along the path. He shook his head, exasperated, his finger off the PTT switch. 'Who the fuck does he think he's fooling? I can see him right there.'

'I can't,' Archie said, squinting, his eyesight considerably worse. 'Probably thinks he can dart off for a smoke.' He flashed a look in the side mirror. 'We're good to go.'

Jack unbuckled his seatbelt, put a hand on the door. He depressed the switch again. 'Brady, we're heading out. Keep a look out. Stay frosty.'

No answer.

Jack glared out the windshield, but his brow lost its furrow immediately.

Brady wasn't there anymore.

The trail was empty.

Archie said, 'What?'

Jack shook his head. It had been a long day. A long year. 'Don't worry. Fuckin' seeing things.'

18

B rady hated feeling used.

Lately, that's all he felt.

He didn't mind being the low man on the totem pole. He was unique in the sense that he knew how dumb he was. Other idiots kid themselves, think they're smarter than they are, that it's the world holding them back instead of themselves. Brady had been the only one to ever hold himself back, but at least he could see that, and play to his strengths. He was big, all his gifts physical. He couldn't think clearly about much of anything, but he could do what he was told, and he didn't mind where it sat morally. That was a gift in itself.

But they used him, tried to make him seem more important than he was.

He despised that.

When Jack said, 'Go patrol the perimeter for hostiles,' what he really meant was, 'You're useless here, so go keep busy.' He should've just told the truth. Brady would've accepted that. Being fake rubbed him the wrong way. He'd never been pampered or coddled in his life and he wasn't about to let it start. He'd found that autonomy and independence made being dumb more tolerable.

His earpiece squawked: Jack's voice. 'Brady.'

He didn't answer, but turned on his heel and started back toward the fleet of vehicles. No doubt the boss wanted him for some menial task. He could be frustrated, but he would never say no. This wasn't the place for disobedience.

He walked past the dead space between two huge tree trunks and sensed something large and physical.

Something that wasn't natural.

Right there in the dark.

He nearly leapt out of his skin and twisted on the spot, bringing the AR Five Seven submachine gun up. He'd never been scared like that, and he could only liken the crushing squeeze in his chest to what a heart attack might feel like. He aimed into the darkness and hesitated for what could only have been milliseconds, trying to make out any sort of target. It would do him no good to fire impulsively into the woods, drawing unnecessary attention to this place. Jack might execute him for it.

So he squinted.

He peered.

He saw nothing.

Then a big figure detached from the wall of black, like it had shed a snakeskin by bursting into motion, and ripped the gun out of his hands like it was a plastic toy.

A hand seized Brady's throat, more pressure than he'd ever felt in his life, and wrenched him forward off his feet.

Dragged him into the woods.

19
_____

King had been merciful enough tonight.

Against his better judgment, he'd let Sam walk free, but at least the worker hadn't aimed a weapon at him. As King stood statuesque in the undergrowth, the big bulky sentry brushed by him, then turned and spun, panicking, aiming a big AR SMG shakily into the dark. The barrel drifted closer and closer toward King, and only when it was inches away from tracing a line across his chest did he reach out and wrench the man off his feet, pulling him out of sight.

He shoved him down into the undergrowth and tried to get a hand over his mouth but the guy kicked and thrashed and tried to scream. King put crushing pressure on his lips, pressing down so hard it was a surprise he didn't break both rows of teeth.

The man reached up and tried to claw King's eyes out. The way he expertly jabbed with his thumbs suggested he'd done it before. The tips of his outstretched fingers brushed King's lashes, scarily close. The man's physical presence was fearsome, even though he was underneath King, restrained.

It took all King's might to keep him there and keep him quiet.

You've been merciful enough. He'd already forgotten.

It was now a constant reminder, eating away at him.

King pressed harder.

The man snatched at the AR Five Seven, which had dropped on the forest floor beside them.

Which sealed his fate.

King let go of the man's head and he sat up with a gasp, elated to be free, but King dropped a vicious elbow into his throat as he sucked in air, using all the power he could muster. With a noise that resembled a wounded animal, the guy fell back to the cold dirt, clawing at his throat, and King dropped another elbow to put him out of his misery.

He was dead in seconds, his airway destroyed.

King dropped to his knees beside the body. He was grateful to be cloaked in darkness, relieved that it hid the savagery. There was nothing pretty about what he was good at. Never had been. The business was thankless, and it left nothing behind but ruination. Happy endings were few and far between.

He was okay with that.

He left the corpse like he had Ethan's, moving on, letting the night keep its secrets until morning. He made his way silently to the edge of the path. It afforded him a better view of the shoreline. No sooner had he shuffled to a vantage point along the tree line than one of the Sprinter vans came to life, its front doors opening in unison.

Two men stepped out into the chill.

If not for the wind coming up off the moody ocean, you could hear a pin drop.

One was taller than the other and looked rougher, meaner, more weathered (not that that meant anything.)

King had been in this game long enough to know appearances were deceiving, but the shorter man was morbidly obese, and his face was kind. The taller man's fair hair was thinning; he wore it forward to mask where his hairline truly lay. His cheeks had the texture of sandpaper, indicative of a life spent mostly outdoors. They were both in their forties, although King guessed the fat guy could be younger, his weight having aged him prematurely.

There wasn't much else to see, not under faint moonlight.

Intricate details were lost to the dark.

The fat guy turned and trudged in the direction of the cigarette boat, bobbing a couple of dozen feet offshore. It was hard to discern, but King counted three silhouettes onboard already, their shapes black against a blacker backdrop where the night sky met the water.

The taller man loitered, staring up the trail, concerned about something.

The fat man looked over his shoulder. 'Jack.'

The fair-haired man shook his head slightly, tearing himself away from his thoughts. 'Yeah.'

King thought, *So you're the boss.*

The fat man said, 'You're gonna hold this up for *Brady*?'

Jack turned on his heels. 'Nah. But when we get back, he's done. You answer your fucking radio.'

'Yes, you do.'

Jack signalled out to the boat. A couple of seconds of lag time, then the motor spluttered to life, its guttural chug taking a knife to the silence. King figured he understood; they wanted to keep noise to a minimum. The boat sliced toward the shore. Jack and the fat man only had to wade knee-deep into the arctic waters. In seconds, they'd be climbing aboard.

King made frantic decisions.

Then, steadily building into something audible before amplifying dramatically, came the distant *thwop-thwop-thwop* of rotor blades.

He'd been about to make a break for the boat, but now he stood perfectly still as the racket grew louder, until finally the helicopter roared into view overhead. Its searchlight pierced the night, the beam like an explosion compared to the darkness that came before. It swept over the forest, missing King's position by a hundred feet or so, before tracing a path directly over the cigarette boat.

Lighting its occupants up like a Christmas tree.

King peered up at the belly of the swooping chopper and immediately recognised it. His heart crashed in his chest at the shock.

It was a big Sikorsky MH-60 Jayhawk.

More importantly, it was red and white.

Coast Guard.

20

K   ing turned away.

Of course he was morbidly curious to see it play out, but life doesn't always give you the answers you want. Sure, he'd never find out what was happening here, but it wasn't worth hanging around and getting caught in the carnage. The Jayhawk would raise the alarm, Jack and his men would scatter, and the authorities would descend on this place in droves, arresting whoever they could round up. King didn't need to see it, let alone risk arrest.

Violetta and Junior were waiting for him.

So he walked away.

But he heard nothing. No alarms. Not so much as a whisper from the boat itself. King was in earshot; he should have made out shouts, curses, pandemonium.

He looked over his shoulder.

His stomach dropped.

The chopper continued its northward journey. It hadn't slowed at the sight of the cigarette boat, not even when its searchlight illuminated the five men like sitting ducks. The light was now out past them, trained on the swaying surface of the ocean, the swells stark and gleaming.

Now King saw it for what it was.

A guide.

Lighting a path across the sea.

His blood ran cold. Disbelief competed with anger, both fighting to overwhelm him. He allowed neither to take control. The boat chugged away in the shallows, its occupants milling about, shifting gear around, preparing for *something*.

King had time, but not much of it.

Without hesitation, he pulled out a satellite phone slotted in a holster at the back of his waistband and punched in a number given to him in Boston, at the FBI Field Office in Chelsea.

Besides walking into the government's hands again, it was the only way he could think of of getting hold of Grey.

It was answered on the second ring by a slow, gravelly voice. 'Is this who I think it is?'

King said, 'Are you at a computer?'

A pause. 'I am. Luckily for you. It's late—'

'There's a Coast Guard MH-60 Jayhawk over Lubec, Maine right now. Find out which station they launched it from, and find out who authorised it. Do it now.'

Another pause. But Grey's career was built on crisis response. He was perhaps the best in the world at processing new information and reacting before his emotions could get in the way, before he could think to ask questions. *Act, don't think.* 'One moment.'

'It's urgent.'

King watched the boat. Jack's silhouette looked irritated,

talking animatedly at each of his men and occasionally jabbing a finger in one of their faces. Probably something along the lines of, *'You better be more professional than Brady.'* King couldn't make out a word over the distant thrum of chopper rotors, but that was a relief, as the same went for them. They wouldn't hear him on the phone, wouldn't sense his presence.

Vital seconds ticked by, and the boat didn't move. The chopper receded into the horizon and came to a hover far from shore, its bulk no more than a dot in the night sky. It fixed its spotlight on a specific point in the ocean. Only for a few seconds, but long enough for Jack to stop lambasting his crew and register the target. He nodded, more to himself than anyone else, and turned back to the men in the boat. The searchlight died moments later, indicating this was a familiar procedure. It had to have been done countless times before.

The sound of the chopper receded into nothingness until all that was left was the chugging of the boat motor. Thankfully, that was still loud enough to mask voices.

Someone on the boat stepped toward the wheel.

King said, 'Now, Grey.'

Maybe ninety seconds had passed since Grey requested a moment. The old man added another couple to that before he spoke. 'The Jayhawk was launched from Air Station Cape Cod. They also launched a boat from Coast Guard Station Southwest Harbour, but it's already been recalled. They mustn't have needed it, or its work must already be done. I don't have anything on why they were launched—'

'Don't worry,' King said. 'I'm looking at why they were launched.'

'The chain's complicated, but it seems to be a personal favour for Noah Dubois.'

King blinked in the dark. 'The fucking *governor* of Maine?'

'As far as I can tell, yes. He has some sort of personal connection to a petty officer. Is that—?'

'Thanks. That's enough.'

'Why do you need this?'

'I'm deciding what to do.'

'About what?'

'I'll be in touch.'

King ended the call, tucked the phone away, and worked rapidly through the information he had. There was so much to comprehend, and such little thread to make connections with. He'd been willing to leave it, to walk away from what may very well be a suicide mission, but with the governor and the Coast Guard in the mix, he simply couldn't let it fly.

He'd made a promise.

He drew his SIG, left the AR Five Seven behind, and took off sprinting.

It was only a few dozen feet from the tree line to the shore, and far less than that from the shore to the boat, through water only knee-deep. Jack was wrapping up his chastising, and one of the men had a hand on the wheel, ready to speed off. The motor still throbbed, though, loud enough to drown out King's steaming charge over the pebbles and through the water.

Finally their ears perked up as he sent geysers of water churning off his trouser legs with each step. By that point, he was feet from the boat's lip. They spun, panicked at the complete stranger hurtling toward them, but no one had a drawn weapon. There'd been business to attend to onboard, and they must have decided simply being armed was enough.

Now hands snatched for holsters.

King lurched forward and hurled himself up into the boat.

———————

21

King sent one of them flying as he tumbled in, knocking the man aside as the boat rocked violently underneath them.

The swaying made them all stumble.

It gave him that vital second to scramble to his feet, snatch Jack by the collar, and jam the SIG barrel into the soft flesh above the man's ear.

Everyone stopped what they were doing.

'Good,' King said, both projecting his voice and deepening it, hoping to instil fear. 'That's the right idea.'

It was suppressed, subdued chaos. A chorus of imprecations came from the four men, their profiles outlined under moonlight.

'*Shit—*'

'*What the fuck—*'

'*Oh my god—*'

The fourth man said nothing, just bristled. Same went for Jack. King stood behind the tall man, using his frame as a human shield, choking him hard with his own collar to dissuade him from getting any smart ideas.

King muttered in Jack's ear, 'Tell them to relax.'

Jack's face was scarlet, visible even in the lowlight. He spluttered, 'Relax. Jesus Christ, relax.'

No one moved.

'They don't want to,' King muttered. 'They want to be heroes.'

Jack gasped for breath.

King said, 'Tell them not to be heroes.'

Jack knew what was good for him, knew the strength of the grip at his neck. Nothing made men more complicit than physical force. Understanding you were outmatched was something primal, recognition of your place on the totem pole. Our egos want to resist, but survival instinct batters them down. It's only temporary, but King didn't need it to be permanent.

Jack addressed his men. 'Toss your weapons over the side.'

Someone said, 'Fuck no.'

King looked for the rebel. It was the fat man, the Sprinter's passenger. Up close, he wasn't as much of a teddy bear as King first thought. Behind the disarming double chin and bulging cheeks, his eyes were cold and soulless. Given that he'd accompanied Jack to the boat, he had to be second-in-command, and it showed. His words carried weight. Encouraged by his resistance, none of the other three followed Jack's instructions.

Things got tense.

Jack hissed, '*Now.*'

He could barely form the words, there was that much pressure on his throat. He was fighting to stay conscious, to keep blood moving to his brain.

King stared directly at the fat man. 'I don't want it to go that way.'

Small waves lapped gently at the hull.

The other three seemed confused at what was unspoken. *Go what way?*

The fat guy knew. It was all there in the eyes, a visceral understanding. King was offering a lifeline. An opportunity to let bygones be bygones. The prior disobedience could be forgotten. All he had to do was fall into line, toss his weapon over the side and pretend he'd never hesitated.

King hoped he was getting the message across: *I don't want to kill you.*

Too bad.

This is the hurt business.

You don't go soft.

So when the fat man whipped his gun up, teeth gritted as he aimed at Jack's face, King shot him through his double chin. The man had been planning to fire through Jack, killing his boss to hit King. He didn't get the chance. King wished he could leave it there, but the gunshots injected the boat with rabid energy, and within a half-second the others were ripping sidearms from holsters, crazed with adrenaline.

King threw Jack aside, took a double-handed grip on the SIG to steady his aim, and popped each of them in the head. He pumped the trigger as fast as he could, firing follow-up shots into throats and chests. Two of them pitched overboard, and one dropped where he stood. The fat man was still in the boat, too, facedown and lifeless.

King ejected the mag, slipped a fresh one from his utility belt with graceful deftness, and reloaded.

He turned to aim at Jack, expecting resistance.

He found the boss sitting on the long wooden bench at the back of the boat, slumped forward with his elbows on his knees. Jack had watched the bodies drop, and was still blinking, still processing what had happened. King aimed the SIG at his forehead.

Jack shook his head. 'Don't worry.'

He reached for his holster with two fingers in a pincer-like grip, the universal signal that he had no hostile intentions. He withdrew his piece — a Glock — between those two fingers like it was hot to the touch, and tossed it over the side.

The black water swallowed the weapon.

King said, 'You're smarter than them.'

Jack scratched his grey five o'clock shadow. He sniffed and cleared mucus from his throat in unison. 'They're dead and I ain't. I plan to keep it that way.'

His voice grated like sandpaper.

King said, 'That's up to me.'

Jack made a face. 'No shit, pal.'

King pointed away from shore with his free hand. 'What's out there?'

'You'll find out, won't you?'

'I'd prefer you tell me.'

'Do I have a choice?'

King didn't answer, and Jack gave a tiny smirk, fatalistic in nature.

King said, 'So?'

'Four men,' Jack said. 'They'll be small. Short and thin s'what I'm saying. They'll have guns, but they won't know how to use them. They'll be old cruddy things, too, probably AKs. It's that part of the world.'

King listened to the spiel in disbelief. He recalled the patch of ocean the Jayhawk hovered over, training its spotlight down onto...

Nothing.

Onto water.

King said, 'Out there?'

'You got it.'

'Show me.'

Jack shook his head. 'I'm not doing your dirty work for you.'

'*Now* you think you have a choice?'

'Yeah,' Jack said, the smirk growing into something genuine. 'Now I do.'

'You—'

Jack rose to his feet.

King trained the gun on him.

The wizened mechanic leapt off the side of the boat. He landed in the knee-deep water with a significant splash. Then, in no hurry whatsoever, he started wading to shore.

One slow step at a time.

His back to King.

King's guts twisted. He didn't want to do it, and he wasn't sure why. Maybe he'd killed enough for tonight. Maybe he was quickly becoming a relic for this line of work. But the classic line still rang true: beware of an old man in a profession where men usually die young.

So, although he hated to, he raised the SIG and shot Jack in the back of the head when he took his first step onto shore.

The boss pitched forward and lay still, having chosen the equivalent of suicide by cop.

22

Standing in the unsteady boat in the dark, with nothing but two corpses and his own thoughts for company, King grimly pulled his satphone back out and dialled Slater.

Who answered with, 'Here we go.'

King said, 'It's really bad.'

A pause of disbelief. 'Every time, man. Where are you?'

'Still in Lubec. But I don't know how this is going to go.'

'You need me?'

'It's too late,' King said, staring out into the darkness. 'By the time you get here, I'll have missed my window.'

'What window?'

'I'm still trying to figure out exactly what's going on. I've been in contact with Grey.'

'Oh, God.'

'I had no choice. I needed information.' King paused to take a breath and clear his mind. Then, carefully, taking care not to misremember anything, he relayed all Grey had told him. Air Station Cape Cod; Coast Guard Station Southwest Harbour; Noah Dubois. Those were the key details. When he was done, he said, 'If I don't make it through this, promise me you'll get answers from the governor. By any means necessary.'

'What are you about to do?'

The ocean at night was a terrifying behemoth, a void of unfathomable depth.

King said, 'I don't know. But seven men from the auto body shop are dead, and they all chose for it to go that way. They could have submitted, complied, and I'd have let them walk. So whatever consequences were waiting for them if they'd walked away, they were worse than a bullet from me.'

'Holy shit. They hit a *dog,* and that's what they got?'

'Tip of the iceberg.'

'Right.' Slater knew all about that. 'You want me to tell Violetta?'

'If you don't hear from me.'

'How long should I give it?'

King pictured the memory of the chopper's path, clear as day in his mind. 'No more than thirty minutes.'

'Good luck.' More to himself than King, he added, 'You're kidding...'

The line died.

King thought about calling her now, getting it out of the way, but it might affect his concentration for what was to come, and that was everything. Fearing a negative result often brings it into reality, so he tried not to think about what might take him by surprise out there. Instead of dwelling, he walked to the front of the boat and gripped the wheel. There was serious power in his hands; he could feel it.

He knew what he was commandeering: a go-fast boat. Made of an amalgamation of fibreglass and kevlar and carbon fibre, vessels like these were used to bring illegal goods to shore from beyond territorial waters. They were long and sleek with a viciously tapered hull, for the purpose of slipping through the Coast Guard's fingers. In this case, though, the Coast Guard was *with* them, and, more confusingly, there was nothing out there, no vessel in sight, no target.

Only a vague checkpoint.

Something primitive gnawed at King. An unshakeable notion of some great beast, hiding in the dark.

Before he could overthink it, he revved the propellor and took off away from the mainland. Maine — and with it, the rest of the continental United States — receded sharply from view, serving only to amplify his dread. Ocean spray came over the top of the glass shield as he picked up speed. The salt stung his eyes. He re-traced the searchlight's path from memory, steering into total blackness.

He was probably the hardest person on the planet to scare, but this struck a chord. Despite his best efforts to impose self-control, his brain drip-fed stress chemicals, making his heart race and the back of his neck hot to the touch. He was ready for a fight to the death with an invisible enemy.

He slowed as he approached the perimeter of the spotlight's final resting place. The surface of the ocean churned like it was angry and alive. He kept a hand on his SIG as he dragged the wheel in a semi-circular arc, letting the lights at the front of the boat pass over the water in a wide, sweeping motion.

Nothing.

Then something.

Out in the middle of the rippling waves.

He corrected course so the boat stopped turning and he leapt up, placing a boot on the hull's lip, steadying himself against the swaying as he took aim at the object. He considered firing a shot just in case, but there was such little information that he didn't trust himself. So he stood there, a statue on a rocking boat, until his eyes adjusted and he made out what it was.

A huge log.

Driftwood.

Ominous seconds passed. The moon shone in a cloudless sky, spreading silver across a surface that lived and breathed. It wasn't romantic. It was horrifying, providing just enough light for King's imagination to run wild.

It wasn't a coincidence. The log bobbed on top of the water, dead centre of where the Jayhawk last shone its spotlight. The chopper had revealed it to Jack and his men. Why? It was an old hunk of wood.

Only it wasn't.

After nothing happened, King revved the propellor and drifted a little closer. More detail became apparent, illuminated by the cigarette boat's small spotlight and the all-encompassing moonlight.

Details like the shiny, reflective surface underneath the wood, revealing it was fake.

It was a buoy, made to look like a tree trunk bobbing on the surface. A huge, hollow container was suspended underneath by winches.

Containing what?

And deposited by whom?

King knew immediately what this was, and the realisation hammered home with a thud in his chest. His view broadened, expanded, taking in things he hadn't noticed before, things he'd glossed over.

Like the enormous shape looming a couple of hundred

feet behind the log, further out to sea. It was semi-submerged, but King knew what to look for.

He'd dealt with the cartels too often for one lifetime.

The shape shifted as a wave broke over it, and ocean water foamed and sluiced off its broad hull.

King saw it for exactly what it was.

A submarine.

23

"Submarine" was too flattering a term.

The government had briefed King on narcosubs multiple times, back when he was in service. Publicly, they'd been a problem for the Coast Guard (and therefore America) since 2006, when the first vessels were "officially" seized, but the covert world had known of their existence since the late eighties. King had never physically seen one, but he knew intimate details of their design, and much about where they came from. It had been more than a decade since those briefings, but certain things are unforgettable.

Certain things strike you with such disbelief that you'll be able to recite them at a moment's notice.

Internally, he did so now, fixated on everything they'd told him.

He couldn't help it.

Anything to offset the dread of the huge semisubmersible hovering out there. It was the stuff of nightmares. He couldn't communicate with the crew, couldn't find out what he was dealing with. He just had to imagine.

He directed the spotlight out that way, and the gleam glinted off something reflective. Glass.

King froze. There was a viewing port out there, built into the top of the submarine, a third of the vessel hovering just above the ocean's surface. So whoever they were, they had eyes on him. But it was pitch black, and they had no lights, and he was shining a light at *them*.

Which meant they'd see a silhouette, same height as Jack. King was a far broader man, dense with corded muscle, but could they make that out with such poor visibility? King had presented his profile for a good thirty seconds or so, standing up on the lip.

And he hadn't taken any action like Jack would.

He hadn't started hauling up packages from the container beneath the buoy, packing the cigarette boat for the first run to shore. King guessed it would have taken Jack and his men a dozen trips to unload it all, maybe more. There had to be at least five tons of drugs down in the depths, most likely resting in a hollowed-out torpedo. The submarine would have towed the torpedo all the way from South America, and when they arrived they would have used winches to release the buoy to the surface, signalling it was time for Jack to come and collect.

The log was a beacon for the payload lurking beneath it, and the submarine was sitting back and watching.

Rage began to burn, deep in King's core.

It was hard enough for the average civilian to resist temptation in this day and age, what with the advancement of technology and the use of both food and dopamine as psychological weapons. The world's best neuroscientists and advertisers were paid by the largest corporations to make life as easy as possible, with the aim of killing the desire to struggle day-to-day. With social media, dating apps, and food delivery services, everything was *right there,* immediately accessible, and that can make you miserable when you realise there's no challenge left in your life. So the cartels were taking advantage of the burden of modern life by making hard drugs — literal poison — as accessible as fast food or porn. Vulnerable, unhealthy people make the best and most devoted customers, so the narcos would do anything (building their own shoddy submarines, for example) to get their product into the country without detection.

The war on drugs was an infinitely complex and likely unsolvable problem, but King was looking at something simple, straightforward. There was at least a hundred million dollars worth of cocaine or heroin below the buoy, ready to be carted off to Lubec Body Works, whereupon it would be distributed all across Maine, up the noses and into the arms of America's lost souls, accelerating their journey to early graves.

Stripping what little hope was left from them, not allowing them something as meagre as a chance.

Hence King's anger.

He waited, in no hurry to be the first to move. The semi-submersible stewed in the water for a long few minutes. King kept the cigarette boat steady. He didn't move another inch toward the buoy, hunching behind the wheel like he was hesitant, racked with trepidation. Hopefully they'd think Jack had cold feet. They'd wonder where the rest of his men were.

Or maybe they already knew that King was an imposter.

The sub rumbled and moved forward. King felt its size in the water beneath him, like some prehistoric mega-shark. Uncontrollable shivers worked their way down his spine.

The sub trawled toward him, drawing parallel with the

buoy. Its nose, invisible below the surface, was probably only a dozen feet from the side of the cigarette boat.

King's brain screamed a clear command: *Don't fucking do it.*

He did it.

Gripped his SIG tight, took a huge, bounding step, and leapt off the side of the boat, arms outstretched, thrusting forward with the hips.

He cleared considerable distance and came down, bracing for impact.

Boots thudded on slippery metal, and he skidded for a moment, but kept his footing. His heart thrashed in his chest.

He tried not to think about what he'd done.

Way out in the Gulf of Maine, on top of a narco-submarine, and already the cigarette boat had drifted away, out of reach. If this went to hell, he'd have to swim for the go-fast boat in all his gear. He'd probably sink and drown before he reached it.

Which made it do or die.

He ran along the top of the sub as it lurched beneath him, beelining for the hatch.

If he didn't make it in time, they'd open it from the inside and cut him down. He had no cover.

Six feet from the hatch, the door swung up and a dark figure materialised.

24

King was first to act.

First to capitalise.

Jack had told the truth about the crew's inexperience. They had plenty of time to empty the contents of an AK-47 into King. They only got the jump on him by a couple of seconds, but in this world, that's enough. Instead of shooting, King saw the man who'd opened the hatch squinting, trying to make out King's features as he charged toward the opening. The guy was wishing for it to all be okay, maybe even praying: *Please be a mix-up. Please be Jack.*

King hurled the hatch door all the way open and aimed his SIG in the man's face.

The guy froze, staring up with his neck craned, one hand gripping the ladder he stood on and the other awkwardly balancing his Kalashnikov rifle on his knee. Moonlight added a touch of silver to the darkness, enough to discern features. His skin was mahogany, his appearance Creole in nature, some blend of African and European. He was a small man, short and lean, all skin and bone. He wore a filthy pullover. His wide eyes gave him the appearance of an addict, but King presumed it was a result of living in a sealed box for two or three weeks.

Indiscernible yelling and the racket of general commotion came from underneath the man, deeper in the bowels of the sub.

The other crew members, panicking, shouting questions.

The man on the ladder stayed right where he was. Horrified, he stared past the gun barrel, into King's eyes.

In one maximum-effort motion, King reached down, snatched a tight grip around one of his skinny arms, and hauled his entire bodyweight up out of the hatch. It took all available physical effort, and at the very end of the action, his boot slipped on the sub's slick hull.

They both toppled.

The ocean reared up in King's vision as he fell toward it. His adrenaline hit its peak. Terrified by the notion of plunging into the sea and losing any advantage he might still have, he held onto the fibreglass for dear life, scratching at it to find any sort of purchase. He found something to stop the slide, some meagre grip, and hurtled back to his feet. The Creole man lay on the other side of the hull, arms and legs flapping for purchase too. He was weaponless, his AK-47 lost to the churning sea.

King did what he could to rectify the situation.

Stomped across the hull, pulled the guy to his feet, and spun him toward the open hatch. No one else had emerged; the mouth was a dark maw.

King aimed his SIG over the man's shoulder. He shouted into the man's ear to be heard over the waves. '*Tell them I don't want to kill them and I mean no harm.*'

The man's lips flapped, too shocked to process.

King hadn't a clue if he spoke enough English to understand. '*Tell them!*'

The man hesitated, then screamed, '*Il ne te veut aucun mal!*'

What? King thought. *French?*

Before he had time to process the unexpected language, a war cry emanated from within the sub.

I don't think they believe you, he thought, but there was no use saying it.

No use doing anything but trying to survive.

A silhouette appeared from the hatch, racing up the ladder and bringing another bulky rifle up to fire. King shot him once in the head and his deadweight clattered against the rungs and off the walls as his body dropped back down.

The man he was using as a human shield panicked, started writhing against King's grip.

King let him go and kicked him away.

The last two men came up the ladder together, sandwiched shoulder-to-shoulder in the impossibly tight tube. They were trying to overwhelm him, but they must have forgotten their own inexperience. In the chaos, gripped by total confusion, they bumbled up into fresh air, and the first man to get his wits about him panicked and emptied a burst of automatic rounds into the first shape he saw.

His own crewmate.

The Creole man, the one whose desperate eyes King had seen something in, something that deemed him worthy of a chance, fell back off the hull as bullets stitched his chest, ripping the pullover to shreds. The ocean swallowed him, all trace of him erased.

King fired two clinically precise rounds: *pop-pop.*

Both heads snapped back, and there was sudden stillness.

The sub continued to rock underneath his boots, but there was no tension, no fight left. Even the ocean seemed to pause, its incessant stewing receding, allowing something close to quiet.

Everyone was dead.

All of them, bar a single warehouse worker King hadn't the stomach to put a bullet in.

He stood atop a now-unmanned narco-submarine, idling beside a hollowed-out torpedo it had carted from South America, the payload packed with nine figures worth of hard drugs and kept afloat by a fake log.

If he told Dawn Cates the truth, he wondered whether she'd believe him.

25

T oo stunned to form thoughts, King looked around for the cigarette boat.

No sign of it, not in the immediate vicinity. It had drifted away, lost to the night.

He crouched on the fibreglass so as not to topple off. Pensiveness overcame him. He tried to think deeply, even as his racing mind fought to make it seem like the world was crashing down around him.

He could call it in. An operation as colossal and unbelievable as this ... Grey could crack it wide open. Squeeze out the corruption festering in Maine's Coast Guard, lock the governor in a room (unofficially, of course) and sweat him until he spilled his secrets...

It was simple enough, and having the old man on King's side would do wonders.

And then? he asked himself.

But he knew what then. Then, nothing would change. The subs would keep coming, three or four at a time churned out of some shipyard each month, somewhere along the north coast of South America. There were roughly five thousand miles of open ocean between there and here, the easternmost point of the United States. It seemed simpler to ship the drugs up to Mexico and then smuggle them over the border, but the extra fuel costs to increase the narco-subs' range must be worth it for some opaque and exclusive deal with the governor here, and by extension (through personal favours) the Coast Guard.

King didn't want to begin deciphering the puzzle, so he used his wicked memory to recall the government briefings from all those years ago. It took an event like this to realise he'd never truly forgotten them.

Back in the pivotal early days of his black-ops career, the focus had been on Colombia. Over a decade ago, the choking coastal waterways weaving through Colombia's jungles were believed to be the only place the cartels dared construct the submarines in covert, hastily-built shipyards. They'd been estimated to cost $2 million each back then, so King couldn't imagine what sort of budget they'd run nowadays. More importantly, they were horrendously profitable.

He estimated the sums in a present-day climate. If this sub cost, say, $5 million, but carried ten tons of cocaine at $25,000 a kilogram, for a street value somewhere around $225 million, then the sub itself cost a measly two percent of the money they stood to make. Which reminded him of what else the government told him: the subs were usually single-use. They were built to get to the final destination, and no further. An onboard "scuttle valve" fills the sub with water, sinking it long before it can become evidence. The ocean floor holds countless untold secrets.

He got curious. Technology had advanced since then. Was this one intended to be reusable? He was no expert, but its size was formidable, and from the outside the design and engineering seemed solid, structurally sound.

An idea began to form.

He didn't call it in, didn't even think of contacting Grey.

His satphone stayed in its holster as he trotted across the hull and mounted the ladder, rungs slick with blood.

He descended before he could think twice.

Down into the belly of the beast.

26

Junior was old enough to comprehend *PAW Patrol*.

A significant milestone, really.

Violetta only made the discovery a couple of days back, flicking through channels on the wall-mounted television until she came across an episode of the kids' show concerning a snow monster. Maybe it was the similarity to his new surroundings, but Ryder and the Paw Patrol seized all Junior's concentration, his mouth hanging open as those baby blues flickered between each of the cartoon canines.

It was three in the morning and they were both up, Junior unable to sleep and Violetta needing something to distract him, soothe him back to slumber. Soft lamp lighting kept the living room cosy, and she'd enabled a setting on the TV that added a reddish-amber hue to *PAW Patrol,* masking the harsh blue light that keeps you awake and disrupts your circadian rhythm.

She was discovering all sorts of tips and tricks these days. Parenthood simplifies life, makes what's good for your child the only thing in the world.

Well, for her, at least.

She'd accepted this new chapter of her life, accepted the phasing-out of what she used to do, what she used to *be*. She couldn't begin to understand how King balanced it all. She'd seen his all-consuming desire to protect his own family, but the need to protect others still blazed in him. He was doing his best to juggle it all, trying to both be there for his son and also help innocent people he'd never met, good folk preyed upon by monsters.

Bleary-eyed, she held Junior and zoned out, drifting away...

Her phone buzzed beside her.

Contact name: KING SAT.

Not a call from his usual number; he was somewhere without reception, using the satellite phone.

Trepidation brewing inside her, she answered. 'You on your way back?'

'Not just yet.' He sounded shellshocked, a tinge of disbelief in his voice.

'Still in Lubec?'

'Sort of. I'm out at sea.'

'What?'

'I'm...' He hesitated. 'I'm in a narco-submarine.'

She sat bolt upright. She was no fool; she'd handled black-ops for much of her adult life. He didn't need to dumb it down or explain what it meant. 'What the *fuck*?'

Instinct told her to cover Junior's ears, but it was too late for that. He was oblivious anyway, smiling as one of the PAW Patrol sped down a ski slope on-screen.

'The auto body shop was storage for the cartels,' he said matter-of-factly. 'Lubec Body Works was owned by some guy called Jack Michaud. He and his men were assigned to unload narco-sub payloads and hide them away until I assume they were distributed all across Maine, at truck stops and street corners and dive bars.'

'How big a payload are we talking?' Her knowledge of cartel submarines was adequate but not extensive.

'I didn't know for sure until I got down here. But the interface was simple enough to figure out, and my French is passable. There's nine tons of weight inside the torpedo, so that's, what, two hundred million dollars of product if it's coke? They were dragging the thing behind them the whole way, keeping it afloat with a ballast system. There's chambers I have control over, on the screen here in front of me. I can pump water in or push air out to sink the torpedo or make it surface. I'm guessing they sink the thing down deep when they're near the authorities, when they're most at risk of detection. And there's some sort of radio-buoy system, but I can't make much sense of it.'

Violetta's brain lit up, dots connecting. 'Is there a buoy above the torpedo?'

'Yeah. They've made it look like a piece of driftwood.'

'That's for if they need to dump the payload in the ocean and pick it back up later.'

A pause. 'Oh. Right.'

'There'll be a transponder inside the buoy for transmitting a signal. That way, if they think they might get intercepted, they can bail on it at a moment's notice. Obviously it's incriminating if they're caught in a homemade submarine, but if there's no drugs onboard, it makes things tricky. And if they evade capture, I'm sure the transponder emits a signal only their boats could pick up, so they're safe to go back and find it and carry on their journey.'

Another pause. She sensed his marvel. He said, 'Sometimes I forget what you used to do.'

'I was in as deep as you and Will were,' she said. 'Just in a different way.'

He sighed, then went quiet. She could tell he was focusing hard. After a long beat, he said, 'The crew could dump this thing at a moment's notice? That means I can, too.'

'And where *are* the crew?'

'Took me forever to get the bodies up the ladder.'

'Jesus, Jason.'

'I didn't instigate it.'

'What, you told them you'd do them no harm if they came out with their hands up?' she said sarcastically.

'Actually, that's exactly what I said.'

'You're serious?'

'Deadly.'

She paused. 'Fatherhood's softened you.'

'I doubt that.' Hesitation. 'Everyone from the auto body shop had to go.'

She'd never had a dramatic flair, but she couldn't help covering her mouth with her hand. 'Same story?'

'I wanted to get to the bottom of it without violence. But … it was me or the cartels. They made their choice.'

She understood. Better a merciful bullet than surviving and having to answer to the narcos. 'Are you okay?'

'I think I'm in shock.'

He never would have confessed that before. As time passed, he was becoming wiser, more in tune with his emotions. She could see him evolving day by day. 'At the killing?'

She already knew it wasn't that. Killing those who deserved it was nothing to him. Nothing to any of them.

'At the scale of this,' he said. 'I've got remote control of a torpedo holding nine tons of coke. Nine *tons*. And this is just one run...'

'What are you going to do with it?'

He said, 'Hold on.'

She heard fiddling, a hand against a lever, fingers against a screen, *tap-tap-tapping*.

He said, 'It's done.'

'What's done?'

'The payload was already cut away from the sub, so I retracted the winches to pull the buoy back down, then filled the ballast system's chambers with water. It was simple enough.'

Her eyes widened. 'You sunk it?'

'Two hundred million dollars at the bottom of the ocean,' he said. 'And the night's still young.'

'Now what?'

He said nothing.

Concern stewed in her. 'Is this one of your infamous bad ideas?'

'Are they bad if I manage to pull them off every time?'

'Yes,' she said. 'Absolutely they are.'

27

D awn.

An important day.

Slater rolled out of bed. Aside from the brief interruption to field King's call in the middle of the night, he'd slept soundly. The first cracks of light materialised in the dark blue sky outside, heavy as a blanket as it hovered over the house. He kept silent, letting Alexis sleep a while longer, and padded quietly to the garage.

He found Tyrell there, already dripping sweat, thrashing himself on a Rogue Echo Bike that Slater had ordered weeks ago and had finally arrived on Friday. The assault bike's handles added resistance, making you work all the muscles of your arms and legs in unison. If you pushed hard, the experience was accurately described as torture.

Slater noted the puddle of perspiration on the concrete beneath Tyrell. 'Relax. It's your first day of school. You don't want to be exhausted.'

Tyrell shook his head, panting. 'I'm good. It's all mental, right?'

Slater smirked. 'To an extent, yeah.'

Tyrell took a hand off one of the grips to tap the side of his head. 'I'm putting it into practice. What you said up Mount Katahdin.'

Slater took a mental step back to afford him an objective look at the teenager. Tyrell was far from the skinny, stooped child Slater had inherited a little over half a year earlier. Slater couldn't take full credit; puberty had broadened the boy's frame, starting to shape him into the man he'd eventually develop into. As for the rest of the changes, Slater and Alexis alone were responsible for those: the young sinewy muscle rippling across his frame, the open, curious eyes, the relaxed demeanour, the decrease in suspicion of everyone and everything. Slater and Alexis had fought like demons to change his worldview, but they'd had to do it subtly. Anything overt, they knew, Tyrell would have rejected. They'd shown him a new way to live, but hadn't forced him into it. They'd led by example and hoped like hell he'd catch on.

He hadn't just caught on: he'd attacked every task they'd suggested with fervour.

Now look at you, kid.

Slater said, 'You worried about anything?'

Tyrell gave the bike a final thrashing, maximising his output until the built-in fan was roaring instead of whirring, then let go of the grips and eased off the pressure. His chest heaved. 'Like making friends?'

'Sure.'

Tyrell shook his head. 'Nah. I'll make friends. Not hard. Just gotta have your shit together and show interest in whatever people are doing. Right?'

'Right.'

'Danielle's asking when I'll be back in Boston. Says she misses me.'

Slater watched the teenager clamber off the bike, stagger across the garage and fetch a towel to wipe his face.

Slater said, 'You miss her?'

A long pause. 'I think I do, yeah.'

'So there's something there?'

'I dunno. Might be. Didn't really get to know her. Was too distracted...'

Slater scoffed. 'Teenagers are usually allergic to talking to their parents about this stuff.'

'Yeah, but you ain't my dad,' Tyrell said with a wink.

The wink said everything. *You know what you are. You're more than my dad.*

'Get through this first week of school,' Slater said. 'Put more effort in than you want to. In every aspect. Then we'll go back to Boston for the whole weekend.'

Tyrell hesitated. 'Really? You'll drive me to another state for some girl? I'm thirteen.'

'That's what most parents would say. *"There's plenty of fish in the sea. Don't be a whiner."* But *I* say that's selfish. You just got the courage to do more than talk with Danielle, and I moved you way up north at the worst possible time. That's my fault. So you keep crushing your goals like I see you doing, and I'll do a whole lot more than drive you to Boston.'

There wasn't a pause so much as an extended silence. Slater could see Tyrell wrestling with emotion under the surface, trying not to let it climb to his face. Finally the boy said, 'I ain't ever had anyone think about me.'

'I know.'

Slater's phone buzzed at his hip, vibrating through his sweatpants. It wasn't even six in the morning. He didn't have to take it out to know who was calling, and his core tightened involuntarily, a reflex reaction to the dark side of the world, the side he couldn't avoid if he tried.

Somehow, Tyrell noticed the microscopic changes in posture. 'You expecting bad news?'

Slater rolled his eyes. 'Get ready for school.'

He left the garage and strode into the kitchen so he was out of earshot before he pulled it out and answered the call. The contact name flashed on the screen: SATPHONE KING.

'You're alive?' he asked.

'I'm in a submarine,' King said. 'I'll be gone for three weeks. I'm taking it back to French Guiana.'

Slater had a learned knack for taking outrageous news in his stride, but even he couldn't help saying, 'You're doing fucking *what*?'

28

S ure, Slater had expected there to be more to it than just the auto body shop, but this...?

'Don't worry.' King's voice came through the receiver, clear and calm. 'I've cleared it with Violetta.'

'Oh, yeah,' Slater said, rolling his eyes to himself. '*That's* what I'm worried about.'

King laughed. The noise was surreal, considering the circumstances.

Slater said, 'Care to fill me in?'

Fifteen minutes later, he was leaning against the marble countertop of the kitchen island, shaking his head slowly from side to side. All he could think to say was, 'French Guiana?'

'I'd only vaguely heard of it,' King said. 'I'm sure most people don't even know it exists. It's an overseas department of France, between Suriname and Brazil. Thank God for active satellite subscriptions; otherwise I'd be down here with no internet connection, swimming around in the dark.'

'What else are you working with down there?'

'It's straightforward enough. A wheel, dials, and a

screen, all for handling navigation and the state of the engine. Enough canned goods, Gatorade, and bottled water to last me more than a month. A cargo hold entirely filled with duffel bags of cash. I'm talking mountains of the stuff. Got to be the two hundred million or so that the drugs are worth, but I don't understand how it's already onboard.'

Slater said, 'The boat.'

'What?'

'You said the Coast Guard launched one, but it was recalled. From the Southwest Harbour station. They'd have brought the cash before Jack's crew arrived to unload the coke.'

King absorbed this. 'Your memory's even better than mine.'

'Why the torpedo? Why not just bring the coke in the cargo hold instead of dragging the payload behind them?'

'The hold's mid-sized. You're not fitting any significant amount in there. Cash is smaller than tons of coke. If I had to guess, they sacrificed cargo space for more fuel. Last I heard of these things, their maximum range was three and a half thousand miles or so. This one I'm standing in can do five thousand plus. And the tank's full, so they already refuelled before I arrived. The Coast Guard boat would've brought the fuel *and* the cash.'

Slater couldn't think straight, his mind too warped by the revelations. 'Wait, Violetta said she was *fine* with this?'

'It's the opportunity of a lifetime,' King said. 'It's simple enough for me to feign an issue with the phones, pretend the crew can only communicate with their handlers back home via their encrypted messaging software. This thing was built in the jungles of French Guiana, for God's sakes. Tech problems are part and parcel of the experience. And they were lazy; the captain's satphone has no password. I already replied in French to a text from an unknown number who appears to be their boss. I said I'm on the way back with the money and the phones are bad, and that I'll be in touch soon. They said "OK."'

'You're doing five thousand miles in an underwater box when you could just jump on a plane.'

'It's semi-submersible,' King corrected. 'So not fully underwater.'

'Not the fucking point.'

'I abandon all this and jump on a plane and the jig's up. Anyone important will scatter long before I land. But if I keep up appearances, the men that matter in French Guiana will come out of the woodwork. I'm bringing them two hundred million dollars, after all, and they have no way to confirm who's onboard other than asking me to send a selfie, which they sure aren't gonna do.'

Slater said nothing.

King said, 'There's a gaping hole in their defences and all I have to do is sit in this piece of shit for three weeks.'

Slater sighed. 'So...?'

'So what?'

'You need to keep up appearances. I understand.' He paused. 'What do you need me to do?'

'Clean up the mess I left behind.'

'How bad?'

'A few bodies in the woods, but that's not so important. They'll rot before anyone stumbles across them. But it's nearly daylight and all their vehicles are still lined up along the shore. Sprinter vans and pickup trucks. Four of them. You still know how to hot-wire?'

'Maybe I remember a thing or two. It'll take me hours to get there, though.'

'That's okay. There's no one left to investigate, not from

Jack's crew. And if the Coast Guard boat was recalled in a hurry, then whoever's behind this is being very cautious with using their resources. Too much misappropriation would be noticed. An occasional favour can fly under the radar if you know the right people, but anything more...'

It turned Slater's thoughts to a different avenue. *Whoever's behind this.*

'Noah Dubois is French, isn't he?' Slater said. 'The governor.'

A moment's silence from the other end of the line. 'He is too.'

'Sounds like I've got three weeks to sniff around. You want me to chase leads?'

'It'd be a help. But don't do anything drastic. You start offing well-known politicians and there'll be nothing left in French Guiana by the time I get there. They'll bail if they smell trouble.'

'An operation as big as this? You think they'll just pack up shop?'

'Did Black Force ever brief you on narco-subs?'

Inwardly, Slater reeled. Any mention of the shadow organisation he served for most his adult life mustered a reflexive recoiling, an allergy to anything that might so much as suggest getting dragged back in. After a pause, he said, 'No. Were you?'

'A couple of times. I never encountered one, though.'

'Chasing submarines sounds a little more espionage-oriented than the sort of work I was suited for. They used me as a wrecking ball, not a dagger.'

'I was far from a dagger.'

'But you obviously had the capacity for it.'

'As you do now.'

'We all get older. Wiser. More patient.'

King said, 'Exactly.'

It made sense. At first, the idea of three weeks in a home-made submarine had sounded like insanity, but the more Slater thought about it, the more the isolation and tension of such a trip seemed an inconvenience rather than a genuine difficulty.

He and King were bred for stressful situations.

If all it took for a competitive advantage was a little discomfort, that was a price they were both more than happy to pay.

Slater said, 'I'll leave now for Lubec. Stay in touch.'

He hung up, and on the way out of the house, he passed Alexis in the hallway. Her eyes, heavy with concern, revealed she'd been in earshot toward the end of the phone call. 'King needs you at the auto body shop?'

He placed his hands on her shoulders and took a breath. 'It's so much more than that. I'll call you on the way and explain, but I need to get going.'

She nodded.

'You okay to drop Tyrell at school?'

'Of course. Will you be in danger?'

Slater shook his head. 'No. Save all your worry for Jason.'

Before she could ask follow-up questions, he was out the door, jogging through the freezing morning air for the Range Rover.

29

Cramped.
Cold.
Dark.

Miserable.

The flat tops of the gas tanks were fashioned that way deliberately, for the crew to use as beds. King rested his bulk on the edge of one of the tanks, taking the weight off his legs as he gently reached out to steer the submarine. Every so often he'd glance through the periscope up the conning tower, steering by sight. The satellite GPS and compass on-screen beside the wheel practically navigated for him; otherwise he'd have nothing to go off but the sight of the churning surface of the ocean and the unchanging horizon, expanding infinitely into the distance.

A few hours in and there was nothing but the tiniest speck of progress on the GPS.

It helped him understand just how small and insignificant he was.

He sat in monastic silence and tried not to think too much.

If he put his mind to the idea of more than twenty consecutive days in this janky underwater tube, with nothing but his own thoughts for company, he'd tear his hair out. Thankfully, he was well-versed in the art of making decisions that came with immense cost to his own sanity and wellbeing, so he knew how to grapple with the intrusive thoughts that rolled in without mercy.

This is so fucking ridiculous. Even if you don't get intercepted by the authorities in international waters and thrown in prison for drug-trafficking, you'll still be relying on a hastily-concocted plan. Who's to say the men responsible will come anywhere near the sub when you get to French Guiana? You're risking your life and your freedom for no guaranteed payoff.

Which didn't deter him.

That's what he'd done most of his life, after all.

So he ignored his brain's negative loop and focused on physical details, better familiarising him with the space. If you were in any way claustrophobic, simply sitting in this mostly-submerged vessel would give you heart palpitations, making your throat tighten, your chest constrict. At six-foot-three, he only had several inches of space between his scalp and the curved roof. Obviously there were no windows, no sunroof. Weak light bars fixed in the roof cast eerie shadow, the electricity that powered them provided by a generator beside the engine. This generator kept everything functioning, recharging the batteries for the satellite and comms, plus the UHF and GPS gear. King had already shut down all the comms he could find, so those back in French Guiana would believe him when he maintained a dialogue about phone issues over the next three weeks.

The intrusive thoughts didn't stop. They switched gears, in fact, tried to find a new angle.

Do you think you're achieving anything? You've said it your-

self a hundred times before: you'll never stop the drugs. Kill every trafficker in South America and they'll be replaced within the week. Your chance of success is slim, and the payoff is pointless. So what the fuck are you doing here? You have a young boy. Go home to him. Be there for him like any sort of decent father should.

But there were decent fathers all across Maine, stuck in dead-end jobs and dead-end lives, trying to resist the temptation to put a line up their nose or a needle in their arm. Fighting to stay away from something that would stop their existential pain. Trying to do right for their families.

This payload alone would have broken hundreds, if not thousands, of them.

So if the cartels were fighting to make hard drugs easy to access, King could fight right back. He could send a message. Show them what might happen in future if they kept getting caught with their guard down. Even though it may mean nothing in the long run, to King it meant everything.

The intrusive thoughts settled, and monotony sunk in. Without stimulus, the brain can sabotage itself; hence why solitary confinement is such a severe punishment for prisoners. King sat and steered and stared into space. He wondered how many of the twenty-plus days would be uneventful.

Suddenly, he drifted, and when he blinked, time had elapsed.

How long, he couldn't be sure.

He was disciplined, but human; not a robot. There were supposed to be four crew members down here: the first man (the captain) to steer and navigate, the second to assist with navigation, the third to watch the engine, and the fourth to watch the cargo. King couldn't give a shit whether the dirty money made it to French Guiana intact or not, so the fourth position was moot, but the second and third were crucially important roles that he'd just have to do without. Maintaining concentration for such a long stretch is next to impossible, especially after the night he'd had. Adrenaline faded, fatigue set in, and his aching body and mind pined for rest.

So he'd lost focus.

And a deep rumbling snapped him out of it.

He wasn't sure if he actually sensed it. He swore he could feel it in the water, a great presence nearby, on the other side of those Kevlar and fibreglass walls. His heartbeat seemed to resonate in the space. It thumped in his throat.

He snatched for the periscope and swivelled it, peering out over the ocean's surface.

He panned past gentle waves, across a still horizon...

There.

A huge manmade object, looming, growing in size each second.

Approaching on the starboard side.

No time to see what it was exactly. A small speaker built into the navigation interface shrieked, warning of an imminent collision far too late. The tinny alarm screeched. King killed the acceleration and pulled to the port side hard.

The sub shook, rattled.

The walls moaned.

Beneath him he sensed the infinite depth of the North Atlantic Ocean. He couldn't help picturing how far the journey down would be, couldn't resist imagining the narco-sub splitting in two upon impact, the walls of water rushing in, battering him and seizing him and dragging him down, down, endlessly down...

The sea trembled and the sub protested but the enormous vessel passed by. King waited with impossible tension for the impact.

It didn't come.

When it was over, he used the periscope again, got a good look at the stern of an oil tanker receding into the distance. The ship was the size of a small island. He wouldn't have experienced the impact so much as been obliterated by it.

And if the tanker had seen the top of his semi-submersible as it passed by and called it in...

It would take tremendous luck for the news to be stifled by the corrupt faction of the Coast Guard.

If they came after him, he was finished.

So began the waiting game.

30

S later followed King's instructions to a tee and was staring at a row of four large vehicles on a pebble shore before ten a.m.

The scene was untouched, deserted. A grey sky hung over the beach, and a body bobbed facedown in the shallows. No blood in sight; the gentle lapping waves had washed away the crimson. Maybe there'd be a handful of visitors to West Quoddy Head Lighthouse today, but they wouldn't dream of turning off South Lubec Road, taking the winding dirt track to this featureless and unimpressive stretch of coast. The only chance of detection was from "Quoddy House," a historic private rental only a few hundred feet west, but in all likelihood it wasn't occupied, and if it was, there was an impenetrable swathe of forest between the green fields and the dirt track that Slater stood on.

He got to work.

The body had keys stuck to the inside of a water-logged pocket, and Slater counted his blessings. In the other pocket he found a drenched smartphone, a very recent model, one he thought might be waterproof. He tried to power it on and the screen lit up, revealing a wallpaper of Jack arm-in-arm with a heavily-tattooed, heavily-overweight woman. Slater grimaced; he tried not to fixate on the second-order consequences of an operation, but now they were staring him in the face. He wondered if she'd known what her man really did for work.

The soggy corpse went in the back of one of the Sprinter vans, and Slater took each of the vehicles cross-country, driving them one by one directly into the woods, squeezing between trees. He hid the vans and pickups so deep in the forest, traversing such rocky and unstable terrain in the process, that not even seasoned hikers would have a chance of finding them. He trashed the vehicles completely in the process, rocks and roots and fallen branches destroying suspension, disfiguring wheels, flattening tyres. Even if he wanted to, he couldn't have driven them out of the woods again.

When it was done, he clambered on foot back to the trail, soaked in sweat. It took thirty minutes to eliminate the tyre tracks, scrubbing the lines in the dirt from existence, and when he finally finished he dumped himself down on the pebble shore and surveyed the scene.

Not a trace of what had happened.

He dialled King's satphone and it stewed his guts, made him nauseous. He wasn't sure why until he realised everything was riding on the phone continuing to work. If something happened to the generator that prevented King from charging it, or it inexplicably stopped working halfway across the North Atlantic, he'd be stranded at sea with no means of communicating his predicament to anybody.

But King answered. 'Made it?'

'Made it. No one got to the scene before me.'

'You sure?'

'Positively. I'm not that rusty. I know what to look for.'

'Good. This might actually be feasible.'

'I have Jack's phone. The water didn't ruin it. It's pass-code-protected but I'll take it back to Violetta and get her to crack into it. From there, I'm sure I can figure out which contacts are related to his side hustle. I can feign some major emergency, send out texts saying I've got the payload but I think I'm in danger so I've gone to ground and won't be popping my head up for a while.'

'You think that'll buy us three *weeks*?'

'Probably not. But all you have to do is get to the top dogs in French Guiana, right? It doesn't matter how frustrated they are with the operation when you show up. Only that you're there when they do.'

'Yeah.'

'You made any progress on that? Sent any more messages off the captain's phone?'

'No. I've been preoccupied.'

'Oh?'

'I almost hit an oil tanker.'

Slater buried his face in his free hand, using the other to keep the phone pressed to his ear. He suppressed a groan. 'How is this going to work? I mean, seriously...'

'One step, one day at a time.'

'You got enough supplies?'

'You already asked me that. There's canned goods, remember?'

'Right, right. Sorry. Forgot. Too much shit to think about.' A pause. 'How are you gonna sleep?'

'In consistent short bursts. Never more than an hour or two at a time, spread evenly across each twenty-four hour period. I'll just kill the engine and get some rest; after the near-miss with the tanker I figured out how to increase the radius of the motion sensors, so I'll get a warning long before anything gets near me. I'm slowly figuring out what this thing's capable of. Turns out it's fully submersible when I want it to be. I can bring it down to sixty feet or so below the surface, but I'm not sure if I want to risk it. It seems straightforward enough, but my worst nightmare is not being able to figure out some simple command and getting stuck down there. I'm taking my crash course on submarining in real-time.'

'You're a lunatic.'

'Maybe. But the worst part was making the decision to start. As always…'

Slater understood that, at least. 'Right. Not so bad once you're in motion.'

'My brain was eating itself alive for a solid couple of hours, but the cobwebs are clearing. I'm settling in.'

'Good,' Slater said, standing up with a sigh. 'Now it's time for me to get to work.'

31

A three hour drive back to Millinocket gave Slater all the time in the world to coordinate a meet.

Rather than heading home, he drove straight to a diner on the outskirts of the small town. An icy afternoon shower fell as he hit the town limits. Dirty sleet accumulated atop the wipers, settling for a few seconds each time before they cleared the windshield with a spasm of motion. He pulled in next to Violetta and Alexis' vehicles, already resting side-by-side in the lot. A dusting of snow encapsulated both rides.

Slater slammed the driver's door as he stepped down and strode inside.

They were at a vinyl booth in the far corner, deep in intense conversation. Junior bounced on Violetta's lap, gazing dreamy-eyed around the busy room, pointedly disinterested in what the adults had to say. Hers was the only face Slater could see as he approached; Alexis had her back to him. Violetta didn't seem stressed, just focused. Slater supposed, for people like them, those two sensations were one and the same. An unusual level of focus meant something was important, and "important" in their world was guaranteed to come with an avalanche of stress.

Most things that matter do.

Slater slotted into the booth, taking the space beside Alexis, and touched her hip in greeting. But he couldn't look at her, couldn't take his eyes off Violetta's. 'You said *yes*?'

She rolled her eyes. 'He would've gone either way.'

'No,' Alexis said. 'He wouldn't have.'

Violetta said to her, 'You know him better than I do?'

Alexis raised her hands, feigning innocence.

'*I* know him,' Slater said. 'Maybe not better than you. But well enough to know if you weren't okay with it, he'd have stayed.'

Violetta gave him a look. 'You sure know what happened between you, him, and Grey.'

Slater stiffened. 'What'd he tell you?'

'That you came to some agreement in exchange for Grey's protective services. That the old man had some small part left of himself that was idealistic, that in some way he was trying to live vicariously through you and King. That he agreed to go back to work, to a job he detested for a country he no longer truly believed in, only if the pair of you took any opportunities you could to make a difference.'

Slater hesitated. 'Yeah. More or less, that's what he said.'

Alexis already knew this. She squeezed his hand under the table.

Slater said, 'King will be fine. He always is.'

'Correlation is not causation.'

Alexis said to her, 'We keep saying it's about time their luck ran out. We keep being wrong.'

Violetta shrugged. 'I *am* fine with it. Really. If I actually had a problem, I'd have protested. I'm not a pushover.'

Slater said, 'We know you're not.'

'But,' she continued, 'it makes me nervous. Because it's not about reaction speed, is it? I'm sure he can get to French Guiana and come up in some clandestine shipyard and massacre everyone there before they lay a finger on him. But three weeks getting there puts him at the mercy of the authorities. Doesn't matter how dangerous he is, if he's stuck in a tube, surrounded by the Coast Guard. And that's life in prison, even if he's dumped the drugs. He'll hardly be able to explain the money.'

'He'll be out of U.S. territorial waters soon,' Slater said. 'And the Coast Guard shouldn't be a problem, huh?'

Alexis stiffened beside him. 'You following that up?'

'As subtly as I can. Don't want to rock the boat before King reaches dry land.' He stared at Violetta. 'What do you know about the governor?'

'I've seen him on TV a couple of times. I know his name. That's about the extent of it.'

Slater didn't respond.

Violetta said, 'Since we got here, I've had bigger things to worry about than state politics.'

'We all have. But you're better at intel than I'll ever be. Can you try to find an opening for me?'

'You kidding? Of course I can.' She winked almost imperceptibly, one eyelash flitting. 'If I've got three weeks, I can probably get you a photo of Dubois posing next to a mountain of cocaine. I'm used to all this bullshit unfolding in the space of hours. When's the last time we formulated a long-term plan?'

It drew a smirk from both Slater and Alexis: the dark humour of shared trauma. Everything had been reactive since the day Slater met Tyrell and Violetta brought Junior into the world. First Mexico to pursue an ex-televangelist preacher, then California to pursue a psychopathic CEO, then Boston to defend themselves from a disillusioned and troubled black-ops crew, then avenging Alonzo, which brought the fight back here to Millinocket. All four events had unfolded uncontrollably, leaving them gasping for breath, surprised they were still alive at the end.

Now they could plan, scheme, put pieces in place.

It felt good.

Slater said, 'So we look for a way to get to the governor, find out what exactly his role is in all this, and we pray for King. That's about all we can do, right?'

Alexis said, 'Right.'

Violetta gave Slater a funny look. 'You've started praying?'

'No.'

She smirked.

He and Alexis rose. Alexis looked down at Violetta. 'You need anything, *ever,* you call me.'

Violetta smiled back, a touch sadly. 'This'll all be worth it. Look what he's done already. There's good people all across Maine who now can't get their hands on what was in the torpedo he sunk.'

'They wouldn't be appreciative,' Slater warned. 'They'll be withdrawing already.'

Violetta shrugged. 'No one who truly needs help is appreciative. They're in too deep for that.'

Slater nodded. 'It's a thankless business.'

'Which is the point,' Alexis said. 'It's why no one wants to do it.'

Violetta said, 'Except you, apparently. King, Slater, and I didn't seem to have much of a choice in the matter.'

Alexis tapped the side of her own head. 'Yeah you did. Doesn't matter where I started. The four of us aren't so different.'

Violetta's smile turned from sad to soft. 'I don't doubt that.'

Alexis left with Slater.

The whole way across the diner and out to the car, Slater couldn't shake a unique discomfort.

It felt strange, having time to breathe.

He almost felt sorry for Noah Dubois.

PART II

32

S even days at sea.

Sixteen hundred miles from Maine.

A third of the way there.

King hadn't gone mad yet, which was about the only silver lining he could find in the mind-numbing sameness of it all. After the oil tanker near-miss early in the voyage's first day, there'd been nothing, literally *nothing,* to the point where he was almost wishing for some tension to alleviate the emptiness. He was far beyond territorial waters, the U.S. Coast Guard a distant memory, such a way out in the North Atlantic that even looking at the GPS filled him with a strange dread.

He was about as far from civilisation as you could get.

In the middle of the world.

The island of Bermuda was the closest landmass, and today he would chug past and leave it behind, killing his last opportunity to bail on this whole plan. It was a straight shot through the North Atlantic from Maine to French Guiana, and Bermuda to his west was the only significant landmass before Puerto Rico and the rest of the Caribbean islands.

He'd considered dumping the sub off Bermuda's coast and scheming his way onto a flight back home, but at some point he crossed an invisible threshold, found himself in too deep, to the point where he wouldn't consider throwing away the effort he'd already put in.

This couldn't be for nothing.

No help would come for him. Distress calls would go unanswered. He had nothing, not an ounce of outside assistance. If he picked up the satphone and called Violetta or Slater, as he had many times over the last week, there was little they could do other than offer him words of reassurance, which meant nothing. He doubted even Grey could mount a rescue operation in a hurry, not without drawing considerable attention to diverted resources.

King was alone in every sense of the word.

Thanks to the absence of razors onboard, his heavy stubble would soon transition into a beard. He was filthy, coated in a dried layer of salt from the endless perspiration. His single pair of clothes reeked, but he'd become numb to the stench. The days had quickly grown muggy and stifling as he left Maine behind, and as he spent most of his time fussing over the engine and the generator and the conning tower, the sweat flowed uncontrollably. He only dared go up the ladder to relieve himself and splash himself with seawater when the sub was stationary. It gave him nightmares to think of slipping off the hull with the sub in motion, toppling into the ocean and watching his only lifeline rumble away.

Treading water until he lost his strength and sunk into the black depths of the ocean wasn't the way he wanted to go.

But it was a double-edged sword, as he was reluctant to stop any more than absolutely necessary. Each time he killed the engine, it meant a longer journey, and right now the prospect of more time in this coffin was enough to make him tear his hair out.

He regretted ever fucking agreeing to this.

It had been that way for three days now.

He'd spent a decade on ops in foreign countries, so canned meals and a lack of hygiene were nothing to write home about. He barely registered the discomfort; that wasn't the issue. It was the total lack of scenery, the fact he could sense the gargantuan weight of the water outside these walls, like an invisible crushing pressure. Days of monotony are fine when you're camped on a hillside doing recon, surveilling some hostile hotspot. You can change your view by simply looking around at the surrounding terrain, even get up and change your position when you know it's clear. There are freedoms you don't realise you have until you're trapped in a cramped box underwater, wishing for literally anything different. To top it off, King's sleep-wake cycle had been in ruins for a week now, compounding the stress, building the anxiety until it was something physical, the exhaustion putting weight on his chest, cooking nerves already so frayed.

He sat on the edge of his bed atop one of the gas tanks and adjusted the wheel a fraction, an action that had become a part of himself now. But he was still breathing. Neither the engine nor the generator had conked out. He didn't know whether that was out of sheer luck or because he was doing everything right, which also drove him mad. If this was a military submarine, with a crew who knew what they were doing, he wouldn't be fazed. Claustrophobia was no problem if he knew it was safe. But this was some home-made project, thrown together in a clandestine shipyard in the jungle, maybe only intended for a couple of uses...

...and he wouldn't know where to start if problems arose.

As he meditated on this, the captain's satphone buzzed an alert. The vibration made his heart leap, such was the shock of a disruption to routine. He snatched it off the top of the console and stared at the little screen.

A message from the unknown superior. King knew enough French to translate.

THINK I CAN GET THROUGH.

King read the words and said, 'Fuck.'

His voice cracked; he hadn't spoken out loud in twenty-four hours, not since he talked to Slater yesterday about leads on Noah Dubois.

A moment later, the phone shrieked in his hands.

An incoming call.

The same number.

The captain's boss.

33

H e thought he'd disabled the ability to receive calls.

He stared wide-eyed at the number flashing on the screen, thinking, *No, no, no.*

The phone kept buzzing in his hand.

He counted out the seconds, in each one wondering whether he was making a colossal mistake, if the only way forward was to answer and impersonate the captain as best he could. But there wasn't a hope in hell it would work. He'd barely heard the man talk, barely picked up any details of tone and inflection, and although he could read a good swathe of French, he'd never practiced speaking it.

So he let the call go, left it until the ringing stopped and the phone idled between his sweaty fingertips.

Another message, half a minute later: FUCKING ANSWER.

King's pulse throbbed at his temples. If he botched this, if seven days of hell had been for nothing at all...

And, he thought, *what if contingency measures are in place?*

It was well inside the realm of possibility. In fact, it made a great deal of sense. If the boss feared foul play, if he thought there might be sabotage, it wouldn't be hard to incorporate a self-destruct mechanism in the sub's design. After all, the crew didn't build the thing, so the narco workers constructing the sub wouldn't have a problem with the feature. It wasn't their lives on the line. If the boss didn't get the responses he was looking for from the captain, he'd electronically activate the device, maybe blow a hole in the side and send all the evidence to a watery grave. It wouldn't take much of a bomb. Such was the nature of a shoddily constructed vessel.

King couldn't play this safe.

It was all or nothing.

He frantically messaged back: J'AI RÉPONDU.

I answered.

A full minute of silence.

He held his breath and considered scrambling up the ladder, diving into the ocean before the sub collapsed on itself and dragged him down into the darkness of the North Atlantic. Both options were horrible, but there was maybe a one in a million chance he could tread water until a boat miraculously passed by, as opposed to zero if he stayed onboard a plummeting submarine.

You don't know anything yet, he told himself. *Cool it.*

But he couldn't.

A text came back and he translated as he read: MY CALL WENT THROUGH. TRY AGAIN.

No sooner had King scanned the words than the phone shrieked again, like an extension of the device he'd convinced himself rested in the sub's walls. This second call was an alarm, a warning, a precursor to annihilation.

Pick up, a voice told King, *or you die.*

He didn't.

He let it ring.

The longest seconds of his life.

When it was over, the shrilling died down for the second time. It felt final. The urge gnawed at him to fire a message immediately, to explain with haste what had happened, but he resisted. Desperation was weakness, and if he did anything suspicious, that might be it.

A text from the boss: ANYTHING?

King almost whooped with relief, but reined himself in. As opposed to an order, a question like that spoke volumes. It signified the payload was important, that the head honcho was willing to work through difficulties to get this drug money back home, willing to make compromises and allowances. King had wondered if there were a fleet of other narco-subs out there, constantly hauling tons of drugs and hundreds of millions of dollars in cash back and forth between continents. And there still may very well be, but it was obviously a big deal that *this* sub made it back. They wouldn't be blowing it to shreds in a hurry.

King spent a couple of minutes composing a message, cross-checking his rudimentary grasp of French with translation programs on his own satphone (a little more state-of-the-art than the captain's.)

YOUR CALL COMES UP, I ANSWER, NOTHING HAPPENS. SOME GLITCH. WILL SORT WHEN BACK. IF YOUR TRACKERS AREN'T WORKING, CURRENT CO-ORDINATES ARE 32°39'45.9"N, 61°27'19.2"W. ENGINE & GENERATOR FINE. CREW OKAY.

A long wait, then from the boss: YOU WILL HAVE TO EXPLAIN THIS TO RÉMI WHEN YOU GET HERE.

King gripped the phone tight.

He needed more information, and there was only one way to go about it.

His heel tapped incessantly against the floor, an unconscious tic. To delay what he knew he needed to do, he looked through the periscope and adjusted course, but there was nothing of note, only endless, roiling sea.

He bowed his head, took a breath and typed: Rémi ne fera rien.

Rémi won't do shit.

Either a horrendous mistake that would implode the operation, or he'd find out a little more about what he was dealing with.

The reply came back promptly, and King sensed the boss angrily typing on the other end: You think the fucking prefect won't do anything? He'll wipe you off the face of the earth, idiot. Watch your mouth.

King smirked in the shadows. If there were witnesses, they might consider him a wild man, the untamed look coupling with the maniacal glint in his eyes. He allowed himself a small celebration. It was all falling into place. He had information, and, more importantly, he was alive. So he could poke and prod without immediate repercussions.

He shot back: Shouldn't be this hard to speak to you over the phone. Fix your tech.

The more he pressed now, the more the boss would buy it. The boss would be furious at the captain, but he'd never suspect the captain was someone *else*. No sane imposter would test the waters like this.

Thankfully, King had never considered himself sane.

The boss replied: We will.

King clenched a fist in wordless victory. In the big picture, very little progress had been made, especially when he turned his mind to everything there was left to overcome. But only a third of the way into the journey, the direction of progress was more important than the scale.

Small wins move mountains.

Then, with a soft chime to alert, a new message came

through: DID THE YANKEES SEEM STRANGE WHEN YOU MADE THE HANDOVER? THEY'RE SCREWING US AROUND.

King leered; a macabre sight in the bowels of the sub, given his dishevelment, but no one was around to watch him gloat.

It meant that back in Maine, Slater was putting in work.

34

K ing once told Slater, *Small wins move mountains.*
Slater had unconsciously followed such
ideology for most of his life, but it was a beautiful way to phrase it, and it stuck. He recited the mantra
now as he stood out the front of the grocery store, waiting
for Dawn Cates to show.

The old lady was a creature of habit, but aren't we all?

It hadn't taken long for Slater to figure out her routine. He
hadn't wanted to startle her by showing up at her house. Hence,
here he was. There were very few customers at eight-thirty on a
Sunday morning, most residents of Millinocket either working
on the weekend, deep in the grind of the vacationless blue-
collar lifestyle, or still pottering around at home if they had a
cushy gig that afforded them days off. Dawn turned her old
Volvo into the parking lot two minutes before Slater thought
she would, but that was close enough to the schedule he'd estimated. She didn't hesitate before clambering out of the driver's
seat, the wind and snow hardly fazing a lifetime Mainer.

She made it all the way to the automatic sliding doors

before she stopped her hobble, noticing the shape out of the corner of her eye. She turned to Slater, her face flat, like the morose expression was permanent after what happened with Louie.

'Hi, Dawn,' Slater said. 'I'm—'

'I know who you are.'

He nodded slowly.

She blinked. 'No one has seen your friend around for a while. Not since I spoke to him at the tavern, actually. That was, what, a week ago now?'

She knew precisely how long ago it was; it wasn't ancient history. Evidently, she considered it polite to be vague. Like hard statistics might be interpreted as an insult, a direct attack.

He said, 'Who's "no one"?'

'People.'

'Uh-huh.'

'Everyone talks. That should be obvious, dear.'

'And what are they gossiping about?'

'Whether Jason's coming back.'

'He is. He's just away for a while.'

Dawn's gaze penetrated straight through the veneer, trying to get to the truth without asking directly. 'Is he ... okay?'

'Yes.'

She sighed. 'That's good. It's a work trip, I imagine? For a while I thought...' She trailed off.

'You thought what?'

A breath. 'Never mind. Thank you for letting me know...' This time it was deliberate, leaving space for a name she didn't yet know.

'Will.'

'Will,' she repeated, as if testing how it sounded. The hint of a smile played at her pursed lips. 'I like "Will."'

'I'm glad.' He gave her a moment to walk away, but she didn't. So he asked again: 'You thought what about Jason?'

She waved a hand dismissively. 'Oh, forget it. I'm too old. I had a silly thought...'

'You thought he went to Lubec?'

She stiffened, the stoop in her shoulders straightening slightly. She tried to stop her eyes from widening, but a sliver of the reaction was uncontrollable, and it leaked out briefly. She coughed in an attempt to cover it up. 'So he told you about that.'

'He had to. You understand, right?'

'You're his...?' She didn't know what to say, and settled on, 'Emergency contact?'

'That's right. That's me.'

'So he went out that way...?'

'He did.'

'And you're telling the truth when you say he's okay?'

'He's fine. He's doing very well. He made some significant progress with your issue.'

'Oh.' She looked everywhere but at Slater. Probably worried this was a setup, fearing incrimination. 'Well, I best get—' She didn't finish the sentence, started shuffling away.

'Dawn.'

She froze.

He was speaking to her side profile now. 'You might read some things. Hear some things. Not now; down the line. Some stuff might come out about the auto body shop. It might sound a little ... theatrical.'

She faced forward rigidly, but didn't head inside. He could tell she was desperate for information, fighting her conditioning that told her to walk away *now*.

Against her better judgment, she asked softly, 'What did you do?'

'Me? Nothing. But if you get any ideas about who might be involved — you know, down the line — maybe you could leave those dots unconnected. Maybe you could chalk it all up to baseless suspicion, and get on with your life. You know what I mean?'

'Yes,' she said. 'I do.'

'And Dawn...'

'Yes, Will?'

'If Louie's up there, looking down ... I think he'd be very happy. If he could comprehend that sort of thing...'

She went a little pale.

But she said, 'Thank you.'

Her tone conveyed everything she couldn't say.

'Be seeing you,' Slater said politely, and turned away from her. He headed toward the lot, but she called out to him. He looked over his shoulder.

'Why tell me now?'

'I might be going away too. Work trip, like Jason. I wanted to make sure you knew, before...' He shrugged. 'Just tying things up.'

For a moment, she got brave. At least, brave enough to stick a finger in his face, scolding him in the grandmotherly role she knew to play. 'I'd better see the both of you back here.'

'You will.'

'Then don't go talking like you're off to your own funeral.'

For a moment, the veil was broken, and he let his guard down. It could have only been milliseconds, but she was paying close attention, displaying none of the senility you'd expect from a woman her age. She saw the truth in his face, saw who he was, and it shocked her.

He said, 'Not my funeral, Dawn.'

He closed up again, nodded politely to her, and walked away.

35

F rom the grocer's, he drove an hour south to Bangor, putting as much distance between himself and Millinocket as he deemed appropriate.

Whatever happened, he flat-out refused to bring this home.

He drove all the way down through Bangor, unable to shake the sensation that this airy and tranquil place, only thirty thousand strong, was the "big city." Enough time in Millinocket had warped his worldview, subconsciously making life seem scarcer, neighbours spaced further apart. The small town of four thousand was dwindling in population with each passing year, hometown employment simply infeasible for some, and necessity made them migrate elsewhere, to larger places like Bangor with better job prospects. But Slater had fallen in love with his home and its isolation, so he figured he'd stay even if the town died around him and his family. He was doing what he could to stimulate Millinocket's economy, spending heartily wherever he fancied, but his influence was limited. He wouldn't be able to keep the whole town afloat.

What he *could* do was protect his neighbours from collateral damage, which is why he'd buried Jack's phone in Bangor a few days ago, deep in the dirt embankment where the Penobscot River diverted into Eaton Brook.

If Jack's superiors could track it, they could dig to their heart's content. The phone was all they'd find. They wouldn't so much as catch a whiff of Slater up in Millinocket. Dawn Cates had been through enough; she didn't need the tranquility of her hometown shattered.

He took State Street over the river and gunned it northeast, parallel to the riverbank, until he hit the brook. He left the Range Rover in the driveway of a vacation home with all the telltale signs of unoccupancy, and from there he set off on foot. North Main Street fell away, replaced by near-impenetrable brush, dusted in a fine coating of powder snow. He forced his way through and jogged down a steep hillside to the bank of the twisting brook. The trickling body of water resisted solidification with all its might, fighting against the elements.

Slater found the right spot and started sifting the loose dirt away with his hands until his fingertips touched something solid.

He pulled out a small metal box, unlocked it, and took Jack's phone out. The battery was dead, but the portable charging bank in his jacket pocket gave it the requisite amount of juice, and ten minutes later he was staring at the familiar home screen: Jack, arm in arm with his partner. Slater gritted his teeth as he tapped in the passcode.

Violetta had retrieved it for him.

She'd cracked the phone days ago.

He opened an encrypted messaging app Jack had installed long before. A trio of numbers with no contact names comprised the entirety of the chat history, each number untraceable. Violetta had already tried tracking them down, but they all led unwaveringly to dead ends.

Jack likely had the same technology installed on his own phone, so Slater hadn't bothered to bury the box too deep. He doubted anyone would come for it: not before, not now.

He fired a message to one of the numbers: READY.

Within minutes a reply came: OUTSIDE CROSBY'S?

Slater typed back: THAT'S WHAT I SAID.

THOUGHT SOMETHING MIGHT HAVE CHANGED.

WHY?

DON'T WORRY. SEE YOU IN 10.

Slater winced to himself as he put Jack's phone in his pocket and dropped the box back in the hole. He was working off next to no intel, but that wasn't anything out of the ordinary. With muted resignation he started back up the embankment and trekked the half-mile northeast along North Main Street to Crosby's Gun Shop, a white weatherboard house with an American flag out front. He took up position on the opposite side of the road and shoved his hands in his pockets, hunching so he appeared shorter and smaller than he was.

Then he made himself look timid. He put his head on a swivel and kept glancing up from the road frantically, like he was terrified of something as simple as eye contact.

In the end, he heard the muscle car coming from hundreds of feet away. It surged up to him and only braked at the last second, tyres screeching on cold asphalt. He forced himself to jolt, widening his eyes. He glanced up briefly. The vehicle was an old Plymouth Barracuda, two-door, low to the ground. The windows were down and trance music thumped from the speakers. Its four occupants were angry-looking, large men, the lot of them. Despite their heavy coats, tattoos were still visible on the backs of their hands and creeping up their necks.

The passenger up front said, 'You sure as fuck are not *Jack.*'

Each syllable *dripped,* his French accent impossibly heavy.

Slater managed a little nervous laugh. 'What gave it away?'

The passenger said, 'You are black.'

The driver made a derogatory gesture to the passenger. 'He is being *sarcastic.*'

The passenger said, 'I know this.'

A scoff. 'You know this? Bullshit, you know this.'

Slater said, 'Jack sent me.' He made sure not to hold their gazes any longer than a second.

The passenger spat on the sidewalk in front of Slater. 'Why he send someone?'

'Because he's a paranoid moron.'

Like sweet honey to their ears. They'd been expecting a list of excuses, and seemed relieved to hear the honesty.

The passenger smiled, flashing gold grilles, and wagged a finger. 'I like you, friend. Come. Get in. We talk.'

'Yes,' Slater said, still sheepish. 'We talk.'

They didn't bother to frisk him, such was their confidence. The passenger got out and tilted his seat forward to allow Slater into the back. It was harder for Slater to minimise his profile as he squeezed through. One guy had to slide over to give him room, and Slater's shoulder pressed against him as he took his seat. The guy looked across, eyebrows raised. 'What you made of, metal?'

Slater shook his head. 'Nah. But this is.'

He ripped the SIG out from underneath his jacket moments after the passenger sat back down and slammed his door. To manoeuvre in such close quarters, Slater had to move explosively, so he brought the gun up hard and jammed it against the head of the man beside him. The impact of metal on bone resonated, a gruesome *clack,* and the guy recoiled, falling over his buddy's lap. Slater kept the SIG pinned to his skull as he reached over the centre console and took a handful of the driver's hair in an iron grip. He yanked hard, pinning him back against the head-rest, preventing him going anywhere.

'Drive,' he ordered.

The passenger up front twisted awkwardly in his seat in an attempt to snatch a better look, but the crush of five big men in a cramped space made things difficult.

Slater saw him going for his waistband from a mile away.

'*No!*' he shouted, loud enough to make them all flinch. He took the gun off his hostage next to him for maybe half a second, only long enough to pistol-whip the passenger in the back of the head. Blood spurted from split skin and the guy crumpled forward. Slater jammed the SIG, its barrel now wet, back above the ear of the man beside him.

'Anyone else goes for a gun and you get it worse than that.' He tugged the driver's hair up, as hard as he could, and the guy yelped. '*Drive.*'

He wouldn't be ignored twice, and he made that clear to them with the tone of his voice alone.

The driver pulled away.

36

S later wanted some privacy.

Somewhere isolated, as far from civilisation as possible, with the lowest chance of bystanders stumbling upon them. Somewhere like where he'd buried Jack's phone.

He ordered them east.

The road veered away from the Penobscot River, putting Bangor in the rearview. The whole time he watched them think about trying something. The guys beside him were uncomfortable and humiliated, one splayed across the other's lap, but the driver and passenger simmered. Slater didn't want to stifle momentum by getting them to pull over and relieve themselves of their weapons, so he kept a close eye on the passenger instead. The guy bled from the wound on the back of his head, and intermittently reached up to smear the blood with his palm. A reflexive gesture. Each time that Slater barked at him, ordered him not to move, he jolted like an abused animal. He couldn't seem to help himself, but Slater knew he'd eventually use the motion as a cover to reach for his waistband and pull his piece.

They'd only been on Main Road for a few minutes, but Slater impulsively demanded a turn-off. The driver slowed and went left, taking a road that weaved through country-side, past grand homesteads and endless snow-dusted fields. The trail culminated at the lip of a vast body of water.

Slater directed them off-road. The old Plymouth bounced over rough ground, its underbelly groaning in protest until Slater pointed between two trees facing the lake, out of view from the road they'd left behind. When they stopped, Slater looked to the water, not so much as a ripple on its surface. 'Anyone know this place?'

The driver mumbled, 'Chemo Pond.'

'Is that a joke?'

'No. That's what it's called.'

'That's unfortunate.'

'Welcome to Maine.'

A wisecrack, despite the nature of the situation, with the passenger's skull gushing blood and the guys in the back statuesque. It told Slater the driver would be the likeliest to talk. His lips seemed the loosest, his composure the best of the bunch.

Slater ordered them all out.

If it was going to get sketchy, now was the time. The passenger had to pop the door, clamber out, and use a lever to tilt his seat forward. His waistband was in view the whole time, and Slater kept his gaze locked on the bulge at his hip. Any attempt to snatch for it and they'd all go down in a storm of bullets.

But the man's bravery had vanished, a magic act spurned by uncertainty.

Slater was first out when the seat came forward. He vaulted out of the death trap like someone lit a fire under him. He twisted at the hips as he emerged from the

Plymouth, turning his body into a low kick. He got enough speed behind his shinbone to knock the passenger's legs out from underneath him, toppling his considerable weight to the dirt. Slater imagined the guy had never felt anything close to that sort of force in his life. If he was as tough as he acted, maybe he'd been in a few street fights, and maybe he'd been caught once or twice, but a lucky punch is a world away from a professional's practiced blow. The guy went down and stayed down, moaning in pain as he clutched his calf muscle. He offered no resistance when Slater reached down and pulled the pistol — a Colt — from the guy's waistband, before slotting it into his own.

He aimed his SIG inside the Plymouth. 'Out.'

No one got brave.

They piled out one by one, rattled, and Slater lined them up between the trees on their knees, guiding them with the pistol barrel. The guy he'd kicked in the legs was still down. Slater hauled him to his feet. The moment the passenger put weight gingerly on his bad leg, he moaned and collapsed again. Slater dragged him unceremoniously over to the other three and laid him out beside them. Then he backed up a couple of steps and trained the gun on them.

An unresisting four-man lineup.

Mission accomplished.

'Alright,' Slater said, taking a breath, channelling the calming energy of the motionless body of water behind them. 'Let's get started.'

The two men from the rear seats closed their eyes and bowed their heads, the fear of God in them.

The driver fought for self-control and succeeded. He simply raised an eyebrow. 'Get started?'

'I don't know who you work for. Let's start with that.'

The driver couldn't hide his confusion. 'You don't—?' He turned to the other men. 'Are you fucking kidding me?'

The guy from the middle seat, the one with the barrel imprint in the side of his head, kept his eyes shut. He muttered through gritted teeth, 'I'm so stupid. I was sure it was Jack. He even texted the same. I just went with it...'

The driver — clearly the ringleader — said, 'You ask for something only *Jack* would know. That is common fucking sense.'

'Yes,' the man agreed, tone laced with regret. 'It is.'

Slater cleared his throat.

Everyone shut up.

Slater let the SIG's barrel dance in the air, making slow, soft circles. 'I'll shoot you once each in the head, weigh your corpses down, and dump you in this pond. Then I'll go get your car crushed.'

They knelt silently, monk-like. Hands trembled. Everyone thinks they're invincible until it's too late and they have to rapidly come to terms with their own mortality. It's horrifying, accepting the end.

Slater said, 'I absolutely will. But I'd prefer not to.'

The guys from the rear seats didn't believe it. The driver did. His gaze whipped up.

Slater said, 'I'd prefer to talk.'

The driver said, 'Let's talk.'

Slater raised an eyebrow. He waited a couple of beats, then gave a small nod. *Go on.*

The driver said, 'We work for Rémi Poirier.'

S later blinked. 'Okay.'

The driver, stereotypically French, shook his head side-to-side and lifted his palms to the sky. He looked to the men kneeling beside him. 'This means nothing to him.'

Slater said, 'You'd better make it mean something.'

'Yes, yes.' A dismissive wave. 'Mr. Poirier is the prefect of French Guiana. French Guiana is—'

'I know what French Guiana is.'

'Ah. So you are *little bit* in the loop.'

'Soon to be all the way in.'

'Yes, of course.' A gulp that barely suppressed mortal fear. The driver seemed to sense the invisible thread his life was hanging by. 'You know what prefect is?'

'I think so.'

'The French president pick him. Set him up at the prefecture building in Cayenne, make him comfortable. Then ... well, there is not much for him to do, because government in French Guiana does fuck-all. There is no infrastructure, very big unemployment, and poverty *every-*

where. Protestors make a scene in 2017, it's a big deal. They demand aid. They get some meaningless fucking accord signed by some meaningless fucking ministers. Lots of money promised and nothing delivered. You know the drill.'

Slater said, 'I do.'

'Yeah, well, Mr. Poirier puts a lot of effort into not doing his job. He, uh, has to find things to keep himself occupied. Keep that brain going, you know? He sure as fuck will not help the people he lords over, no, so he figures out how to smuggle drugs to America—'

As a test, Slater asks, 'And how does he manage that?'

A big shrug. 'I do not know. He would not tell me. Not worth it. No point. I am — *we* are...'

'The muscle.'

'*Oui,* the muscle.'

'Where are you from?'

'Is it not obvious?'

'I mean, did you come from French Guiana?'

'No, I come from France. I meet these guys here in Maine, many years ago. We all come from France, at different times...'

'And Rémi Poirier recruited you because...?'

'We are French.'

'You don't seem to like him very much.'

'He thinks, if you are French, your character does not matter.'

Slater raised an eyebrow. 'And you're so noble?'

The driver flashed a half-smile. He gestured to the rest of the line-up. 'We are sleazy fucking gangsters, my friend. We do — uh, how you say? — small-town crime. And nothing crazy. I mean, you see, right? You get us all here, lined up, no problem. Nothing we can do. We don't know shit. But Rémi ... ah, Rémi... he is the worst. You know why?'

'Enlighten me.'

'They say, "Rémi, you want to be prefect?" He says yes.' The driver tutted condescendingly. 'This is not good. Why? Because he knows he is not right for prefect. You ask any of us if we want to be big important politician, you know what we say? We say no. We know our place. Rémi says yes to something that comes with — how you say? — responsibility. If Rémi is shit at his job, it makes big problems. So fuck Rémi. He get away with all of this...'

'You work for him.'

A shrug. 'Is lot of money.'

And therein lies the problem, Slater thought, though it wasn't a bad speech.

Slater said, 'So who was I messaging?'

The driver's eyes widened. 'Who were—?' He couldn't help himself: he scoffed.

Slater said, 'What?'

'You been talking to the source, my friend. Rémi call us this morning, tell us to pick up some guy called Jack, find out what the fuck he's doing. Rémi say Jack is being very difficult, causing many problems.'

'I wasn't messaging you guys?'

'Before today I never hear of Jack in my life.'

'Jack is dead.'

A pause, like: *Should you have told me that?* 'Oh.'

'But that's not what you saw.'

'Oh?'

'You *saw* Jack. You pulled up beside him and told him to get in the car, and maybe you were a little too aggressive, too intimidating. He bolted. Ran away. You couldn't catch up to him. It's a shame.'

Exuding both calmness and overconfidence in a life-or-death situation practically makes you a messiah. Slater watched it dawn in the eyes of three out of the four men: the driver, and the guys from the backseat. All their past confrontations had been heart-racing, adrenaline-fuelled interactions, but here they were being manhandled, ordered around and told exactly what to do, given clear instructions. It was overwhelming, and Slater knew the trio would do precisely what he said.

The passenger, on the other hand, had too much on his mind to absorb Slater's aura, more focused on figuring out whether he'd be able to walk again. He would, of course, but a well-placed kick to the calf makes the lower leg balloon. The calf is a small muscle, surrounded by nothing but bone and tendons, and the swelling has nowhere to go. It often results in a golf-ball sized lump on the front or side of the shin, and makes placing weight on the limb a living hell.

The passenger pushed himself up on his elbows, wincing the whole time, then levered to a sitting position.

Slater could see his eyes now.

Shock, disbelief, pain...

...and rage.

Slater focused on the passenger alone. 'I'd really prefer not to kill anyone today.'

Which simplified things.

It would push the guy one way or the other.

No middle ground.

The passenger's face twisted, his inner toughness rising up. A look of scorn came over him.

Slater thought, *Goddamnit.*

The guy launched to his feet and took off running.

38

He made it three steps.

Slater didn't have to move a muscle.

The guy hadn't thought through his body positioning, fight-or-flight consuming him, elevating him into a state of obliviousness. When he rose, he planted his bad leg first, and it was clear as day the limb was compromised. An uncontrollable wince came over him, but in the heat of the moment he ignored it. The second step on his good leg propelled him forward. Too fast. Too powerful. When he took the third step his whole leg gave out, the knee buckling, the ankle failing.

He went down grotesquely.

Like he'd been shot.

Landed on his back and rolled into the foetal position and spewed forth a torrent of cursing in rapid-fire French. He yelled through gritted teeth, furious and rebellious.

Slater sighed as he walked over to the man. He grabbed him by the collar and dragged him back in line beside his three buddies, who were now completely convinced of

Slater's messiah status. They couldn't believe their eyes. They'd seen their only mutinous member try to escape and fail within a couple of seconds, like Slater had reached out with an invisible hand and thrust him back down to earth.

Slater stepped back from the groaning passenger, who continued swearing at the sky. He kept his SIG pointed at the ground, but brought it around to face the quartet side-on, so they could see his trigger finger straightened against the side of the guard.

To the passenger, he said, 'Are you going to do the right thing?'

'Fuck you,' the guy spat, his chin resting on his chest so he could make eye contact with Slater. Veins strained at his temples. 'You'd better kill me now, or I'll—'

Slater ignored him, turning to the driver. 'What are we going to do about this?'

Fear consumed the driver, who was clearly smarter than the rest of them.

Slater's eyes asked a silent question. *If I kill him, is this still salvageable?*

The driver answered the question by going for the back of his own waistband.

Slater's stomach dropped.

But when the man came out with another old Colt, one Slater hadn't even noticed under the bulky fur-lined jacket, he didn't raise it or aim it forward.

Still seated, he rolled to his side, jammed the barrel against the side of the passenger's head, and pulled the trigger.

Blood splashed in the dirt.

Slater had brought the SIG up to aim at the driver, just in case, and he remained there, frozen. 'Jesus.'

The driver changed his grip immediately, taking the Colt's stock in a pincer grip to signify a newfound pacifism. With the threat eliminated, he tossed the pistol away, throwing it at Slater's feet. Then he put his hands in the air.

He said, 'I hope that shows I'm serious.'

Slater blinked. He turned to the other two. 'And how about you? Are you serious?'

Two vigorous nods.

The fresh corpse was hard to process, but the more it sunk in, the less Slater was surprised. He should know better than anyone on earth how all-encompassing the survival instinct is, how quickly we turn on each other out of self-preservation. But it wouldn't do to leave it at that. The remaining trio might *think* they were scared of Slater, might *think* they were intimidated into submission, but as soon as there was a little distance between them all, they were likely to get brave, get some big ideas about how to remedy the situation.

They needed the fear of God in them.

Slater walked over and crouched beside the driver, who he knew would influence the other two when this was over. He didn't speak for nearly a full minute. The silence was deafening. He watched them try not to cringe, try not to look away or start whimpering.

Slater said, 'You might think getting on the wrong side of me is better than getting on the wrong side of Rémi Poirier.'

'No,' the driver said firmly, shaking his head. 'Absolutely not.'

'Of course you don't think that now. But you might, a couple of hours from now. Because despite what you might suspect, I'm going to let the three of you walk. Don't make me regret it.'

'We won't.'

'I'm very interested in what's going on between Rémi and the governor, Noah Dubois.'

The driver gulped.

Slater said, 'Don't worry. I won't ask you about that. You won't know much, and what you know is probably wrong. But it's very important that Noah suspects *nothing* for at least a few weeks. Moves are happening that take time. So if Rémi or Noah end up fleeing for their lives before I'm ready to move on them, I'll know who talked. I'll come for you. And that guy' — he jerked a thumb at the body — 'will be the luckiest of you all.'

The driver blinked. The other two looked like they were trying not to cry.

Slater bent down, leant closer. 'And if you get brave, think you can hide from me, well...'

The lake hovered in stillness.

Birds cawed in treetops.

'Truth is,' Slater continued, 'I won't even need to find you. I know about Rémi, and who else could have told me about him? So I'd just track him down and leak my sources. That'd make one very unhappy prefect.'

All three of them looked ready to shit their pants. Hands trembled.

Slater stood up. 'You can dispose of your buddy there. After all, you killed him.'

He got behind the wheel of the Plymouth and fired it up. Soon he'd be back in Bangor; a certain phone needed re-burying. But he noticed only the two from the rear seats had moved toward the corpse. The driver was still on his haunches, gaze fixed forward. Staring at Slater. Refusing to look away. Neither man blinked.

Slater considered himself a keen judge of character. Over the engine's purr, he called out, 'You hate your boss?'

Might be wrong. Might not.

The driver hesitated. Then dipped his chin in a nod. 'You want help fucking them over? Him and the governor both?'

'Get in.'

39

Rémi the prefect.

A satellite Internet connection gave King the answers he needed. An hour of research and he was up to speed, able to visualise all sorts of potential connections between a disgruntled French politician and an American state governor. Of course, there'd be no actual answers until he came out in French Guiana like a bat out of hell, but at least he had food for thought for the next two weeks. He'd skimmed over every interview of Rémi Poirier he could find, and was able to translate the "politician speak." Through very polite and subtle comments, what Rémi was effectively trying to say was, '*Fuck the president for appointing me to this useless, dead-end role in a useless, dead-end territory.*'

And where there was discontent, there was rebellion.

King couldn't wait to get his hands on the slimy little man.

Reinvigorated by progress after a week of monotony, he took himself through a savage hour-long bodyweight workout. The settings were suboptimal, but that didn't matter.

The sub rumbled above the sea's dark belly, ruining his balance and equilibrium, putting that vague sense of primal fear deep in the back of his head the whole time, but he was adept at ignoring the external, focusing entirely on the internal.

Fixating on his locus of control.

Because, really, that's all we've got.

So he ignored the rattling and the creaking, and worked as hard as he could.

Spending all his time trapped in a metal box left him with more energy in the gas tank than he could possibly expend. He was used to thrashing his body to its limits on a daily basis (carefully calculated to prevent overtraining, of course), and now the complete lack of movement for most of the time he spent awake was mind-numbing. It meant, when he decided to flush the energy out, that he could take the suffering to new heights, push himself harder than he thought humanly possible. It was like his whole life had been a training camp for these claustrophobic workouts, his body growing in capability until he cut away all the exercise at once, tapering off into single hour-long sessions each day.

He simply didn't get tired, no matter how hard he pushed.

For forty-five of the sixty minutes, he forced himself through an unbroken chain of burpees, throwing in a trio of push-ups at the bottom of each repetition. He finished at three hundred burpees and nine hundred pushups, then focused on solo martial arts drills, combining shadow-boxing with wrestling sprawls. Something about throwing his two hundred and twenty pounds around the homemade sub scared the shit out of him, but he did it anyway. It was like the whole thing might roll over at any second, the change in gravity bouncing him off the walls as he tumbled to a watery grave.

Down, down, down, into the depths of the North Atlantic...

He shook that off by pushing himself harder. When he finished, he used clean clothes from the bags of the deceased crew to mop the perspiration off the floor. Sweat poured off him, forcing its way from open pores, and he used the cool-down time to power down the engine and coast the sub to a halt.

When it stopped, he used the periscope to check that the coast was clear before taking his satphone up the ladder and heaving the hatch outward.

A clear, crisp morning. A cloudless sky. He'd never tasted air so pure, so far removed from civilisation. The narco-sub bobbed in the middle of the world, the closest landmass a distant memory. He was starting to adjust to the barren emptiness, the feeling of insignificance, and once he got past that, he had to admit it was beautiful.

He felt he had tapped into something the monks spoke of, that feeling you were *part* of the world, not separate from it, not an observer.

So, really, what was a three-week journey?

Nothing, compared to the change he could make when he reached his destination.

The monks might not approve of the way he would enact change, but fuck it, you can't please everyone.

He hooked the satphone to the top rung of the ladder and leapt into the water, swapping sweat salt for sea salt. As he ducked his head under, the ocean's natural rhythm pulled him a few feet from the sub. It wasn't a true issue (he could swim back with little effort), but not all fear is physical. The idea of floating too far from his only means of survival sent shivers down his spine, and his heart pounded as he watched the semi-submersible continue to drift.

He took several powerful strokes and was back on top of the vessel in seconds.

He let the sun beat down on his bare chest and legs, savouring a rare moment of peace, then reached for the ladder and unhooked the satphone.

He dialled Slater.

40

'Who's that?' said the Frenchman. 'Someone important?'

Slater glanced down at his phone screen, driving one-handed away from the crime scene. 'Shit.'

The guy beside him stiffened. 'Bad news?'

'No.' He answered and lifted the phone to his ear in a single motion. 'Urgent?'

'I'm not in danger, if that's what you mean.' King's voice was shockingly clear, considering he was over a thousand miles from the nearest continent. The advancement of technology never failed to baffle Slater.

Slater said, 'I'm just in the middle of something.'

'Chasing the governor?'

'In a roundabout way. Don't you worry; I'm being careful. I only killed one man today when I could've killed four.'

Beside him, the Frenchman sat ramrod straight. Didn't move a muscle. You could cut the tension in the air with a knife.

'You're an angel,' King said. 'Listen, I've got a lead in French Guiana. Name's Rémi Poirier.'

Synchronicity.

Slater shook his head. He couldn't help but scoff. 'You're kidding.'

'Why would I be kidding?'

Slater glanced across. 'I'm looking at Rémi's man in Maine.'

'As in...?'

'He's in the car with me.'

'And you haven't killed him yet.'

'He's on our side.'

A pause. 'Bullshit.'

Slater raised his eyebrows. Addressing the passenger, he said, 'My friend doesn't believe you.'

'He should.'

Into the phone, Slater said, 'He says you should.'

'Be careful.'

'How'd you find out about the naughty prefect?'

'I'm messaging the guy the captain reports to. He still doesn't suspect anything. Which means you successfully covered up the mess I left behind. So thank you.'

'Anytime. So, what, this guy in charge of the narco-subs told you all about Poirier?'

'He said "Rémi" and "prefect." I've got an Internet connection. I can fill in the blanks on my own.'

'You tech guru, you.'

'You quizzed your new friend yet?'

'About to. Like I said, I'm in the middle of something.'

'I'll leave you to it.'

'Stay sane.'

'Hasn't been easy.' *Click.*

Slater hadn't had a moment to pause and take stock since the Plymouth first pulled up in front of him in Bangor. Now he looked over at the Frenchman, getting a proper look at features he'd glossed over. The guy had a full mop of light brown hair with blonde tips. He wore it messy and waxed it sideways, the fringe draping his right eye like a frayed curtain. His eyes were intense, stark green like Slater's. He was handsome. All the sharp lines of a model. The tattoos lacing their way up his neck gave him that edge most people associate with toughness, but men like King and Slater see straight through them, as the performance it truly is. If you need to puff your chest and shout from the rooftops that you're a gangster, all you're doing is masking insecurity. But from everything Slater had seen so far, the guy was sharp and switched on, able to pivot at a moment's notice. He had impeccable survival instinct, and from what he'd already said about Rémi, he was a no-bullshit truth-teller, too.

Slater said, 'What's your name?'

'Timothée.'

'Will.'

Timothée cracked a smirk for the first time.

Slater said, 'What?'

Silence.

Slater said, 'Spit it out.'

Timothée waved a hand in the air, searching for the right words. 'I think I get you.'

'You do?'

A long pause. Then, 'You are what I pretend to be.'

'You're smart.'

'Or a fool. Depends how this goes.'

'You're not a pretender.'

'Oh?'

'Not the way I first thought. You just shot your friend and you've still got your shit together.'

Timothée shook his head. 'He was not my friend. No

friends in this world. Everyone is a scumbag. Everyone will stab you in back. Me included.'

'Will you stab me in the back?'

'No way. I know my place.'

Ordinarily, Slater wouldn't have a bar of it, but after Timothée's condescending rant about Rémi, he believed the man.

He said, 'Why would you help me?'

'Because … what I said about Rémi. This was not me trying to save my own ass. This is what I think.'

'And the other two?'

'They'll do whatever I say. I'm the boss. If I think they wouldn't hide the body and keep their mouth shut, I would have shot them too.'

Slater nodded.

Rémi said, 'So tell me how you got in this mess.'

Slater took a deep breath. He momentarily wondered if he was making the right decision, then shook it off. 'Okay.'

41

T he Plymouth rumbled down lonely backwoods roads.

Slater said, 'Jack unloads the drugs Rémi sends over.'

Timothée scoffed.

'What?'

The man hunched forward in his seat. 'Rémi does nothing of the sort. He is ... too dumb and weak to be involved. He only grants permission.'

'To who?'

'Da Silva.'

'You'll need to fill me in.'

'Alain Da Silva. I've never met him. I should not know anything about him. Like I said, Rémi is dumb and weak, and one night he called me for, uh, usual debrief, and there were things he wanted to get off his chest. He said he shouldn't be telling me this but he told me anyway. This is number one sign of an idiot, yes?'

Slater smirked. 'Yes.'

'He tell me all about Da Silva. This man sounds like ... ah, how do I put this? Like evil version of you.'

'Not a pretender.'

A vigorous shake of the head. 'No way. He is cartel, born and bred. He come from terrible place, Rémi say, and he do anything to not go back there. *Anything.* Rémi give him access to important coastline in French Guiana, let him build shipyards, let him make submarines in the jungles. You understand what sort of person it takes to coordinate this? It takes ... destroyer. It takes ruthless man. Rémi tell me too much about it, and I know he's scared of Da Silva. Da Silva organise bringing all materials into jungle; generators, tools, supplies, everything. He do what Rémi could only dream of doing. He's the one who handles it all. Rémi sits in office and says "yes."'

'Okay. So Jack unloads the drugs Da Silva sends over.'

Timothée nodded. 'Yes.'

'Jack isn't around anymore. My friend and I got involved.'

'Why? Rivals pay you?'

'No.'

Timothée seemed to sense it again, that essence he would never understand, that invisible *thing* that made Slater different to anyone he'd encountered before. So he moved on. 'Okay.'

'I have Jack's phone,' Slater said. 'We cracked the passcode a few days ago. I got into an encrypted messaging app Jack uses for business. He was only communicating with three numbers, and he must have thought he was smart, because he had no contact information saved. Any efforts we made to find out more about the people behind the numbers led to dead ends, so I messaged all three of them simultaneously off

Jack's phone. I said I was fed up with the bullshit and was going to ground, and if they wanted me to crawl back out of the woodwork, things would have to be done very differently going forward. It was vague enough that I was sure I wouldn't give away the fact Jack's dead. It's very important that these people believe he's alive for the next couple of weeks.'

'Why?'

'I don't trust you that much yet.'

Timothée shrugged.

Slater said, 'One number said nothing. From what you've told me, I gather that was Alain Da Silva. I doubt he'd care about a dumb Yank throwing a temper tantrum.'

'He would not.'

'The second number came back bluntly. Just "OK." I'm still figuring things out, but I'm going to assume it's the governor. He has to be very careful about leaving a paper trail.'

'I do not know anything about the governor. Rémi keep me in the dark. He only tell me about Da Silva because he gets fucked around by the man.'

Slater believed him. 'The third number came back immediately. Sent me an entire fucking paragraph of questions. He was seriously worried.'

Timothée didn't need it spelled out for him. 'This is Rémi.'

'I know that now.'

'He call us and tell us we need to go pick you up. He tell us we need to do whatever possible to fix things, to get you back to work. If this does not work, he tell us to kill you, shut you up so you stay quiet.'

'Would you have done it?'

'Probably. No one in bed with Rémi is clean. I don't think

very hard about what he tells me to do, because no one is innocent, yes?'

'Sure.'

Timothée stared openly across the car. 'You despise me.'

'I don't like you.'

A hand waved in the air, a broad circular motion. 'What you no like about me, *specific*?'

'I think you do what idiot gangsters do, only you're not an idiot gangster.'

A pause. 'You are what you do, no?'

'Usually. Sometimes there's an exception to the rule. You're smart enough to sort your life out, but you fall back into what's easy.'

'Yes,' Timothée said. 'Yes, this is true.'

Silence.

'If I was you,' Timothée mused, 'when this is all over, I'd kill me.'

'I could kill you now.'

'You could, yes. But you need me. And I'll help you.'

'And then?'

'Why are you asking me?'

'Because I want you to make the choice. I don't want you to be forced into it. That doesn't work. I want you to help me do this, not because there's anything in it for you, but because it's the right thing to do. Then I want to let you go, let you get your shit together. Because this will give you a taste of what you could do, rather than serving little boys like Rémi Poirier.'

'You want me to serve *you*?'

They'd been trawling through Bangor's outskirts for a few minutes. Slater turned into the same street they'd picked him up on and beelined for the stretch of road opposite the gun shop. He slammed the brakes, pulled to the kerb, and threw his door open. Only then did he look over. 'I couldn't think of anything worse, Timothée. I've got enough problems.'

'So...?'

Slater was out of the car by then, and slammed the door shut behind him as he turned and lowered his elbows to the windowsill. He jabbed a finger at Timothée. 'So get convincing your boss that Jack's still out there hiding.'

'I can do that.' Timothée looked around, somewhat disbelieving. 'I can keep the ride?'

'You think I'm some scavenger?'

'I don't know what to think about you, my friend.'

'Good.'

Slater slapped a palm twice on the sill and walked away.

42

W aiting was hell.

Slater hustled through the woods on foot to bury Jack's phone again, back where he'd dug it up that morning. After smoothing the dirt over, rendering the burial site invisible, he jogged back up to the Range Rover, consumed by his thoughts.

The landscape was taking shape, puzzle pieces slotting into place. Noah Dubois, Rémi Poirier, Alain Da Silva: a sticky web of evil, growing clearer the more he thought about it, the more he visualised connections and backroom deals.

And there wasn't a thing he could do.

Given his expertise, it'd be simple enough to track down the governor's residence and nullify whatever meagre security Dubois might have lying around before storming in and executing him in the dead of night. Slater had pulled off far more dangerous feats than anything Dubois could throw at him. The governor could have more than just the Coast Guard on his side. Police, Army, it was irrelevant. Whatever it was, Slater had faced worse.

The only catch: it meant King would spend three weeks in solitary confinement to arrive at a deserted shipyard, with nothing to show for his troubles. If anything went sour in Maine, everyone in charge of the operation in French Guiana would abandon ship.

So, patience.

Far from his defining characteristic.

A little over an hour on snow-dusted roads carving through inhospitable terrain put him back in Millinocket in the early afternoon. He gunned it straight to the Scootic In Restaurant, a staple of the small town, in operation for well over a century. The wooden building stood tall and sturdy in the falling snow, a refuge from the elements. Warm light blazed in its windows.

Slater parked out front, strode inside, and found Tyrell easing his way into a booth. He drew alongside the table just as the teenager's rear end touched the vinyl.

Right on time for their lunch appointment.

Slater said, 'You ever going to suggest anywhere else?' as he sat opposite and picked up a menu.

Tyrell shook his head. 'You kidding?'

In Tyrell's eyes, far more important than the establishment's treasured history was the caloric density of its food. He didn't care that it had been open since 1901, only that it served pizza and pasta in giant quantities to satisfy his needs. Slater didn't blame the kid; he seemed to be expanding each week, adding lean muscle across his ever-growing frame, and puberty coupled with the sheer amount of calories he burned each day meant he was eating enough to fuel a family of five.

One of the major downsides of following Slater's approach to life was the strain it put on the food budget. A monk's existence — sitting still all day in the search for truth — was more cost-effective.

After they ordered food, Slater said, 'I'm sorry about this past weekend.'

'It's cool,' Tyrell said, drumming his fingers excitedly against the tabletop at the prospect of a big meal. 'Really. I wasn't lying when I said it was no stress.'

'I promised we'd go to Boston if you applied yourself, and I didn't follow through. That's on me.'

'Shit comes up. I get it.'

'Yeah,' Slater said, nodding with a sigh. 'Shit comes up.'

'You authorised to tell me about it?'

Slater stared vacantly down at the table's chipped surface. 'I don't think that's a good idea.'

'No, me neither. I don't wanna get sucked into your world. Not yet, anyway.'

Slater's ears pricked up at the last sentence. He snapped his gaze up to meet Tyrell's.

Tyrell laughed. 'I'm kidding, man. I get it. You lived the life you did so I don't have to, blah, blah, blah...'

'Something like that.'

'Yeah, well, you ain't doing a good job of pushing me in other directions. I mean, look at me.'

Slater did. Tyrell was still thirteen years old, freshly a teenager, but had grown a couple of inches since he came into Slater's life. Another few months and he'd be six foot, seeing eye-to-eye with his surrogate father. Slater figured the boy might catch King eventually. Hell, there was a chance he'd just keep going, and end up towering over the both of them.

In contrast to the stooped, lanky, stick-limbed twelve-year-old Slater had inherited, Tyrell's frame had hardened in the months since. He was still long and lean, held back by the unavoidable time it takes a boy to become a full-grown man, but there was an added weight to his build, a presence that couldn't be ignored. Lean, tight muscle clung to him in all the right places: shoulders, thighs, an ever-broadening chest and back. He didn't look ludicrous compared to other boys his age — it's hard to balloon when puberty is still bringing adult musculature into existence — but there was a hard edge that set him subtly apart from his peers.

Slater said, 'I pushed you to do Harvard Summer School, and to take Lexington High seriously. That's not so you can grow up to be a soldier.'

'You weren't a soldier.'

'Technically I was.'

'*Technically* you weren't. I looked it up. A soldier serves in an army.'

'Army of one.'

Tyrell rolled his eyes. 'Whatever. Call yourself what you want. I don't know ninety-nine percent of the shit you've done and I still know you done more for the world than any Harvard snob.'

'You think they're all snobs?'

'Nah, I'm playing. I know education's important.'

'I can tell you know that. You've been given high praise. This town's small enough for the principal to make home calls. The guy rang and talked you up to Alexis on Friday afternoon—'

'He only made the call 'cause he knows what Alexis looks like.'

Slater scoffed, then feigned a shiver. 'Think I should be worried?'

'I think *she* should be. I was walking out Thursday after-noon and overheard two moms saying something about you. They were, like, drooling...'

Slater waved a hand dismissively. 'My ego doesn't need that. So first week went okay?'

'Went good, man. Made a couple friends. Got talking to a girl.'

Slater's turn to roll his eyes. 'So we don't even need to go back to Boston? Danielle's old news?'

'Nah. She isn't. I'm, uh...' He trailed off.

Slater honed in on the hesitance. 'Say it. Never fear sharing that stuff. It's us men who bottle it up that turn out the worst.'

Tyrell nodded, eyes clearing in resolve. 'I'm excited to see her.'

'Alright. When what I'm dealing with is over, we'll make a week-long trip out of it. To make up for the weekend I promised you.'

'It ain't that big of a deal.'

'Trust me, it is. It's important.'

'Why?'

'We both stick to our word. You work hard, fulfil your end of the deal, and I give you the best life I can. Yin and yang. And that comes from the little things, like a weekend in Boston that might be easy to sweep under the table, let go and leave unsaid. That's where it matters most.'

Tyrell reverted to shyness, to his base conditioning. Slater comfortably accepted the silence, and when their meals arrived they ate quietly. Finally, when Tyrell had processed what he was feeling, he said, 'I know I keep saying this, but I never had this.'

'I know.' Slater offered a fist as he took a bite of pizza, and Tyrell bumped it. 'Me either, kid.'

43

Another night at sea.

If the depths of the ocean weren't enough nightmare fuel, the total darkness above the surface would do the trick. Each glance King took through the periscope revealed nothing but a void of black. He'd gotten used to it after the first couple of nights alone, but even still, it tested the limits of his stoicism.

He paced the length of the sub, clutching the captain's satphone, trying to work up the courage to send the message. Earlier that evening, Slater had called to provide an update, and the new information acquired from Rémi's goons had given King an idea that ended up festering in his mind.

With the lack of stimuli aboard, it had been about all he could think of for the last few hours.

It'd be bold, but he desperately needed to do something bold. This murky limbo about "communication issues" couldn't last forever without raising suspicions.

So this little move would kill the doubt, or, if he was wrong, blow the whole thing up in his face.

He couldn't find the nerve to press SEND, not if it risked destroying everything he'd already worked toward, so he called Violetta instead.

She answered sleepily. 'At least this means you're alive.'

'Give me the scoop.'

In the early days of the voyage, he'd asked her to feed him every painstaking detail of Junior's waking life. It was something warm to fill the cold void of the narco-sub, no matter how trivial the updates. He relished hearing how Junior babbled unintelligibly at *PAW Patrol,* how he knocked his bowl off his high chair and then smiled when it splattered across the floor, how he gazed all around, looking deep into the corners of each room, like he knew something was missing.

'Nothing of note today,' she said. 'Junior's been an angel. No fuss, no crying. Alexis dropped in for a couple of hours of gossip this morning, and she roped me into a hike up Mount Katahdin tomorrow. I've sorted a babysitter. You know, I'm actually looking forward to feeling that physical burn again. It's been six months of downtime.'

'You've still been exercising like crazy.'

'I've been *exercising.* But you know we have different definitions of "crazy" to most people. Several thousand feet of elevation gain makes me giddy with excitement. Might run up the mountain.'

King smiled; an odd sensation. He was aware of the emptiness of the gesture, the fact that no one was around for thousands of miles to so much as catch a glimpse of it. But in its own small way, he felt it bring some light to the dank and gloomy surroundings. 'Soon you'll be spouting Slater's philosophy like Tyrell. He's a whole different kid since Slater took him up Katahdin.'

'Alexis tells me he's crushing school. The principal

called her on Friday to laud his efforts. Sounds like he's settling in smoother than you can imagine.'

King managed another fond smile. 'That's Will, alright. *"Control what you can, discard what you can't."* Tyrell probably loves the fact he's the new kid in town. I'm sure Slater's taught him to lean into difficulties, embrace them.'

'Well, if Junior can learn half as well as Tyrell…'

'He will.' He heard her smile through the phone. 'What?'

She chuckled softly. 'I've never heard you sound so sure.'

'He's got our blood. There's nothing in this whole world he won't be able to do.'

'He's got *your* blood.'

'And it's a miracle he's got yours, too, or he'd get himself killed before adulthood doing something monumentally stupid.'

She sensed his tone. 'Like you're about to do now, maybe?'

'Mmm.'

'What's that mean?'

'It means, "Yes, but I don't want to admit it."'

'So go on. Run it by me.' She clearly knew why he'd called.

He talked her through it, then finished with, 'If I'm wrong, this whole thing is dead in the water. Literally. And it could be worse than that. They could have some sort of self-sabotage feature. Wouldn't be hard. One press of the button, the engine dies and the evidence is wiped…'

'They don't have that,' Violetta said sternly.

'You're sure, are you?'

'They'd already have run you through a gauntlet of questions if they had a means of ending you before you reach French Guiana. They want the money, so they're being cautious. I mean, they took your insult this morning, swearing at them to fix their tech. They don't want to piss the captain off to find out he's disappeared with the money.'

'That doesn't change the fact it'll be over if I fuck it up.'

'So? Sail to Bermuda and come home.'

'Without a passport?'

'You'll figure something out.'

'That's optimistic.'

'When *haven't* you figured something out?'

She had a point. 'You miss me?'

'Yeah.'

'You're supposed to play it cool.'

'If I play it cool and don't say how I really feel, then wake up one morning and you're gone forever, I'll beat myself up for the rest of my life.'

'I'll be fine. I promise. Junior's not growing up without me.'

'Send the message,' she said. 'Your logic is right. They're putting up with the aloofness for now, but as you get closer to the coastline, they'll get more and more concerned. You won't be able to do much if you go up the ladder when you arrive and find yourself staring down the barrels of a dozen AK-47s. You need them on your side, so you need to take a risk.'

'I'll let you know how it goes.'

Neither of them said, "I love you." They didn't need to vocalise it; they knew, deep down. He hung up and switched from his phone to the captain's. Took a deep breath and stabbed down with a grimy finger on the SEND symbol on-screen.

It fired off a one-word message to the unknown number: ALAIN.

He couldn't help but hold his breath. He knew if he was wrong, any follow-up messages to the number would

bounce. As soon as the contact was addressed by the wrong name, he'd snap the SIM card and bail, fleeing with his money and his freedom.

But if King was right...

The few minutes it took to receive a response felt like hours, but finally the phone pinged. King surveyed the room before he glanced down, savouring what might be the last moments of peace before everything potentially imploded.

He looked at the screen.

THOUGHT YOU'D FORGOTTEN MY NAME. WHAT IS IT?

King sighed as he rested the back of his head against the side of the sub, and the rattling fibreglass massaged his skull. The knots of tension bunched through his neck and shoulders started to disintegrate. Tight muscle fascia loosened, alleviated by relief.

Whatever he said now, whatever excuses he used to hide the fact he was an impostor, Alain Da Silva would eat it up. Even if the man suspected sabotage, he'd never allow himself to be convinced, because there was no way in hell the crew would give out his name. They would have died painfully before giving away information about their cartel overlords, and he would never imagine someone had provided his name from another source.

When King arrived in French Guiana, they'd be waiting for him.

Guards down.

Weaknesses exposed.

He couldn't think of anything better.

In short bursts spaced across the night, he had the easiest sleep of the whole journey.

PART III

44

Three figures jogged in sync down the gently sloping asphalt.

On the outskirts of Millinocket, traffic was a non-factor. Anyone travelling down the road, which was long and straight and entirely unchanging, would see them from a mile away, and adjust their trajectory accordingly. Slater always veered onto the shoulder anyway, as a courtesy. Each time he did so, Alexis and Tyrell fell in behind him. He was ten miles into a planned fifteen-mile run at an easy aerobic pace, and he hadn't expected company. He was accommodating, though, and never set in his ways. If someone asked to tag along, he'd never deny them the opportunity, but he wouldn't slow down to wait for them. Which meant for Alexis and Tyrell the pace wasn't exactly leisurely or aerobic...

Barely breathing heavy at an eight minute per mile pace, Slater looked over his shoulder. 'How we faring?'

Alexis scoffed between breaths. 'Bullshit this is an easy pace.'

'It's all relative.'

She was sucking air like her life depended on it, her defined quads and hamstrings puffed up, already full of lactic acid. Despite the adversity, her form and stride were still measured, her Nikes seeming to glide gracefully over the asphalt. With a perfectly proportioned physique like hers, it was hard *not* to look good running.

Tyrell couldn't even respond. He was breathing harder than both Slater and Alexis put together, and his running form paid the price. His feet slapped the concrete, and he plodded forward with only determination as fuel. At least there was a built-in excuse: he was still adjusting to his physical transformation, no longer a prepubescent boy. It made sense that he'd need to grow accustomed to moving his larger frame around.

As Slater trotted along, using each muscle as efficiently as possible to conserve energy, he said, 'Five miles left. You should both slow down. You're not getting much use out of a run if you spend the whole thing trying to survive.'

Tyrell gulped down the winter air, summoning the energy to turn to Alexis and say, 'He's so damn smug, isn't he?'

She managed a pained smile.

Slater's phone buzzed at his hip.

The only phone he took everywhere he went.

The one for emergencies.

He reached across and pulled it free from its armband holster, peeling it off his bicep. One look at the screen and the wince became a stare, eyes widening. His heart noticeably sped up in his chest. If he checked his fitness watch, he'd be well above the aerobic zone: the power of adrenaline.

He slowed to a walk and as Alexis and Tyrell moped past him, he said, 'I'll catch up.'

Alexis said, 'No shit.'

It drew a laugh out of Tyrell, even though he was deep in the pain cave.

Slater slowed to as slow of a walk as he could manage without completely stopping, and trudged along until they were both out of earshot. Then he dialled the number back.

Timothée picked up on the first ring. 'We need to meet.'

'Today?'

'Right fucking now.'

'It's been a whole week. You couldn't have warned me in advance? I'm with my family.'

'*I* didn't get any warning, man.'

'Alright,' Slater said. 'Better be good.'

'Good for you, maybe. I'm fucking scared. I need advice.'

'And you can't take advice over the phone?'

'It's *serious*.'

'Uh-huh.'

Silence.

Slater said, 'What, you're scared to tell me?'

'If I tell you, it makes it real.'

'I don't have time for this shit. I'm hanging up.'

A sharp inhale, then Timothée blurted out, 'The governor!'

Slater froze. 'What?'

'Rémi called from Cayenne. He, uh, he is not happy. He wants me to meet with Dubois. Today. This afternoon. Two p.m.'

Slater glanced at his watch: almost eleven. 'How am I supposed to give you advice in the flesh? You've got to be in Augusta by now if you're planning on visiting the governor.'

'I am in Bangor,' Timothée said tentatively, the French

accent stronger than ever. 'He is … coming to me, I think. He's here in town in hotel. That's all I've been told.'

Slater sensed the fear in his tone. 'Surely you've sweet-talked Dubois before. It can't be that hard to alleviate his concerns.'

'What?'

'What do you mean, what?'

Timothée cleared his throat. 'This, uh, this is why I call you. I never met governor before. And Rémi … Rémi doesn't have my photo. He never come to America, obviously. He first get in touch through mutual contacts and I do good work for him, so he keep me on. But … I don't think he know what I look like…'

Slater scratched the stubble at his jaw as he listened, turning in a slow half-circle by the side of the road. 'Oh, shit.'

'Yeah. So, like, if you want to meet Noah…'

'You're goddamn right I want to meet Noah.'

'You might need to do French accent.'

Slater changed up his voice in an instant. '*Is 'zis good enough for you?*'

A long pause. 'Pretty fucking good, actually. Most people exaggerate too much.'

'*Voilá.* I'll be there as fast as I can.'

He hung up, put his hands to either side of his mouth, and shouted, '*Alexis!*'

A few hundred feet ahead, her figure slowed and turned to face him.

He yelled, '*Business!*'

She nodded and waved a hand dismissively. *Go.*

Part of the terms they'd agreed upon for this three-week period. As long as King was aboard that sub, Slater could drop everything at a moment's notice to help. Which, really, was no different from their ordinary lives.

He returned the emergency phone to his armband, turned back toward Millinocket, and took off fast.

This wasn't the time for an easy aerobic pace.

45

As he gunned the Range Rover south to Bangor, Slater's thoughts turned to King.

As they did during most of the downtime he had these days.

The man had spent two whole weeks in the narco-sub, and was well into the home stretch of the trip. They'd last spoken the previous day, and everything appeared to be running as smoothly as it could be. Da Silva hadn't made any significant interrogation attempts via satphone message, not after being addressed by name last week. King was still chalking the inability to make phone calls up to tech issues, and there didn't seem to be any serious resistance to that idea.

So, externally, all was well.

King wouldn't go into detail about the mind-numbing monotony, but Slater had to imagine that internally, it was a different story.

It sure would be if it was *him* in the submarine instead of King, forced to sit in a box for a little over five hundred hours. Their lives were all momentum and forward progress; the sudden shift would be brutal on the soul.

As he entered Bangor's limits he drove one-handed and fired a text to Timothée, who came back immediately with an address. Slater copy-pasted it into Maps, which revealed a grainy top-down satellite view of a small dwelling on rural Kittredge Road, north of the Bangor Mall and the commercial supercentres surrounding it.

Could be a trap, but it fit with the living conditions Slater had pictured for the gangsters. Timothée took work far beneath what he was capable of for a boss he detested, so it made sense he lived in squalor. He probably had the money for somewhere better; it could be a form of self-punishment. It still turned Slater's stomach as he studied the satellite images and eyed the acres sprawling in all directions away from the shack.

No fencing, no perimeter, no tree cover.

A thousand different angles to approach for an ambush.

He called Timothée, who answered with, '*Oui?*'

Slater turned his voice to ice. 'I found your friends. They're all dead. I'm coming for you.'

'*What?!* What the fuck are you talking about? What friends? Will, I swear—'

'Don't worry,' Slater said. 'Just a test.'

A pause, then a hard inhale. 'You're a bastard.'

'Needed to know I wasn't walking into a death trap.'

'You should hurry. I have to be there in an hour.'

'Where?'

'Some budget hotel by the river.'

'Is it wise for the governor to be staying somewhere cheap?'

'I don't fucking know. That's where I was told to go.'

'By Dubois personally?'

'Yes. He's not going to go through an intermediary. He is, uh, too paranoid.'

'Did he call you?'

'Text message.'

'Okay. Good.'

'Listen, Will, I don't think it's a good idea for you to go in my place or anything. I think it will get us both killed, no?'

Slater said, 'See you soon,' and hung up.

He slipped north-east onto Stillwater Avenue, passing titanic industrial developments: a Home Depot, a Walmart supercentre, a Best Buy, a Target, a Petco. The mammoth warehouses loomed under early afternoon cloud, and something about his surroundings put a pit of unease at the bottom of his stomach, a wholly uncomfortable sensation. Contrasting with the Maine wilderness he'd grown accustomed to, this stretch of barren concrete was alien in its modernity.

Then, as quickly as the city-sized shrine to capitalism appeared, it was gone, replaced by fields and trees and the occasional long and winding driveway to secluded homesteads. The GPS told him the Northeast Penjajawoc Preserve lay ahead, but he pulled off before that down a dirt trail leading to Timothée's residence.

Instead of driving the Range Rover up to the gangster's front door, he pulled off-road and parked it deep in a copse of trees. He'd much prefer manoeuvring his own two hundred pounds of bodyweight over the SUV's four thousand. It made for a quieter approach, which, in his world, was total peace of mind.

Glock at the ready, he ghosted along the tree line until he found the shack. It wasn't hard to spot, planted dead in the middle of an impressive number of acres, without a single tree nearby. He'd rather wait ten minutes and ensure no one was lying in wait for him than rush to make the appointment with Dubois and take a bullet in the back of the head for his troubles, so that's exactly what he did.

He counted out a long, measured six hundred seconds.

Not so much as the tiniest movement from anywhere in his peripheral vision. The only disturbance was Timothée himself, who emerged onto the rundown porch at the eight-minute mark, squinting down the trail and wearing a concerned frown. At the nine-minute mark, he stormed back inside, swearing to himself. The cursing carried across the empty fields, and Slater picked up every word. Finally, his count complete, he jogged fast across the grass, leaping up onto the porch less than a minute after Timothée went back inside.

He hurled the screen door open and strode down a dark and cramped hallway into a musty living room.

His sudden appearance quite literally terrified the three occupants. Timothée was the only one standing, dressed in a white pullover and baggy grey sweatpants. He twisted on the spot and recoiled backwards, nearly tripping over the coffee table. The other two — the guys from the back of the Plymouth — were sprawled on the sofa, and reeked of weed. They didn't even notice Slater, only flinching at Timothée's sudden movement, then when they turned and noticed the huge shape looming in the doorway they shouted in unison. The one whose head Slater held a gun to the previous week instinctively snatched for a heavy glass ashtray on the coffee table, and feigned to throw it at the intruder.

Slater raised the Glock in response. 'Throw it. See what happens.'

46

W hen they figured out who it was, they settled.
Tutting disapprovingly, Timothée waved at his buddy to put the ashtray down. The guy complied. Timothée turned to Slater and said, 'Jesus Christ, man. I thought you bailed. What took you so long?'

'Had to see whether you were bluffing. It'd be a lot easier to tell Dubois about me than to tell me about Dubois.'

'Bullshit. He's some useless politician. You're ... a ninja or something. How you sneak up on us like that?'

'Practice. Now give me everything you were scared to tell me over the phone, and make it quick.'

'Okay. Okay, shit.' Timothée had broken out in a full sweat, and he crossed to a tattered armchair and dropped himself down on its ripped cushion cover. 'So...'

The stench in the room was awful, a mixture of body odour, stale food, and bad weed. Slater crossed to the window and opened it.

Timothée composed himself, spine bent like a hunch-back as stress sunk him into the chair. 'So Rémi called me this morning. Said there's a lot of people very interested in talking to me, because Jack's still AWOL. I cannot say that I know Jack's dead, of course, so I tell him there's not much I can help with. Rémi says it doesn't matter. No one else seen Jack or any of his men since that night when they unload the drugs. Rémi not supposed to tell me this, but he say Jack take something like ten tons of coke off that submarine, and now him and his crew are gone and their warehouse empty. No drugs. Rémi says the governor is furious about all this shit and is already on his way to Bangor because Rémi told him I was there. I must report to Riverside Inn in forty-five minutes. That's all I know.'

Slater nodded to himself. 'Alright. And you're positively sure the governor has no way of knowing who you are?'

'Rémi doesn't even have my last name. He operates on trust alone because he is idiot. So there's nothing he can pass to Dubois. I make sure of this. I don't like interference. I like my privacy, my life out here.'

Slater gazed around the shithole of a living room. 'Right.'

Timothée straightened up to stare at Slater. 'You...?' He trailed away.

Slater raised an eyebrow. 'What?'

'You have the drugs, no?'

Slater shook his head.

Timothée said, 'Then where are they?'

'At the bottom of the ocean.'

One of the guys on the sofa swore in French and feigned spitting. In English, he said, 'Idiot.'

Slater turned to Timothée. 'He's brave saying that to my face.'

Timothée's face was a pale mask of shock. 'It's just, uh, he knows how much money you lost...'

'Two hundred million dollars,' Slater said. 'Cash.'

'How do you know...?'

Timothée trailed off before something flared in his eyes, a sudden, visceral understanding. He rocked back in the armchair, awestruck, before he found the right words for the question he wanted to ask. 'Where is that submarine?'

'Wouldn't have a clue,' Slater said, sarcastic. He crossed the room and walked behind the sofa, and the guy who'd cursed and mock-spat at him made to get up, but Slater grabbed him by the shoulder and shoved him back down. He pushed the Glock into the side of his head again, holding him in place as he addressed Timothée. 'Can I trust you to keep this idiot's mouth shut?'

'Yes,' Timothée stammered. 'No problem. Yes you can.'

'That's good.' He took the gun away, but the guy remained transfixed, rigid. 'Only one more thing I need to know.'

'*Oui*?'

'How close are Rémi and Noah?'

Timothée shook his head vigorously. The other guy on the sofa, now cowered in the corner, shook his head too.

Slater said, 'What's that mean?'

It was all too much for Timothée. He fetched a pre-rolled joint and a lighter from the coffee table and used a hand to protect the flame from the cold wind whistling in through the window Slater had opened. After lighting the end, he took a long pull, drawing the smoke into his lungs and holding it there before he exhaled. After that he straightened up a little, nerves steadied. 'They, uh, they no get along anymore.'

'Anymore?'

'They used to be tight. Obviously, no? They took the risk of getting in touch with each other way back when. I don't know who contacted who first, who suggested this whole crazy business. But it was them against the world, y'know. And they did it. Obviously. They made it happen. But, uh, now ... now they don't really speak. Which is why Rémi is angry that Noah's making me show up at his hotel like servant...' He trailed off, winced, and sucked on the joint again. 'This is complicated, okay? Very complicated. It's not good idea for you to go.'

Slater let everyone shift uncomfortably around him. He kept unnervingly still, a port in the storm.

Timothée's eyes clouded over, thinking something through. 'Wait, why you want to know how close they are?'

'If afterward Noah tells Rémi that the Timothée who showed up was black, this is all over.'

Timothée scoffed. 'No chance. Noah not going to say shit. He thinks Rémi is ... moron.'

'Sounds like most people do.'

'But Rémi has the power,' Timothée said, tapping the side of his head as if sharing a secret of the universe. 'The power to say, "Yes, you can do this. I allow it." So Noah play nice, stay in touch, keep the money flowing. But talking about anything unnecessary? No. Noah will say, "Meeting go fine." He not gonna want to tell Rémi a thing.'

'Good,' Slater said, flashing a glance at his watch. 'I've got twenty minutes. Riverside Inn, was it?'

The skin around Timothée's eyes stretched. He'd worn more of a strain as the conversation progressed, and now the expression reached its apex. He'd been clinging for dear life to some notion that he was ultimately in control of the final decision, but that was gone. He brought the joint to his lips and puffed away most of it in three consecutive draws, then sat back in the armchair and brought his knees to his chest like a child. 'Yeah. That's it.'

Slater said, 'Don't go anywhere.'

He walked out through the haze.

47

A black oval sign with neon yellow writing read: RIVERSIDE INN.

The building behind it was a great ochre slab, four storeys tall, all the windows fixed into its otherwise featureless façade sporting white trim and spaced evenly apart. It sat surrounded by concrete, dumped next to the hospital. Northern Light Emergency Care loomed to the west, and the Penobscot River churned behind it in the early afternoon gloom.

Not quite where you'd expect perhaps the most important politician in the state to hole up.

Right away, Slater knew Noah Dubois hadn't waltzed in through the front door.

He approached on foot, so he had all the time in the world to absorb the dreariness. He'd parked at the very top of nearby Bellevue Avenue. The governor might know next to nothing about Timothée, but if he glanced out his window and saw Slater getting out of a Range Rover, he'd get suspicious. There wasn't any way around Slater's intimidating physicality, but he'd left his expensive jacket in the car and tugged and wrenched at his shirt and pants with his bare hands until they were stretched, loose-fitting enough to give him a dishevelled look.

It'd have to do.

There wasn't time.

Hesitation made him freeze several paces before he crossed the threshold to the lobby. He pulled his phone out and consulted the black screen so he didn't seem unhinged, his mind stewing the whole while.

You fuck this up and King's sacrifice has been for nothing.

He only dwelled on this for a couple of seconds before the solution presented itself, beautiful in its simplicity: just don't fuck it up.

He strode inside. Armed with the information Noah had passed to Rémi, who'd passed it to Timothée, who'd passed it to him, he approached the reception desk. He greeted the ashen-looking, grey-haired man who couldn't have been far into his forties with a disarming smile.

'Room 214,' he said with a powerful French accent overriding the English. 'I am told they called down to let you know to expect me.'

'Ah,' the guy said, leaning forward to consult his laptop. 'Yes. Name?'

'Timothée.'

'Timothée.' He tutted. 'Yes. Very well. Up you go.' He hesitated. 'Good luck.'

Slater gave him a knowing look, wondering how much they paid him to sneak them in through the back.

Wondering what they threatened him with.

He walked through a drab space to a drab stairwell, and climbed up through shadow, the lights spaced too few and far between. The second floor corridor seemed to extend forever. Briefly, he wondered how many times he'd done this. Walked down the same hallway to the same door, anticipating total carnage.

Often avoiding it, but sometimes not...

He found the right door and knocked.

Seconds later, a heavy, deep voice demanded, 'Name.'

Not Dubois. Slater had heard the man speak at televised press conferences. The French tint to the governor's accent was barely detectable anymore, but his voice was naturally high-pitched, yet somehow still firm and reassuring. A good fit for politics. You don't want to come off too aggressive, but you can't seem soft, either.

Slater said, 'Timothée.'

The door swung open.

A large dark-skinned man stood there, a couple of inches taller than Slater, a little wider. He wore a tight-fitting dress shirt tucked into suit pants. Slater had wrenched his own clothes out of shape competently enough to hide the impossible hardness of his physique, so at least the bodyguard would think he had the upper hand, but not by much. Clearly Slater's appearance had already set the guy on edge. The man broadened his shoulders, tried to fill more of the doorway.

Slater waited for the pin to drop.

This guy isn't Timothée.

The bodyguard stepped forward.

Slater braced to unleash a colossal uppercut.

The guy said, 'Arms up.'

Slater held his arms out straight while the guard patted him down. He tried to soften his musculature, but it was impossible. You can't create fat that isn't there.

The guy found no weapon, but as he took a step back, there was something in his eyes.

Again, Slater prepared for the inevitable.

The man said, 'You're in scary shape, brother.'

Slater shrugged, nonchalant. 'I do my best.'

The guard nodded and looked over his shoulder, meeting someone's gaze at an angle that masked them from Slater's view. 'He's clean.'

That nasally, slightly accented voice from the TV came back. 'Thank you, Winston.'

'You sure about—?'

'Yes. Thank you.'

Soft-spoken, yet intense.

Trademark Noah Dubois.

Winston slipped past Slater, out into the corridor. For the briefest of moments, their eyes met. Slater hoped he might read something there, but he found a blank slate. You work protective detail for a politician with a double life, you learn to hide what you're thinking.

Slater stepped inside and turned to shut the door.

When he turned back around, the governor was there.

Noah Dubois. Five-eight or so in thick-soled dress shoes, slim build, excellent posture. He stood to his fullest height with his shoulders back because he had to. Without the attention to detail he used to make the most of his slight frame, he'd seem impossibly small, too weak to govern Maine. With the sharp, angular face of an ageing Calvin Klein model, it was no wonder he was a hit with the female demographic. He was old enough for his looks to be a weapon rather than a hindrance; any younger and he'd seem too attractive, too air-headed for a serious position. The grey hairs and the wrinkles as sharp as his jawline leant an aura of wisdom, making his blue eyes and long lashes seem trustworthy rather than arrogant.

In summary, he had the look.

Sometimes that's all you need.

Slater glanced at the thin carpet every couple of seconds, feigning intimidation. The room was four yellow walls and a bed with a scratchy duvet, stretched taut as a board across the mattress. The single window in the far wall let very little natural light in. The gloom outside didn't help. The overhead light was somehow both too harsh and not bright enough. Directly over the governor's head, it made Dubois seem older than his fifty-five years, accentuating wrinkles and illuminating the oil in his pores, but its downward spotlight didn't extend to the rest of the room, leaving shadow in the corners. It gave Dubois a Messianic air.

'Thank you for coming,' the governor said, his words carefully chosen and his gaze a laser-beam.

Slater shoved his hands in his pockets, glancing nervously all around. 'Uh, yeah. No problem.'

He wanted nothing more than to return the icy stare, but the performance was necessary. Some second-rate gangster like Timothée wouldn't be so confident. He fixated on getting his accent right.

Dubois looked him up and down. 'I can see why Rémi hired you.'

'Yeah?'

Dubois spaced two palms apart in the air, the exact distance between Slater's shoulders. 'You got some weight on you, my boy. You lot are reliable.'

Slater shrugged.

Dubois jerked a thumb at the closed door, right where Winston had stepped out. 'I have one of my own.'

I fucking wish you'd talk this way in front of the cameras, Slater thought. He wanted to punch the governor's teeth down his throat. He refrained. 'Rémi told me you want to talk. I'm, uh, happy to help. Whatever you need.'

'Sit down,' Noah said with a smarmy politician's smile, gesturing to the edge of the bed. 'I want to tell you a story.'

Clearly wanting to nullify the obvious height difference.

Slater thought about breaking the man's neck and calling King, letting him know he needed to come home.

Instead he crossed to the bed and sat.

48

'That's better,' Dubois said, pacing the room.

Slater's shirt clung to him. It was stiflingly humid. The hotel room felt like a cage, a prison. What he despised most in the world was knowing he could snap this slimy piece of shit in half, and not being able to.

That old enemy of his: patience.

Dubois reached the windowsill, turned around, and rested against it. He pointed a finger across the room at Slater's face. 'Your accent.'

Shit.

Slater said nothing.

Dubois tutted, shaking his head slowly. 'It's a beautiful thing, isn't it?'

Slater shrugged. Internally, a weight lifted. He did his best to hide the rollercoaster in the pit of his stomach, apprehension and relief alternating with each reveal.

Dubois said, 'French is best, isn't it? You know it's the second most spoken language in this beautiful state of mine? And our country itself? My God. The scenery shits on

Maine. I should know; I was born in a tiny little commune, St-Guilhem-le-Désert.'

Slater raised his eyebrows. 'No way.'

He'd never heard of the place. The governor didn't need to know that.

Dubois flashed that charismatic smile and pointed at Slater again. 'You are a worldly man, Timothée. I knew it. Have you been?'

'No. But I hear it's beautiful.'

Slater's heart thrummed steadily in his chest. He rested his palms flat on his thighs so Dubois couldn't see the sweat beading on them. The nerves came from the threat of Dubois, at any moment, switching to French. Slater had a shaky grasp of the language, much the same as King, but imitating a fluent speaker? Forget it. The governor would sniff him out in a heartbeat, but Slater had to imagine Dubois hadn't consistently practiced his first language in decades. If Slater remembered correctly, Dubois moved with his parents to America at a very young age, and was granted U.S. citizenship by way of derivation. Being a foreign-born citizen prevented him from an eventual ascent to President or Vice President, but it didn't seem like he'd want that sort of scrutiny down the line anyway. Speaking English all day, every day, had whittled his accent down to practically nil, so Slater figured the chances were low, but the threat was there.

And he wasn't nervous for himself, but for King.

Dubois kissed his joined fingertips and threw them outward, a gesture so cliché it came full circle. 'Beautiful. Correct. Only way to put it. And the history? My God. The square alone dates back to medieval times. And the Clamouse Grotto? You know they only uncovered those caves in the 1940s? For *millions* of years, they were untouched. I grew up surrounded by beauty like this. But my parents wanted more for me than life in a rural commune, so we came here. I did well in school (this is humble, I assure you), got all my degrees, yada, yada. As I'm finishing my PhD, you know what they tell me?'

A long pause, at the tail end of which Slater realised Dubois actually expected a response. 'What?'

'That I can do anything.'

You're a sleazy, uneducated gangster, Will, Slater told himself. *This is impressing you.*

He said, 'Wow.'

Tried to act like he meant it.

'But,' Dubois said with a cock of the head, 'you know what I realise during my studies, over the course of my time in this picturesque state?'

'What?'

'That Maine is a cesspool. I hate what I govern. Isn't that funny?'

The air became uncomfortably still. Sounds from outside amplified: the blare of a distant horn, a bird cawing, a siren descending as an ambulance pulled up to the neighbouring ER. Slater had more experience with terrorists than he could remember, but it was different when a wolf in sheep's clothing stood before him, a man wielding significant power in a country he despised. And what twisted Slater's insides, made him sick to his stomach, was that until King was out of that submarine, he couldn't lay a finger on the governor.

The *governor.*

Who despised his state.

It scared Slater in a way that self-preservation couldn't. His own life wasn't as important as the innocents Dubois could destroy under the guise of kindness.

You'd think you'd get used to seeing the worst of humanity, up close and personal, but for decades now it had maintained its novelty.

And here he couldn't channel his rage into anything productive.

'My very first degree,' Dubois said, staring out the grimy window into the grey, 'was in Education and Human Development. That had to be, what, thirty-five years ago now? They sent me to some school I can't even remember the name of now for placement, and you know what I saw?'

Another pause which Slater found insufferable. 'What?'

Dubois looked over his shoulder and moved away from the window, as if summoned deeper into the room. 'If French kids spoke French, it was a fucking sin. That language ... our gorgeous language ... such a rich and deeply-rooted history in this state and those kids were *segregated.* I saw it with my own eyes. I downplayed my own accent because I feared judgment. Can you believe that shit?' His right fist clenched as he strode. 'It was then that I pivoted from teaching aspirations to political ones. Before that, I thought a good life in America is a nine-to-five and a comfortable existence. But I see what is happening to my culture, my *place,* and I think if I'm in a position of power I can change that. And you know what?'

I've barely said a fucking word, Slater thought, *and you're giving me your life story?* It spoke to the accuracy of his faked accent, which appeared to have drawn a deep nostalgia from Dubois.

For the fourth time, Slater said, 'What?'

A shrug. 'I make it my life's work to reach as high as I can, and I get here. And I realise no matter what I preach, no matter how they spin the PR, no one gives a fuck about some old guy, who by this point sounds American, waffling on about embracing French culture.' He spread his arms wide, exposing wide sweat patches in his pits. 'So I think, why should I give a fuck about them? Right? I tried altruism, and ended up nowhere. So why not see what I can do selfishly? Why not pivot a wasted life, put it to use for myself? And guess what?'

Slater strained, about to ask it a fifth time, but to his relief Dubois pressed on before he had to.

'Turns out,' Dubois said, 'there's a whole lot I could do. All it took was one idiot prefect in an overseas department of my beautiful homeland, and suddenly I had the might of international organised crime at my disposal. You come to learn a lot of things, being thrown in the deep end. You learn the price of humans. They all have one. Blue collar, white collar, Coast Guard ... you only need to know where and when to push. A learned talent, of course.'

Slater was a dumb gangster. He offered a shrug and a confused smile.

Dubois tutted, waved a hand indiscriminately, shook his head. 'I apologise. I don't talk to anyone about this anymore, so I take the opportunities I can to vent. I used to speak to your boss about it, but, well...'

Slater took a risk. 'Well, Rémi is a fool. It seems all his relationships implode. I'd go so far as to say if you get on his bad side, it means you've got your head screwed on properly.'

Dubois froze.

Slater blinked.

A smile spread wide on Dubois' face, flashing perfect teeth that had to be veneers. 'You are excellent, my friend. Fucking *excellent. Pouvons-nous parler un peu français*?'

Slater used every ounce of brainpower available. He focused as deeply and intensely as possible without letting a speck show on his face. Wheeling back through decades of memories, scraping together what little he'd learned, he loosely translated.

Can we speak a little French?

His heart dropped.

49

Slater smiled to buy a little time.

Dubois didn't offer any sort of response. Just stood there, staring down at him, watching him perch uncomfortably on the edge of the bed.

A wall clock ticked by the door.

Slater made a decision and stared right back at the governor. 'We've shot the shit enough, no?'

Dubois gave nothing.

His face betrayed nothing.

His eyes were glassy.

Suddenly, like magic, he snapped out of his trance. Shook his head again like he'd freed himself from the clutches of passion and said, 'You are right. You are not here for us to muse on our heritage.' A pointed pause. 'You are here because you are the only person on this planet who's seen the man who ran off with my drugs.'

Slater nodded, injecting some relief into his own expression. 'Yes. That's why I'm here.'

Dubois pulled the chair out from the small desk in the

corner of the room and sat facing Slater. He hunched forward. 'Are you going to lie to me?'

'No.'

'How do I know?'

Slater shrugged. 'I know what you're capable of. You just made it clear, no? Did you say the Coast Guard's on your side? Why would I mess around with someone like you?'

Dubois wagged a finger in his face. 'I know I've said this too much, but you are *excellent*.'

Slater lowered the guard he'd invented, the caution Timothée would have if he were in this room, facing this man. Unavoidably, this lowered his own guard. Only a touch, but enough. He was a tad rusty in the method-acting department.

So when Dubois turned and reached over the seat-back and pulled one of the desk drawers open, Slater hesitated. Only milliseconds, but by then Dubois had come out with a 9mm Springfield Armory XD pistol. Dubois had it aimed at Slater's face before he could blink.

'But being excellent,' Dubois said, some wild glint in his eye Slater had never seen before, 'makes you smart. And being smart, you would see advantages in lying to me.'

Slater couldn't show the truth: that his pulse had barely risen. He put the fear of God in his eyes, widening them as he held up his hands. 'Whoa, whoa, whoa. My brother. You just tell me we so alike—'

'That's right,' Dubois hissed, his eyes ice. 'And if I were in your position, Timothée, I'd sure see the appeal in making it look like Jack ran away. I'd offer a serious favour to the guys from Lubec Body Works in exchange for a tiny percentage of the cocaine profits.'

Slater kept his hands up. In fact, he inched them higher. 'You want the truth?'

'Of course I want the truth.'

The gun drifted closer, and Dubois slipped a finger inside the trigger guard. The first real spike of panic flooded Slater's bloodstream, making him genuinely jittery, ready to tear the man apart with his bare hands. How confident was Dubois? He'd paid off the guy at reception, and Winston was just outside, but the other guests...? Maybe this room was the furthest in the whole complex from another occupied one. Still, a gunshot was a gunshot. It was clear as day that the governor was wholly inexperienced handling a weapon, but it would be simple enough to hit a target from that range, and if Slater lunged for the Springfield it might go off inadvertently.

He was trapped.

Boxed in.

The tunnel rapidly narrowed, his chances closing.

Slater said, 'I didn't even know about the cocaine.'

Dubois watched him closely. 'No?'

'Is it my job? My business to know? Rémi alludes to something, sure, and I can connect the dots, so I guess if you ask me, I guess coke. But no one ever tell me that. I hardly know what *Jack* do, for fuck's sake, let alone you. I'm told to sort Jack out, so I pull up. He see me, he take off. That's it.'

'You never seen him before?'

'No, but it like he see me before.'

Dubois hesitated. He drew the gun back a little, which had been Slater's intention all along. Curiosity usually kills aggression. 'What do you mean?'

'He look at me and I see this terror in his eyes. Like he know who I am and he think I'm going to cut his abdomen, gut him. That sort of fear. Like he never been more afraid for himself, but I wasn't even doing anything. I had no weapon. I don't get it. But if it's, you know' — Slater raised his eyebrows, pursed his lips — 'cartel-related, then I see why he shit his pants. He think I part of that, but I just some nobody some prefect like 'cause he French.'

Dubois traced a gentle line in the air with the pistol barrel.

Slater tensed up, preparing to make a snatch for it. He brainstormed the maximum amount of punishment he could dish out with a single lunge, and ended up landing on a decision to blind the man by raking his nails across his eyes. From there, Dubois would panic-fire blind, and it should be simple enough to pluck the gun off him and beat him to death.

His pulse thudded in his ears.

Dubois lowered the gun and put it on the floor. 'Well, I like you, too, Timothée. You ever been to the Astor Platinum Lounge in Augusta?'

Slater thought, *Like Timothée would have ever been within a fucking mile of a place with "Platinum" in the name.* He shook his head, acting dumbfounded. 'No. I no hear of it.'

'Well, you did good work, kid. It's a favourite of mine. I have a discreet arrangement with management there, if you know what I mean. After I sort this bullshit out, we'll have a drink there. Maybe buy ourselves a little fun. The way they smuggle their VIPs in through the back ... it's professional.' He scoffed, waved a hand dismissively. 'You won't have to worry about that, of course. My bad. Sometimes I default to thinking everyone in the world has a public profile to uphold.'

Slater's blood hummed as he tasted opportunity.

Cautiously, wearing a sly smile, he said, 'How often you find yourself in a place like this? I see you on TV, I picture you in boardroom. Not ... you know...'

'Every Saturday night. It's tradition. It's the only night of the week I can justify being uncontactable under the guise of family time. And, really, once you're in politics, "family" is just PR spin. I got a robot for a wife and two teenagers that hate my guts, so it's better I'm out of the house anyway. Sometimes I'm ready to put her head through a wall, and *that'd* be bad PR. So I'm doing them a favour, you know?' A confused pause. Dubois rocked back in his seat and shook his head. 'Well, there's no fucking way I should have told you any of that, but we can trust each other, can't we, Timothée?'

Slater said, 'Absolutely.'

Saturdays, he thought. *You're on borrowed time, Noah.*

50

A fter a painstaking twenty seconds of silence, Slater rose from the bed.

Dubois held up a hand. 'What are you doing?'

Slater shifted his weight foot to foot. 'Leaving.'

'Did I dismiss you?'

It took all Slater's willpower to act scared when he wanted to shove the governor's teeth down his throat. He sat back down. 'I'm sorry.'

Dubois laughed. 'Don't worry, kid. Just playing. But, look, I really only brought you here to talk about Jack, and we've barely touched on it.'

'What's left to touch on?'

Dubois wagged a finger. 'There's that fiery streak. You're a good egg. I see myself in you.' He looked around, sighed. 'Truth is, I don't trust these Americans. I knew you'd be telling the truth. I just had to confirm it. You wouldn't lie to me, would you?'

'Of course not.' It was extraneous; Slater already had Dubois hook, line, and sinker.

Dubois stared, and the seconds ticked by.

One, two, three, four, five...

'Good,' he said, supposedly convinced. 'That's very good.' He slapped his thighs as he stood up. 'Off you go, then. Scram. You were never here.'

Slater said, 'Do me a favour.'

Dead silence.

Only the faint backing track of sirens.

Evidently Dubois didn't hear those words often. 'What *favour* do you need from me, Timothée?'

Slater scratched his stubble and stared at the floor. 'How do I put this?'

'However you'd like.'

'Rémi ... you know Rémi. He's intense. You either his best friend or worst enemy. I don't like to say this, but he has zero emotional intelligence, no?'

Risky as hell.

But Dubois smiled.

Conspiratorial.

In silent agreement.

Slater said, 'So ... we talk about things here that Rémi wouldn't like to know about. He thinks he owns me. I think ... I think he's lonely in French Guiana. I think he rely on people like you and me, but he push too hard. Push us away. It sounds like you two not on good terms...'

'We're not.'

'Well, I still work for him. So I need to be in his good books. So if you and me talk more, if we go to Astor, if we become close, you no tell Rémi about this. Please. That's all I ask. Otherwise he get jealous, like a bitch.'

By now, Dubois wore a grin from ear to ear. 'Your concern is misplaced, my friend. I only talk business with

Rémi Poirier. This meeting was only for my own reassurance, so the big idiot doesn't need to hear a word of it. Okay?'

Slater smiled back. 'Perfect.'

He made for the door.

When he placed his hand on the doorknob, Dubois called out. 'Hey.'

Slater looked over his shoulder.

'Does blood make you queasy?'

'No.'

'If I need that sort of work carried out, can I call you?'

'Of course. You always count on me, sir. Us against the world. *Oui*?'

'*Oui*.' A wink. '*Ils ne respectent pas notre culture, nous ne les respectons pas.*'

Slater smiled and nodded and walked out without a clue as to what Dubois had said. Something about respecting culture.

He passed Winston without looking him in the eyes and continued down the corridor. It felt like he was floating. He couldn't wrap his head around the incompetency of the system, at how a man like Dubois could slip through the cracks and come into tremendous political power without his true stance coming to light. If all it took was Slater feigning an accent to draw vitriol from the governor's lips, how useless were the preventative measures that were supposed to stop someone like him becoming influential?

Or maybe, just maybe, the system was designed that way deliberately.

As he left the Riverside Inn, stepping back outside under a blanket of storm clouds, Slater knew the truth. Deep down, he always had. He'd seen enough of the inner workings, glimpsed the industrial nature of corruption.

The world was all sick and wrong.

Front was back.

Up was down.

Good thing there were a handful of outliers like him and King to do something about it.

51

A terrifying groan tore King from slumber, pulling him from dreamworld into a different kind of darkness.

The walls moaned.

It was like some beast from the depths had awoken and surfaced for food, the sub caught in the jaws of some mammoth predator. He fell off the gas tank in his haste to roll over, then rubbed the skin off his palms in desperation as he leapt to his feet. A frantic look up the periscope revealed only early afternoon gloom; not a manmade object in sight. When the noise subsided, he chalked it up to the shoddy construction. No telling how long this thing could last without repairs.

Hopefully another week.

He no longer had any control over his adrenaline, a surprising side-effect of the solitary confinement. For decades now he thought he'd mastered the stress response, thought he could fight down fear as required, but it turned out he'd simply never dealt with uncertainty for any significant amount of time. Operations were usually over in a matter of days, if not hours.

Weeks in a cramped box that could disintegrate at any moment was a whole new level of "fuck this."

It took him a few minutes to clear the cobwebs. Once he was lucid he took the captain's satphone off charge and checked the notifications.

One message from Alain Da Silva.

Which read in French: DON'T TEST YOUR LUCK.

He groaned and slid down the side of the gas tank, sat on the damp metal floor.

He couldn't take much more, but he'd have to.

Which, when he thought about it, was the story of his life.

Everything becomes simple when you eliminate options.

You either do it or you die.

For days now, he'd pressed for an end destination, a set of GPS coordinates along the French Guiana coastline to dump the sub. At first he was elated when Da Silva avoided the question, because it meant there wasn't some predetermined drop-off point the captain was already supposed to know. But the delays stretched out, first for twenty-four hours, then forty-eight, and steadily King grew panicked.

King shot back with: WHAT LUCK? YOU'VE GOT TO GIVE ME SOMETHING TO WORK WITH. I'VE GOT YOUR MONEY.

Minutes passed, which meant nothing. Time had become so distorted that Da Silva could have made him wait hours and it wouldn't have felt any different. It was all the same in here, just a long unending nightmare he couldn't wake up from.

Finally, a response: NEAR CAYENNE, OBVIOUSLY.

King rolled his eyes. *No shit.* French Guiana's capital city was about the only cluster of civilisation on its coast; the rest was impenetrable jungle and winding rivers. The only alternative was the town of Kourou, further north than Cayenne, but King doubted they had the infrastructure in place to handle a billion-dollar semi-submersible empire. Kourou was built around the Guiana Space Centre, which carried out rocket launches for the European Space Agency. Reading about the space centre's history over the course of the last two weeks, King was intrigued to see it with his own eyes, but this was a business trip.

Once he stepped foot on solid ground, there'd be zero time for pleasure.

King wrote back: WHERE? OBVIOUSLY NOT WHERE YOU BUILT THIS THING.

Da Silva wrote back: OPEN WATER, MAYBE.

Maybe a test. Maybe not.

King's blood ran cold.

If Da Silva forced him to pull the sub up short of the coastline and sent boats out to intercept and collect the money in the middle of the ocean, it was as good as over. Even if King laid a trap and gunned down all the goons Da Silva shipped out, no one important would dare venture out into open water. Alerts would be raised long before King made it to the mainland, and the people truly behind this operation would be gone.

No, he needed to explode out of the sub with Da Silva *right there.*

But the more he pushed, the slimmer the chances of getting what he wanted. Such was the nature of humanity: often the less you care, the better you do.

So he fired back: NO CHANCE. SPEAK SOON.

With everything on the line, he lay his aching body and its stiff joints down atop the gas tank and went back to sleep.

PART IV

52

Rémi Poirier stepped out of the black Chevrolet Tahoe.

The first step he placed on the jungle floor splashed sun-heated mud over his dress shoe, ruining it and soaking his sock in the viscous muck. He obviously had experience with the region's stifling weather, the heat and humidity like a solid wall, enveloping him in a giant, invisible hug as he left the SUV, but he'd grown accustomed to the air-conditioning of the French Guiana Prefecture Building in Cayenne. Life was better indoors; this godforsaken land had nothing for him. Not even the allure of drink and drugs and women of the night could coax him from his insulated routine.

Such is the life of an introverted coward.

At least he could admit it. Most couldn't. He considered that victory enough.

He bowed his head against the sun, squinted, and followed his heavily-armed, heavily-armoured entourage into the jungle.

Clad in Kevlar and brandishing automatic carbine rifles, his quartet of bodyguards made a fearsome sight. Drenched in sweat as they stormed through the mangroves, leaving perspiration coating fronds and branches they brushed aside, they didn't say a word to Rémi for the entire one-mile trip. He followed meekly, somehow sweating harder than they were despite being weighed down by nothing but his clothes. By the time they finished the fifteen-minute trek, his dress shirt was soaked through, draped off his stooped shoulders like some sopping rag, tucked into black suit pants and held around his flabby midsection by a belt.

He wiped miniature rivers off his forehead. Drops ran over pockmarked skin into his eyebrows.

'How much further?' he gasped in French.

The first words uttered since they left the Tahoe.

One of the bodyguards, Thibault, glanced over his shoulder. At the sight of his boss, the man laughed like a jackal: *Eh-eh-eh-eh.* 'Look at this fucking guy.'

He was the only one with the nerve to mock; the other three faced forward, didn't so much as acknowledge the conversation. Thibault had only been with Rémi for two months, but had already figured out the prefect was pliable like putty. You could beat him around with your words, knock him into any sort of shape, and he'd take it.

Rémi considered trying to change that. 'What's so funny?' he snapped.

'You're the one,' Thibault said, slicking his black hair back, 'who said the shipyards needed to be inaccessible by vehicle. Right?'

'Right.'

'And now you complain about walking.'

'I didn't complain. I asked a simple question.'

'In just about the whiniest tone I've ever heard.'

'You work for me. You answer.'

Even the mercurial Thibault understood his limits. 'Less than five.'

'Good.'

'Hey,' Thibault said, unable to resist another jab. 'You ever think about doing this ten times a day carrying construction materials?'

'No,' Rémi said, sweat dripping off his chin. 'I don't.' He brushed a frond aside.

'Maybe you should. That's what has to happen when some suit in a cool office far, far away makes decisions that don't affect him in the slightest.'

The bodyguard next to Thibault physically winced. He was new; he'd soon learn. Rémi's power carried little weight when you saw past the artificial reputation preceding him. He was a tool, nothing more, and what's worse was he knew it.

Rémi scowled. 'You don't work construction. Quit bitching.'

'No,' Thibault conceded. 'But I come from the same place as the labourers. We come from the muck.'

'You're a labourer.'

'I'm a labourer in the same way that a lion cub's a predator. I stand around and make weak men look important.'

Rémi spat at the man's back. 'Fuck you.'

'Yeah, swear at me.' Thibault smirked over the other shoulder. 'Just words. You won't fire me. I keep you alive out here.'

The other three bodyguards might as well have been back in childhood, waiting to be scolded by their mothers. They looked terrified for their lives. But for all Thibault's rebelliousness, he was right. No one could protect their client the way he could. He was switched on in a way his colleagues could only dream about. Soon he'd be moving up the ladder, but for now he was guarding Rémi Poirier.

The quartet led Rémi around an impenetrable wall of mangroves. At the edge of the barrier, they squelched through mud, and the river opened up before them. The sight of the water offered little relief; it simmered under relentless sun, providing no escape from the way the jungle choked the air.

On the opposite bank lay the shipyard.

The three warehouses were more frames than buildings, skeletons of great structures that, together, comprised a half-finished factory. But even in their ramshackle state, they offered all the protection from the elements that was needed for the submarines within. A semi-submersible was under construction in each warehouse, each vessel slaved over by lean-limbed workers plucked from the poorest regions of French Guiana. Sparks spurted from power tools and men hurried to and fro across the warehouse floors, heaving materials all over the place. Like chameleons slinking through the surrounding undergrowth, paramilitary soldiers paced the complex's perimeter, itchy trigger fingers ready to mow down anyone who showed their face without prior authorisation.

On Rémi's side of the river, a small fishing boat bobbed in the shallows.

Alain Da Silva was its sole occupant.

The cartel killer's sudden presence and beady eyes startled Rémi. He fought down the urge to swallow nervously. He hadn't seen Da Silva in nearly a year, not since the man made his last ill-fated trip to Cayenne. If there was anywhere Da Silva didn't belong, it was in civilised society.

He'd come to the capital to talk business at cafés, bars, and, if he proved himself in those preliminary arenas, maybe the Prefecture Building itself.

Da Silva bailed the first time they got coffee, went crawling straight back into the jungle.

Order, pleasantries, laws and customs ... not his cup of tea.

Rémi got a good look at him. Da Silva's leathery skin baked in the sun. He was a squat, compact brute of a man. Five-eight, maybe, but heavier than Rémi, which was saying something. Rémi was six-one and out of shape, pudgy around the midsection. The other day he'd topped the scales at two hundred pounds, none of it good weight. Da Silva's weight, on the other hand, was all muscle, with the firmness of concrete.

Like the strength of an adult gorilla that had been squashed down, beaten and shaped into human form.

Da Silva smiled with a mouth full of brown teeth and leapt from the fishing boat. He waded through shin-deep mud, up the bank toward Rémi. The sludge didn't seem to slow him down one bit, offering no resistance, suggesting mind-boggling strength.

'Rémi,' Da Silva sneered, extending his arms wide. 'Oh, how long it's been—'

He must have approached too quickly.

Thibault stepped between them and put a hand on Da Silva's barrel chest. 'Easy.'

Da Silva stopped in his tracks. When he turned to face the bodyguard, his hands started shaking, and not from fear. His eyes nearly bugged out of his head as he stared at Thibault, who was a seasoned combat veteran in his own right, far from easily intimidated.

'What did you say to me?' Da Silva said softly.

Thibualt took his hand away and took a step back. He lowered his eyes to the mud. 'I'm sorry, sir.'

The air hung still.

53

Rémi could have stated the obvious.

That on paper, he had twenty times the influence of some jungle cartel servant. A single order handed down back in Cayenne and this shipyard would be torn apart by the authorities. The guerrillas and the paramilitary forces employed by the cartels were fearsome, but Rémi had control over the *Les forces armées en Guyane,* the troops of France's military base in the department. They were two thousand strong, and if push came to shove, Rémi could use them as he pleased. All it would take was a phone call back home to the French president. Their ties ran deep; it was how Rémi landed this gig in the first place.

But power means nothing if you don't use it.

Real power lies in the subtle details, in the way a bodyguard can defiantly shun one man but bow at the feet of another.

Da Silva waited a few seconds so they all got a good look at Thibault's stance and posture. It seemed to set the tone amongst the group. Then he walked forward again, this time unobstructed. 'Rémi.'

He wore that same smile, the sort that said, *I'm in control.*

He opened his arms wide again, suggesting an embrace, but when he got within reach of Rémi he grabbed him by the shoulders and looked him up and down. 'You need a change of clothes.'

'It seems so,' Rémi said, his ordinarily pale complexion now bright red. He could feel the heat in his cheeks, feel his skin roasting as his pores continued to leak. He wanted to be anywhere else. 'It's good to see you.'

'Sure it is.'

Da Silva released his grip, which had been firm as iron, and walked back to the fishing boat. He gestured for them all to follow.

They chugged across the waterway in a matter of seconds. Da Silva wielded the tiller as he gunned it for the opposite bank. Rémi savoured the roar of the motor; conversation was impossible, and for that he was grateful. Before they reached the shipyard, Da Silva swung the tiller around, changing course suddenly. As Rémi gripped the hull's lip for stability, riding out the swing of his stomach, he figured the manoeuvre was unnecessary, just a way to make him more uncomfortable than he already was.

But when he looked down into the rancid, muddy water, he saw a huge shape looming, only a couple of feet below the surface.

Like some dormant beast.

He couldn't help himself; he recoiled.

Da Silva laughed at the top of his lungs, then shouted to be heard over the motor. 'We've got to store them somewhere once they're finished!'

Rémi squinted as the water reflected the sun into his eyes. 'Shouldn't they be out at sea as soon as they're done?!'

'Rémi Poirier, everyone!' Da Silva roared. 'The resident expert on submarine supply chain logistics!'

Rémi looked to Thibault for a reaction, knowing his other men wouldn't dare crack a smile. But the chief body-guard was staring vacantly at the water churning against the hull. It made Rémi's heart pound harder. Thibault had the fear of God in him, all from Da Silva asking one simple question.

You have the power, Rémi reminded himself. *You. Not them.*

It didn't help.

Two guerrillas with olive camouflage streaks across their pockmarked cheeks helped pull the boat up onto the muddy shore. Rémi's bodyguards clambered out first, as stiff and wooden as robots. His men had significant combat experience and even *they* were out of their depth here.

Rémi clambered down, nearly turning an ankle in the soft mud. Insects buzzed and hummed all around him. A *whomp* sounded behind him and he flinched. It was only Da Silva, the last to leap from the boat. He clamped a powerful hand down on Rémi's collarbone, the dress shirt squelching under his palm. Like some voodoo magic fell over him, Rémi became a statue.

Da Silva muttered in his ear. 'Your men will go with mine, yes?'

Rémi didn't answer.

He couldn't.

'Nothing sinister,' Da Silva assured. 'There is beer in the guards' quarters. They would appreciate a drink in this weather, no?'

Rémi looked at Thibault, who delicately met his gaze. Rémi had never before seen the man intimidated, but Thibault wore the expression of a guilty puppy. His eyes pleaded with his boss to do whatever Da Silva said, to offer no resistance. That way, they might all make it out of this in one piece.

Rémi said, 'Sure. They're here for appearances anyway, right? We trust each other.'

Da Silva laughed.

Down the riverbank, a bird shrieked.

Wordlessly, like a procession of monks, the camouflaged guerrillas led the bodyguards away.

It was the prefect and the cartel boss, alone in the mud, overshadowed by the warehouse skeletons and the general commotion within.

Rémi couldn't look at Da Silva. He stared up at the shipyard. 'Am I getting the tour?'

'Would it mean anything to you?'

Rémi suppressed a gulp. 'Of course. I'd ... love to see what we built.'

As soon as the words left his mouth, he regretted them. He knew exactly what was coming, but was helpless to stop it. Da Silva sauntered up to him, taking his sweet time, letting what Rémi said hang in the air.

Rémi shook his head in embarrassment, looked at his feet. 'I'm sorry—'

'*Shhh*,' Da Silva said, so close Rémi was sure the man could smell his sweat. 'It's okay. It's fine. Just ... pay attention to what you say in future. Don't forget your place.'

'Yes,' Rémi said, chin bowed, holding back tears.

'What *I* built,' Da Silva said. 'Never forget that. You said "Yes," on a phone call. That's *it*. I took years off my own life making this happen. You see the result, but you don't see the work. You couldn't fathom...'

'I know.'

Like flipping a switch, Da Silva stepped back and smiled,

the psychopathic glint in his eyes gone. He clapped his hands together, raised his voice again. 'You're not here for a tour anyway. Come. I have important news from Maine.'

He strode up toward the jungle, toward whatever lay behind the shipyard.

Rémi followed meekly, like a dog.

54

Saturday morning.

Slater surveyed Mount Katahdin from the rear porch, phone pressed to his ear. He relished the freezing air.

It cleared his mind, and right now that was the most important thing in the world. All else was useless.

He wore a grimace. 'Look, it doesn't matter if you end up having wasted the last three weeks of your life. It doesn't matter how uncomfortable the days were. If you do what they're telling you to do, it's a one-way trip. There's no out.'

'Is that an order?' King's voice sounded crisp, shockingly clear for transmitting from just off the coast of South America. 'Or a recommendation?'

'I can't live your life for you.'

'Wait,' King said, 'so you think it's *better* to have them intercept me in open water?'

'Infinitely.'

'No chance Da Silva makes the trip out to sea.'

'You're right. He won't. But now it's a matter of what you *can* achieve. Isn't something better than nothing?'

'If I go through the waterways and find that swamp, I can have it all. Everything. The whole lot. Alain Da Silva and Rémi Poirier both. And when I've got them, that gives you free rein to go for Dubois.'

Slater sighed. He couldn't find the words, wasn't actually sure they existed. He sat in the deck chair and dragged a palm over the top of his head, a kind of meditative gesture. 'We'll have to leave Maine, won't we?'

'Who said anything about that?'

'King...'

'What?'

'The *governor*. There's no coming back from that.'

King snorted. 'Why? That's the easy part. What do you think will happen when they find his body in Astor? There'll be a whole lot of hush-hush about it. They'll swear in a new one as quietly as possible. What does a governor even do? A state can go a few days without advancing a legislative proposal.'

'Depends how he dies.'

'Then make sure it's unsuspicious.'

'Easier said than done.'

'Yeah. I know all about "easier said than done." "Three weeks in a sub" doesn't sound so bad until you've lived it.'

'Settle down. You set off on a Sunday night, and it's Saturday, so you're at twenty days. Be a little more dramatic, why don't you?'

'Fuck you.'

Slater smirked, but a little silence wiped it away. 'I just don't think it's a good idea. Bottom line.'

'When is it ever?'

'Have you thought it through?'

'Do you really think there's *anything* else to do in this shitbox other than think?'

'Well, if you're comfortable...'

'I'm not. But it's the right call.'

Slater couldn't fathom what lay ahead for King. He'd survived the journey; whether his psyche would emerge unscathed was another story. In a couple of hours, he would reach the coastline of French Guiana, and via satellite message Da Silva had ordered him into a complicated web of waterways, the mouth of which lay just south of Cayenne. Somewhere deep inland, at one of the most rural and isolated points of the winding Comte River, he was to bring the sub to a halt in a deep swamp to allow Da Silva's guerrillas to unload the money. Da Silva had assured King any officials posted along the river had been paid to look the other way.

King said, 'He thinks I'm the captain, and he trusts the captain. I've got him. Believe me.'

Slater connected the dots out loud, for reassurances' sake. 'Because I got his name off Timothée for you.'

'Right.'

'He might think you got it from the crew.'

'You haven't seen this operation. The crew wouldn't have talked, not under the most egregious torture. Whatever I could do, Da Silva could do a hundred times worse.'

'Okay.' A pause. 'It's your call.'

'I'm going.'

'They'll seal it off behind you.'

'I know. I doubt I'll even be able to turn the sub around when the river narrows.'

'I'll wait to hear from you.'

'You ready to move on Dubois?'

'At the drop of a hat.'

'Good.'

They'd had these conversations too many times to count.

By this point, there was barely a need for a *Good luck.* Time and time again they defied the odds.

One day it would end.

One day there'd be nothing but radio silence.

Slater said, 'Keep me posted,' and hung up.

He stared at the horizon. Inhaled through his nose, held it for a beat, exhaled slowly from his mouth.

Calm. Control what's controllable.

Alexis stepped out onto the porch, hair flowing behind her, tossed by the wind. Her eyes blazed. 'He made it?'

'Couple of hours and he's there.'

She shook her head. 'I couldn't imagine.'

'I could. In some ways I envy him.'

She stood there frozen in disbelief.

He shrugged. 'After three weeks like that, once he gets back, normal life will be heaven. The air, the sky, the smell of the trees. Priceless.'

'Oh,' she said, raising an eyebrow. 'No happiness without suffering?'

'Something like that.'

She jerked a thumb at the looming horizon. 'Just run up Mount Katahdin again. That'll sort you out.'

He smiled.

'You heading out tonight?' she asked.

'If King pulls it off. Quick trip to Augusta.'

She nodded soberly. 'I doubt Tyrell would notice.'

'Oh?'

'You didn't hear? He's been talking to some girl from school for weeks now. They're at the Northern Plaza today. He sounds infatuated.'

'What about Danielle?'

'I think he's still talking to her. He still wants to go back to Boston.'

A pause. Slater bowed his head to mask a smirk. 'I didn't teach him that.'

'Maybe not consciously. But you taught him to be desirable.'

Slater raised an eyebrow. 'You think?'

She stepped closer. 'Of course. I thought I knew what desire was until I met you.'

She kissed him, and the rest of the world washed away. In moments like these, without fail, he thought, *Are my priorities in the right place?*

His phone shrieked, tearing him from her lips. He fished it out, recognised the number, and darted a finger to the screen to answer. 'Timothée?'

Heavy breathing; no words.

Slater knew mortal fear when he heard it. 'Are they leaning on you?'

'They don't buy cover story,' Timothée muttered, his voice raspy. He sounded disassociated, too high to think straight. 'I'm gonna tell Dubois everything. I thought I should let you know. I owe you this, I think. You deserve warning.'

Keeping the phone pressed to his ear, Slater left Alexis on the back porch and sprinted maniacally through the house.

He snatched his car keys off the kitchen countertop on the way out.

55

K ing spotted a solid dark line on the horizon.

The periscope lens was foggy and unclear, grimy after weeks of neglect, but the sight lined up with the GPS. There was nothing else it could be.

Land.

He had zero flair for the dramatic, but he almost shed a tear.

Couldn't help himself.

He stood there, face pressed to the periscope, gripping the handles of its metal pylon. He was filthy. Seawater only keeps uncleanliness at bay, doesn't eliminate it, and the bandaid-job nature of salty water had become less and less effective as the weeks dragged on. He was oblivious to the odour, his nose adjusting as the smell got worse, but his clothes were stiff and dirty and encrusted with salt. Oil and muck covered his skin and made his long mop of unkempt hair disgustingly greasy. His pores were clogged, and acne had sprouted across the length of his upper back.

He'd given up on the bodyweight workouts a few days ago.

That's when he knew it was getting dire.

He'd always prided himself on unrelenting self-discipline, and he'd always been able to push himself to his limits regardless of motivation levels. But all that theory took place on dry land, with beds and showers and clean air and some semblance of routine and sanity.

At some point on day seventeen, he'd thought, *Fuck this,* and abandoned everything that required he bring the sub to a halt. Washing, exercising, extended naps: out the window. He realised he'd rather get to French Guiana a day early with stiff joints and aching muscles, smelling slightly fouler, than bother dragging this godforsaken voyage out a moment longer than necessary.

And here he was.

All this, he thought, *just to die on arrival.*

He made sure not to listen to thoughts like those. The internal vitriol toward himself and his idiotic plan had grown worse over the journey, but he'd expected that. In dark times he detached himself from the negativity, recognising it for what it was: his own brain trying to stifle his progress. He wasn't about to start giving in to that voice; he never had before.

Just because it was harder to do in a situation like this, didn't make it any less straightforward.

It all boiled down to a simple truth: *Keep going.*

No quit.

The sub rumbled forward. Eventually the solid line became a coast with discernible terrain. King sailed closer still, until he could see the lush green of the jungle, make out a sea of trees responsible for the colour.

South America.

Another continent, halfway across the globe, and he'd made it in this creaking, groaning, rattling piece of shit.

He couldn't believe it, doubted it would ever feel real.

Another half hour of paying careful attention to the GPS and he was where he wanted to be. The mouth of the Mahury River lay ahead, wide and inviting. On the right, Cayenne sprawled along the coast, a thriving, vibrant peninsula with beaches and hotels and palm trees. Something shook him whenever he looked at civilisation through the periscope, a reactive shiver that touched the core of his being. He felt like a nomad, a rōnin, a creature from the deep. He feared if he bailed on the narco-sub and crawled up the beach into Cayenne, its inhabitants would recoil in fear at the monster from the ocean. He feared he'd never get home, that he'd repulse people for the rest of his life. He knew it was nonsense, but three weeks in a cage at sea had conditioned him to be totally, completely alone. He wondered if he'd need to relearn how to talk to people.

Five minutes, he thought, staring through the periscope. That's how long he had before he started down the river, before there was no going back.

Before it was either destroy the cartel operation, or die trying.

He clutched the captain's satphone in his hand, and before he knew what he was doing (before there was time for any conscious deliberation at all), he tapped out a message in French and sent it to Da Silva.

Reached Mahury. See you soon.

In the end it was anticlimactic. No grand gesture, no gearing up with heavy-duty firepower or throwing himself into the fray.

He just didn't touch the wheel.

The sub entered the river and started sluicing through increasingly muddy water. On either side the banks narrowed, until the open ocean was but a memory. He swivelled the periscope, turning the conning tower, and watched the sub pass the point of no return. There was no turning around, forward the only way. Cayenne passed by, and a boatful of official-looking men below a guard tower pretended not to notice the top of the semi-submersible trawling past.

He was through, and he was untouchable.

The authorities wouldn't stop him.

Only one thing left.

War.

56

S peeding one-handed down the long and empty
rural road, Slater was on the outskirts of Millinocket
before Timothée finished his paranoid rant.

'It's just,' Timothée finished, 'there is nothing you can
do. Rémi is leaning on me hard about exactly what
happened with Jack, and I have nothing to say. He's asking
me to send a photo of my ID, probably to see what I look
like. Soon he will call Dubois. All they need is a conversation — *one* talk, no? Just to say, "Hey, describe who showed
up at the Riverside Inn." And that's it. It's over. I'm dead,
man. Just sitting here at home, waiting for it. I don't want to
die, but I'm too weak to run...'

'Timothée,' Slater said. 'Shut the fuck up.'

He brought the Range up near a hundred miles an hour.
Terrain flashed past the windshield, an endless sea of white.

'I'm doing you favour, man...' Timothée grovelled.

'Sit on it for half an hour.'

'Why?'

'Because I said so.'

'I've already decided.'

'*Don't!*' Slater smashed the wheel. 'Don't you dare.'

'Just get ready. You can handle yourself, but I can't. So this is the right call. If I say nothing, that's it. I done enough for you...'

'Thirty minutes,' Slater said. 'You *wait* thirty minutes, or I swear to God...'

It struck him that every moment he spent on the phone to Timothée only gave the thug more of an outlet to convince himself he was doing the right thing. Radio silence was better than letting him make up his mind. It was the only thing that would breed indecision.

'Listen,' he said over Timothée's panicked breaths, 'you'd better have thought this through. You've seen what I can do. You're either choosing me or some snivelling, spineless diplomat on the other side of the globe.'

'I'm sorry.'

Click.

Slater took the phone away from his ear, stared at the ended call in disbelief. Trying to shake it off, he threw it down on the passenger seat and gripped the wheel double-handed.

He zoned into a tunnel.

Time sped up. He covered the seventy miles south to Bangor in something close to a meditative trance. He was sure he'd surge past a cop while doing dozens of miles over the speed limit, but fate must have been on his side. He barely slowed as he rejoined civilisation, as the woods and unending snowy plains merged into residential neighbourhoods and, finally, the industrial super-centres. Then he was back on the outskirts of Bangor. He veered onto the dirt trail leading to Timothée's shack. Rubble and dirt flew everywhere, the tyres jettisoning a plume of dust into the sky behind him.

He didn't bother with surveillance.

No time for caution.

No time for anything.

He roared up to the small house, barely managing to brake in time. The SUV skidded to a stop mere feet from the front porch. He'd come abhorrently close to driving straight up the little flight of steps, smashing the hood through the front door. Adrenaline firing, he leapt out, pulled his Glock, and charged inside, shouldering open the unlocked door.

Thirty-nine minutes since Timothée hung up.

Too late.

Feet thudding on floorboards like miniature earthquakes, he tore past a small sitting room before reaching the larger living space. The door hung open, and as he went past he spotted a motionless silhouette, planted on a chair inside the room.

He skidded to a halt, pulse racing.

Timothée sat in a fold-out camping chair in the corner of the spare bedroom. The rest of the space was devoid of furniture. A couple of old video game consoles lay scattered across the floorboards, cables strewn everywhere. Remnants of food scraps littered the dead space between the junk. The man was hollow-eyed, plagued by chronic stress, bloodshot veins in his eyes from a permanent marijuana prescription.

But he was completely still. His phone sat in his lap.

He watched Slater like a hawk.

Slater caught his breath, holding the Glock down by his side. 'You didn't run?'

Timothée shook his head.

Slater sensed the total lack of urgency. His eyes drifted to the phone resting between his thighs. 'You didn't call Dubois?'

'I was never going to. I'm sorry.'

He sounded genuine.

Slater buried his face in the crook of his elbow, wiping the sweat away. Moment by moment, his heart rate stabilised. 'Then what the hell is this?'

Timothée couldn't take his eyes off the gun. 'Are you going to kill me?'

Slater didn't answer.

Timothée said, 'I'd understand if you did.'

Slater glanced back up the hallway, out the open front door. The grounds were still. Subtle patterns of behaviour in Timothée's face told him this wasn't an ambush. It'd be different otherwise.

They'd already have trapped him in the house.

Timothée would have hidden.

Slater turned back and, for the first time, noticed the awe in Timothée's face. At once, he understood. 'That was a test?'

'You're not real,' Timothée said. 'You can't be.'

Slater knew what he meant. Timothée and his two buddies were impulsive gangsters, carrying out menial tasks for a boss a world away, the rest of their time spent chasing a high. Timothée couldn't comprehend Slater, didn't believe he was truthful, loyal. Men weren't like that, not in his world. They were liars, thieves, opportunists.

Slater said, 'You thought I'd run?'

'I thought you were no better than Rémi, than Noah. Maybe I still don't.'

'I'm here.' The house was quiet. 'I gave you my word. I'm seeing this through to the end.'

'To get power of your own?'

'No.'

Timothée took a breath. 'I'm sorry I did that. I thought if

I told you I was betraying you, you'd show your true colours.'

Slater said, 'Do I seem angry?'

'No. You don't. I do not understand.'

'These are my true colours.'

Timothée looked like he might cry.

In the silence, Slater's attention turned to the phone Timothée cradled. It was an older-model smartphone, scuffed and chipped, fingerprints smeared across the screen. Slater pointed to it. 'Is that what you called me from?'

Timothée looked down in a daze. '*Oui.*'

'Your personal phone?'

'*Oui.*' A touch quieter.

'Does Rémi call you on that phone?'

A long pause. Softer still, '*Oui.*'

'You got any sort of encryption on it?'

'Shit,' Timothée whispered, eyes watering. 'Oh, God. I wasn't thinking...'

He shot to his feet and hustled out of the room, brushing past Slater, striding deeper into the house. His breathing became frantic. He stared out windows as he moved, taking paranoid glances out into the still mid-morning.

The tension in the air reached a fever pitch.

Does Rémi know?

Slater waited for the world to come crashing down.

57

B ack from the jungle and newly enlightened, Rémi Poirier hunched over his desk.

He offered a silent prayer of gratitude for whoever invented air-conditioning.

Cayenne hummed outside, the city alive and buzzing all around the historic monument from which he worked. The *Hôtel de préfecture de la Guyane,* or the French Guiana Prefecture Building, had housed his seat for the six years he'd now spent in South America. His large office was cushy and temperature-controlled. What was most important, he'd realised, was that it was predictable, insulated. A tense diplomatic phone call was the worst of his problems in here, where all unrest could be solved from behind a desk. He could spend the rest of his life in this single room and die happy.

He would never go into the field again.

He'd made up his mind.

For now, Da Silva's predicament was on the back-burner. Rémi slumped over his laptop, staring at an audio file, silent in stunned disbelief.

For the fourth time, he pressed play.

The snippets of English blared through the laptop's tinny speakers, from both Timothée and a deep male voice he didn't recognise. Key lines rolled over him, sinking in deeper each time he played the recording.

'...*They don't buy cover story ... I'm gonna tell Dubois everything...*'

'...*Timothée ... Shut the fuck up...*'

'...*I done enough for you...*'

'...*You'd better have thought this through ... You're either choosing me or some snivelling, spineless diplomat on the other side of the globe...*'

Was Timothée speaking with Jack? Rémi didn't know. He'd never spoken to anyone in Maine other than Timothée and his boys.

That was Da Silva's business, all the messy details on the ground floor.

Noah's business, too.

Rémi felt the chill up his spine, felt his blood curdling. He was going to have to call the governor to report this. Describing their relationship as strained would be an understatement. For years now, Rémi had avoided conversations with Dubois. He knew what the governor thought of him, knew what *everyone* thought of him. He didn't care. As long as he was able to maintain the power that kept him in this comfortable existence, he'd happily serve as everyone's bitch. It was a level of self-awareness that eluded other men, made them play their silly power games that put them in the heat of the action all for the sake of a bit more money. He would never stoop so low, sacrifice his comfort so foolishly.

From the Prefecture Building, he could say "Yes," to a deal between Alain Da Silva and Noah Dubois and make a handsome percentage of the profit from uttering that one syllable.

That was wisdom. *That* was success.

Not all this effort.

God, he hated effort.

He pulled out a drawer and fished through the eight smartphones lined up within. He tapped each black screen as his finger passed along the row, mentally eliminating each device. When he came to the sixth phone, he nodded to himself and pulled it out. He unlocked it, scrolled through the contacts, and found an anonymous number, saved only as: MAINE PLAN B.

He dialled it and lifted the phone to his ear.

It rang once, twice...

Click.

No voicemail.

The person on the other end had killed the call before answering.

Rémi bowed his head and sighed. *You don't need Plan B. You need to call Noah.*

He decided to stop delaying the inevitable. He'd wanted to handle this himself, probably for ego protection. He could admit that. Da Silva had bossed him around like a child at the shipyard, told him exactly when and what was happening, and he'd stood there and received orders like the good servant he was. After grinning and bearing *that,* it was too much to now call the governor — a man who despised him — to tell him Timothée was a traitor.

But he'd have to.

He had no other choice.

Then the phone chimed in his hand. A message from the same contact: MAINE PLAN B.

He opened it. It read: CAN'T TALK ON PHONE. JUST TEXT ME. I'M AT YOUR SERVICE.

Rémi grinned.

Started typing away.

58

S later had to warn King.

Had to do it *now*.

But as a location to defend, Timothée's shack was a worst-case scenario, and Slater wouldn't be alive to make the call to King if he didn't secure the perimeter. He followed Timothée out of the spare room, down the hall, and into the central living space. Timothée's two buddies, the tattooed gangsters, were still sprawled on the long sofa against the far wall. It was as if they hadn't moved since Slater had last been here. Like they were permanent fixtures of the room, same as the furniture. The stink of weed radiated off them. Neither looked up from their phones to greet him. Just from the movement of their fingers, he knew they were mindlessly scrolling social media.

Slater grabbed Timothée's shoulder with one hand, spun him around, and reached for the man's phone. Timothée offered no resistance. He knew he'd fucked up. Slater popped the SIM card from the device and crushed it. He let the broken pieces fall through his fingers, vanishing amidst the mess on the carpet.

Timothée stared at his phone in Slater's hands, his teeth gritted. 'Will that work?'

'If it's digitally bugged, yes,' Slater said. 'It might have been constantly recording so long as it was charged, picking up everything you three said to each other in this room.'

Timothée went pale, started blinking like he was trying to communicate morse code. The other two didn't so much as look up from their phones. One man closed his eyes, electing this the most pertinent time for a nap. Slater wasn't sure anything would faze them, not even a grenade through the window.

Timothée said, 'This is bad...'

'Rémi might not be that smart, though. He might have only been recording calls.'

Timothée paused for thought before going paler still. 'That's still bad...'

'Obviously.'

Slater crossed to the window facing the vast empty fields out back, and stood to the side, hiding his bulk behind the wall. He leant over and peered out, exposing only a sliver of his face. The grass and trees and snow were still. Far in the distance, a bird took flight.

He was sure there was no one out there. Decades of surveillance and reconnaissance had opened his vision to all the subtle signs of an imminent ambush, and here there were none. Maybe Rémi knew, and maybe Rémi was scrambling to alert everyone of Timothée's betrayal, but these things take time, not thirty-nine minutes plus the time Slater had already spent here. Calling the governor, pleading with him to amass forces, keeping everything under wraps...

A couple of hours, at least.

He moved away from the window, pressed himself to the

wall, and dialled King's satphone. Timothée was immobile in the centre of the room, probably in shock. His two pals seemed oblivious to the fact they might soon be under attack. One tapped away at his phone. The other slept peacefully.

Timothée said, 'Am I screwed?'

'Probably,' Slater said as ringing sounded in his ear.

King didn't pick up.

Slater held his phone at arm's length and stared at it with a grimace. Was it the end of the world, or was King in the middle of something banal and mundane? No way to know. He went to dial again.

The guy napping surfaced from unconsciousness with a groan and peeled himself off the couch. He slumbered lackadaisically across the room, heading for the bathroom. Half-closed eyes blinked over and over again. Clearing the cobwebs. Slater reminisced on his own years of substance abuse, making that very same walk each morning with a pounding head, preparing to vomit what he'd consumed the night before so he could throw himself back into training.

A different life.

A world away from the man he was now.

When the guy disappeared through a doorway, Timothée shook himself out of his trance. 'Man, I had all these ideas...'

Talking to himself.

King didn't answer a second time.

The muscles around Slater's neck knotted, tension creeping in.

Timothée pressed on despite the lack of reception. 'I saw future for myself. I know this sounds silly, but you show me this. That I can be something more than this, you know?'

Silence.

Slater wondered what to do about King, Rémi, Noah...

What a mess.

Timothée's gaze bored into Slater now. 'I'm sorry I tested you. I was ... insecure, no?'

Slater said, 'It's okay.'

'I was making sure...'

Slater finally gave Timothée his full attention. Only for a moment, but enough to get a read. The young man being genuine.

'It's okay, Timothée,' he said. 'You did the right thing.' A pause. 'You have potential.'

Timothée beamed. 'You mean that?'

'I do. You didn't give me away intentionally, even though you could and maybe should have. You've got a good head on your shoulders.'

The beam petered down to a smile, but the hope remained in his eyes. 'There is time to fix this. *Oui*?'

Slater said, 'Oui.'

Somewhere in the house a toilet flushed, and the guy who'd slunk off came moping back, passing behind Timothée to get back to the sofa.

Slater blinked.

Something in his demeanour was different. It wasn't overt, but he was deliberately trying to look lazy now. It was forced.

Before Slater could say a word, the guy turned, revealing the rest of his profile and the gun in his left hand. His eyes were still bloodshot, but now clear with purpose.

He shot Timothée through the back of the head.

59

The river continued to narrow.

A physical manifestation of how trapped King felt.

There was no hiding now. Fishing boats chugged past the rattling sub every couple of minutes, their occupants smirking wryly at the conning tower, as if they could actually see through to King standing below deck. After three weeks in an ocean so vast as to be beyond comprehension, sailing through this muddy brown water was akin to having a hand closed around his throat, squeezing tight, building the pressure to a fever pitch. Everyone knew he was here, and no one seemed to care. At the least, it opened his eyes to the hugeness of the operation.

This narco-sub was a speck, a tiny cog in the bigger picture. Its great shape, looming mostly below the surface, seemed like nothing but another part of the scenery to those using the river. They might not know its true purpose, but they were conditioned to look the other way.

Da Silva hadn't lied.

A little under ten miles inland, the shape of the

waterway changed again, narrowing further as the Mahury became the Oyak River. As the open ocean receded from memory, the heat began to build inside the sub. The sun beat down on opaque water thick with silt, and the hull started to cook. The generator whined, its racket amplifying along with the temperature. King figured he had nothing left to sweat, but as he sculled a couple of water bottles in an attempt to stay hydrated, his pores pushed out newfound perspiration. Each time he pressed his face to the periscope, he left a ring of droplets on the metal sight.

He didn't dare look away.

He swivelled the conning tower between the riverbanks as he steered, making small and frantic adjustments like a man possessed. If he ran aground, or snagged the sub on low-hanging branches, he'd be forced to bail mere miles from the end destination. It would all be for nothing...

Finally, after what felt like years of accumulated stress, the Oyak became the Comte River. He cruised for a few minutes down a long straight, savouring the chance to calm himself down...

When he swivelled the periscope dead ahead, he found himself staring at a line of trees.

Fuck.

A sharp U-turn in the river.

He slowed to a crawl and worked the wheel slowly, slowly, slowly to the left. The vessel creaked and groaned, and, finally, it began to turn.

He turned the periscope hard to the right as he turned left, keeping an eye on the riverbank at the top of the U. The first row of trunks were so close he could make out the texture of the bark, the way the air hummed with heat...

For a terrifying moment he thought he'd miscalculated

and braced for impact. His mind went haywire. *You'll need to hike for dozens of miles...*

The muddy bank receded.

The sub groaned through the turn.

Stayed on course at the speed of a sloth.

Probably the slowest near-miss in human history.

Another twenty minutes of cruising. It felt like days. The jungle condensed on either side, trees bending toward the water. The occasional civilian cigarette boat tore past, each one giving the sub a wide berth. The desolation grew, until King couldn't shake the sense he was on another planet.

How'd you end up here?

He reached the end.

A waterway branched off from the body of the Comte, taking him to a swamp surrounded by impenetrable shrubs and bushes. Clouds of bugs flitted around the top of the periscope in frenzies. The heat was close to unbearable, pushing at least a hundred degrees inside the sub. He was grateful that over decades of exertion he'd trained himself to sweat profusely, acclimatising his body to the worst of conditions. If he passed out from heatstroke now, he'd hand himself to them on a silver platter...

He coasted the sub into the middle of the swamp, only a few dozen feet from the bank ahead. Almost disbelievingly, he killed the engine for the last time.

It didn't seem final.

Seemed like the beginning.

As the engine powered down, the generator continued to whine, keeping all the navigation equipment alive that had, in turn, kept him alive. The need to escape the furnace was overbearing now, the heat crushing his chest. He fired off a quick text to Da Silva — "I'M HERE" — and downed a final bottle of water. In a strange moment of finality, he gazed all around the sub. Its cramped, stuffy interior had caged him for three weeks, but he knew he'd likely never have an experience like it again as long as he lived. An inexplicable part of him wanted this last pause, to burn it into his memory, to make sure he never took life in Maine for granted.

Often he thought of his life as nothing but pressure, exertion, and pain, but this journey had taught him something significant.

That on a global scale, no matter how hard it got, he had it comparatively easy. For billions, each morning was a fight to survive. He didn't want to think about what meagre sum the crew would have been paid for this job.

He shook himself out of his stupor and gathered his things to leave. The jungle air, no matter how humid and impenetrable, called for him. Sky and sun and fresh air; the light at the end of the tunnel. The swamp was deserted, so he had plenty of time to burrow down and wait for Da Silva and his men to approach the empty sub.

A text came back from Da Silva: STAY PUT.

King turned the captain's satphone over and over in his dirt-encrusted palm, thinking. There was no doubt the cartel was tracking its location; not a chance they'd let themselves lose track of two hundred million dollars. The question was: how accurately? If he brought it with him to stay in contact, would they be able to narrow in on the coordinates, realise the phone was on dry land?

Better safe than sorry.

He left it resting atop one of the gas tanks, where he'd slept for twenty-one days.

He reached for the ladder.

Something stopped him.

Rattled by some vague suspicion, having to wonder

whether paranoia was seeping in, he crossed back to the periscope and pressed his face to it. The air above the swamp's bank simmered between tree trunks, the heat distortion blurring small details. But he was very close, and for three weeks now he'd spent most of his waking life staring through the periscope, his vision all-encompassing. He could look hard and see things that weren't intended to be seen.

Like the small box-shaped camera, painted dark green, fixed onto one of the trunks maybe ten feet off the jungle floor. He'd glanced over it when he first scrutinised the landing area, and that memory had stopped him ascending the ladder, made him do a double-take.

The fish-eye lens was aimed directly at the centre of the swamp.

Watching.

His world caved in.

There'd be no escape without them knowing everything.

60

A bove all else, Slater was most stunned by the reaction of the goon still lying on the couch.

Still tapping away at his phone screen, the guy simply glanced sideways with a raised eyebrow as the execution unfolded in the middle of the room. His brain had to be permanently broken from the drugs, all sense of danger expunged, moving through reality in a fugue state. The guy stayed put as Slater locked his aim on the other one, the man who'd blown Timothée's brains across the room.

'Lower it,' Slater ordered, cutting all emotion from his voice.

The man wasn't stupid. He let the pistol hang by his side, staring directly at Slater. He refused to look down at the body of someone he'd probably considered a friend. They lived together at the very least. They were bonded through their work.

Then again, Timothée had killed the insubordinate one back at the lake without a second thought.

Dog-eat-dog world.

Slater stopped himself pulling the trigger. 'Rémi told you to do that?'

A slow nod. Zero hesitation. You admit anything when there's a gun in your face, when you're milliseconds from instant death.

'Rémi told you to kill me, too?'

A shrug. 'If I could. But I can't. You're too fast. I knew that.'

'So why'd you put yourself in this position?'

'If I no try, it no go well for me.'

'It won't go well for you here.'

Another shrug. 'We no speak, but I been figuring you out. Just watching. Listening. You good person. You no torture me. Not in your blood. But Rémi...'

'Rémi's a weakling.'

'Exactly.' The bloodshot eyes didn't blink. 'He no do it himself. No spine. But he pay the worst people. That's what you no understand. We just one little group. And we small-timers. He pay real killers. This not my world, not our world. So if Rémi say Timothée got a big fucking mouth and Timothée gotta go, then...' He gestured to the bleeding body between them.

'Even if it gets you killed?'

The man laughed. It was brittle, harsh on the ears.

Slater said, 'What?'

'I know you. Or people like you. Got everything figured out. The rest of us do work like this. Live like this. All we got. You don't sign up to this thinking you'll make it out alive. You get money for weed and dope and you make pain go away until it's the end of the road.'

Slater didn't respond.

The man said, 'Just shoot—'

On the sofa, his buddy rolled to one side, reached for the

small of his back, and came out with a gun. He whipped it up lightning-fast, and before Slater could decide who to shoot, the guy aimed and fired.

Hit Slater centre-mass.

The right idea: it's unwise to risk a clean headshot across a crowded room unless you're an expert marksman.

The bullet smashed into the Kevlar vest under Slater's shirt and he went down, propelled back by the force. It took a shocking amount of power to decelerate a bullet, all of which transferred into him, carrying his legs out from underneath. Which was better than the alternative, and he thanked his lucky stars for slipping the vest on as he sped to Bangor.

Before Slater could aim from his back, the guy on the sofa rolled all the way to his side.

The man in the middle of the room saw it coming.

Didn't mean he could stop it.

He closed his eyes.

The exit wound blew out the back of his skull, and he collapsed on top of Timothée.

Slater measured trajectories and timing in a matter of milliseconds. If he brought his Glock up, they'd probably hit each other simultaneously. He didn't want to risk taking a shot to the face, so he curled into a ball, putting his back to the sofa, and lay deathly still. Everything had happened in a couple of seconds, and the last guy hadn't taken stock. He'd shot Slater in the heart, seen him drop, then shot his buddy.

Slater feared he'd made a terrible, fatal error.

Then he heard it over by the sofa.

Feet planting on floorboards, one by one.

With a groan, the final assassin levered himself up. He crossed the room slowly, Slater now forgotten. Slater heard him bend over his two housemates, checking they were dead, and the man heaved a sigh from his very bones. It sounded genuinely remorseful.

Too bad.

Slater flew to his feet with every ounce of athleticism in his frame. He practically teleported, using all his plyometric power, and he was behind the guy before he could blink.

Facing forward, the guy said, 'Oh.'

Slater planted the Glock to the back of his skull and pulled the trigger.

A three-corpse pile-up.

All was still in the house.

Slater realised his error. Because the guy on his phone hadn't killed Timothée, Slater had assumed he wasn't in contact with Rémi. But he must have been Rémi's first option, texting back and forth the whole time, while the other man had gone to the bathroom and contacted his boss from there.

A trifecta of betrayal.

Rémi covering all bases.

No one leaves.

Slater went to the sofa and plucked the last man's phone from between the cushions. The screen was open; no password required. A text conversation was open with an unknown number, discussing imminent killings. Slater typed out a message and sent it off.

GOT IT DONE. THEY WERE MY FRIENDS. DON'T EVER CONTACT ME AGAIN.

He went back through the shack, wiping any surface he may have touched, and left.

A single train of thought allowed him to maintain some slight hope.

Dubois still might not know.

61

GOT IT DONE. THEY WERE MY FRIENDS. DON'T EVER CONTACT ME AGAIN.

Behind his desk, Rémi stared at the message open on the screen.

He called them again, one by one, first "Plan B," then "Plan C." Neither answered, which was hardly a surprise. The text said as much: "Plan B," the first man he'd texted, was the survivor. Timothée and the other guy were dead, as apparently was the mystery man Timothée had been colluding with.

Rémi needed more.

Needed an explanation.

Over and over and over again, he called "Plan B," a man whose name he didn't even know. A message like that wouldn't cut it. He didn't know if he bought it. He had to hear audible confirmation, a shaky voice through a telephone. Then he'd believe it.

Maybe.

But there was nothing.

Radio silence.

AWOL.

Not good enough, Rémi thought. At least he'd tried. He could find solace in that. With regret, he drew a new phone out of the desk drawer — fourth from the end — and did what he should have done all along.

Called Noah Dubois.

As he scrolled to find the contact information, he couldn't help but reminisce. The memory of what he once shared with the governor of Maine burned a hole in him, a bond that carried across continents, a palpable excitement that they were *making shit happen.* The President appointing him prefect all those years ago had been the first defining moment of his life, and his discreet allegiance with Noah had been the second and last. They'd shared everything: a general nihilism toward the world, a burning desire to use their positions for personal gain, and a bitterness and disillusionment toward anyone and anyplace that didn't give France and its culture the respect it deserved.

Which had culminated with Dubois asking a simple question, all those years back. *'If I wanted to open the gates of Maine's coastline to certain deliveries, would you be interested in helping me make that happen?'*

All Rémi had to say was, *'Yes,'* and that's what he did.

Which was good, because anything else would have overwhelmed him. All he'd done was reach out to Alain Da Silva, a ruthless and cutthroat coordinator of French Guiana's cartel members, and recommend he drop a line to a certain private number. Da Silva and Dubois had organised the rest, and Rémi sat back and accepted his millions for doing nothing besides looking the other way.

So what had happened since then?

Nothing, really.

That's the way most friendships go...

They spoke less and less, until about a year ago, when they stopped speaking at all unless on crucial business. Resentment had festered from the governor's end over the years, likely frustration at Rémi wielding such power without having to lift a finger. Dubois probably saw him as a spoiled, entitled brat, and for good reason. It was only luck that Rémi knew the President of France so well, first school-mates and then political allies. The prefect job opened up, and Rémi slotted neatly in. He was no stranger to people considering him soft, weak, unmotivated and undisciplined. He accepted all these labels. They were true. How was he to deny what was so utterly obvious?

He was many things, but he was sure to never add "deluded" to that list.

He knew who he was.

Now, the back of his neck burned hot, raising his core temperature and rendering the air-conditioning useless. Sweating freely again, he was reminded of the jungle. His teeth clenched involuntarily. Every part of him dreaded this. What would he say? *'I know what you think of me, but you need to hear this.'* That was good enough.

On the third ring, something flashed at the base of his peripheral vision. He looked down into the drawer. The very last phone in the row vibrated against the wood, its screen flaring to life.

Oh, God, Rémi thought. *Oh, no...*

That was the phone for serious emergencies, for when the world had gone nuclear. Only Da Silva knew to call him on that number. An agreement existed between them, that no matter what Rémi was in the middle of, he'd drop every-thing to answer that phone.

The phone pressed to his ear stopped ringing as Dubois

answered. His cool, composed voice came through. 'Yes, Rémi?'

Rémi couldn't take his eyes off the drawer, transfixed. He stuttered, 'I'll call you back.'

'What the f—?'

Rémi hung up on the governor. There'd be hell to pay later, but Noah was a politician a world away, whereas Alain was in-country, and a killer to boot. Da Silva would have no qualms about storming the Prefecture Building and gunning Rémi down behind his desk, consequences be damned.

He was first priority.

Rémi answered the nuclear phone. 'What?'

'It's beginning,' Da Silva said softly.

Rémi's blood ran cold.

He'd been briefed in the jungle, in the shadows of the shipyard.

He knew what was coming.

He said, 'Got it. I'll stay ready.'

'Good. Might need you.'

'You mean my forces, right? Not...?'

Da Silva cackled. 'What use would I have with *you* in a firefight, exactly? You'd shrivel into a ball and cry your eyes out.'

'That's what I'm saying.'

'Ahhh, Rémi,' Da Silva purred. 'I guess if you tell everyone you're weak, it's not a weakness, huh?'

'Something like that.' He didn't let his voice waver, even though it's all he wanted.

Da Silva blew a kiss through the phone and hung up.

Rémi dropped the phone and put his head in his hands.

The other phone shrilled on the desk. Noah calling him back, eager to chew him out for wasting his time with the prior call. Rémi didn't think he could stomach it. *Does he need to know about Timothée?*

No.

Not yet.

It could wait a little longer.

Rémi got up, walked away from the phones and the chaos, and locked himself in the bathroom.

Safe and quiet.

An escape from the world.

62

King noticed he'd missed calls from Slater.

It was the last thing on his mind.

He paced the length of the sub, soaked head to toe in sweat, implementing every technique he'd ever learned not to panic. Making sure not to come off as flustered, he messaged Da Silva: HURRY UP. HOTTER THAN HELL IN HERE.

Within seconds, Da Silva fired back: GET SOME AIR, THEN.

King roared a guttural sound that bounced off the walls, his frustration reaching fever pitch.

Checkmate.

He tried to visualise what lay ahead without the dread overwhelming him. Coming up out of the hatch would give the game away, render all the groundwork useless. The narco-sub journey would be for nothing; he may as well have flown here. With the deception revealed, he'd be on foot in the jungle with limited firepower against endless cartel forces who knew the terrain intimately. He had no resources, little remaining food and water, and no survival supplies besides an onboard first-aid kit.

French Guiana would eat him alive.

It wouldn't be competitive.

So he resorted to taking advantage of the only reason that the operation existed in the first place. He wrote: CAN'T. PROBLEM WITH THE MONEY.

Da Silva came back even faster: WHAT?

King sensed the urgency.

He left it.

Didn't respond.

Each minute felt like an hour below deck, but at least Da Silva would be feeling the same. Within minutes Da Silva followed up, the dreaded double-message. The clearest sign of restrained panic. JUST SIT TIGHT. I'M TEN MINUTES OUT FOR THE SKIM.

The skim?

Oh, King realised. He lit up with a smile. *I've got you now.*

He wouldn't believe it until he saw it. Too good to be true. If he was right, it was the opportunity he'd been searching for all along, the mother-load of good fortune. He bounded down the length of the sub and pressed his face to the periscope.

Watching.

Waiting.

Ten minutes passed.

Like an angel descending on the putrid swamp, an open-topped jeep bounced into view, taking an off-road course that didn't seem traversable. It skidded to a halt in the thick mud up the bank, front bumper facing the swamp.

The driver was its only occupant.

Alone.

No help.

The man clambered out, and King fixed the periscope on him. It had to be Alain Da Silva. Short, stocky, built like a barrel. Wide, crazed eyes, a squashed nose, full lips. A bald head — freshly buzzcut — covered in white scars. King soaked in every detail. The man waded forward, staring straight into the top of the periscope. It felt like he was looking right at King. He raised both arms, each thick and bristling with hair and veins, and beckoned the sub forward.

Closer to shore.

For "the skim."

Da Silva had arrived alone, before any of his men, to take money off the top of the haul. A prearranged agreement between the cartel leader and the narco-sub crew. No witnesses, no foul. And, really, who was counting? The amount of money in the hold defied belief. Accounting wasn't a priority, not in a cash-only business. And what's the visual difference between a hundred and ninety-eight million and two hundred million?

Nothing noticeable.

That's for sure.

As King powered up the engine and inched the sub forward, details in Da Silva's face grew clearer. The greed in his eyes; the soft smirk at the corners of his dry, cracked lips. This was better than any drug on earth, the result of a mind-boggling amount of groundwork. This was a man who appeared to have crawled up from the trenches into his place in the underworld, and was finally reaping the rewards of his sacrifice.

Above all else, it was a man with his guard down.

King coasted the sub to a stop only when he was sure he was mere feet from hitting the sloped swamp bottom. At the speed he was travelling, it wouldn't have been anything significant, but the slightest inconvenience could jeopardise everything.

Da Silva waded knee-deep into the swamp. Muck on the surface of the water gripped his dark brown khaki trousers. King clutched the periscope as tight as he could, palms slick. He tried to measure distances, but he'd never get it totally accurate.

Fifteen feet, maybe, from Da Silva to the nose of the sub.

He had to be sure.

If he came up short...

The fat leather pistol holster, faded by sun exposure, rested at the front of the man's utility belt. He could draw, aim and fire in a couple of seconds, at most.

Everything banked on this next minute.

King took three uninterrupted, measured breaths. Deep inhale, hold, long exhale.

Go.

As he readied his SIG and gripped the first rung of the ladder, he envisioned a caged tiger, ready to be unleashed, amassing energy to explode out of the gate. He'd need to utilise every training session he'd ever put himself through, charge all that up into a single series of movements.

Anything else was death.

An Olympic Games with lethal repercussions for second place.

He clambered slowly up the rungs. Sweat ran from the back of his neck down his spine. A few drops fell from his beard, splashed the floor at the bottom of the ladder. He maintained the same rhythmic breathing.

He paused right at the top of the ladder, the top of his head pressed to the metal hatch door.

He closed his eyes, centred himself, and opened them again.

Reached up and smashed the hatch open with a fist and came up out of the sub like a freight train.

63

He gave himself two seconds, beginning to end.

Any longer and he'd be a sitting duck.

One hand had to stay wrapped around his SIG, so he used the other to haul himself up over the top rung, pushing off with both feet from a lower rung. His athleticism propelled him up out of the hatch, and he hit the hull running. Three massive, leaping bounds worked him up to a sprint, and in just those strides he covered the full length of the top of the sub. Da Silva, standing in the shallows, saw the giant shape darting toward him, but the sudden explosion of movement gave him a jump-scare, made his heart leap and his limbs freeze.

He was a hard, cruel man, though, and clearly nothing frightened him for very long.

Within a second, he was reaching for his holster.

King used the third stride of his sprint to launch himself off the sub. He pushed off the nose, forcing his head and shoulders forward, throwing his legs back. He'd need to be practically horizontal to clear the distance. If he botched this, it would be a monumental failure, and he'd splash down in the shallows in front of Da Silva, all so the man could put a bullet in his head.

This is what it had to be.

An Olympic long jump with zero regard for how he would land.

If he went feet-first, he wouldn't make it.

Thick jungle air washed over him as he leapt. In mid-air, he watched Da Silva extract the Taurus PT145 pistol from its holster, ripping it free. He started bringing it up to aim, but simple physics limited how fast he could move. He had milliseconds.

And not enough of them.

King dropped his shoulder at the very end of the dive and threw his head to the side so the impact didn't snap his neck. His two hundred and twenty pounds came down with staggering momentum.

His shoulder struck Da Silva's chest.

Anyone else would be mortally wounded, their sternum caved in by the monstrous hit, but Da Silva was inhuman. He was still fighting and clawing as King came down on top of him. They plunged back into the shallows, brown water splashing over them in a torrent. King landed on Da Silva, whose lower back hit the riverbank hard enough to shatter his spine.

Da Silva didn't seem to notice.

They fell on each other in the knee-deep water, coated in mud and filth and grime. Da Silva's Taurus was gone, and King sensed opportunity and brought his gun hand out of the water.

No gun.

He'd tried with all his might to hold onto it through the impact, but it had been pure chaos. Adrenaline tore through him, masking any injuries he may have sustained. No way to tell in the midst of the carnage. He could barely feel his limbs, and the muddy water spraying in his eyes blinded him.

He grabbed Da Silva by the throat and smashed a colossal elbow into the man's forehead.

Like hitting a brick wall.

Da Silva snarled and seized King's wrist with a grip that defied belief. King was always far stronger than anyone he met in combat, a physical freak of nature, but Da Silva held his arm in place like he was a child. The man's stubby fingers were like metal, knotted scars on the backs of his hands, dirt buried under his fingernails.

King headbutted him full in the face.

Two coconuts cracking together.

It concussed them both. King saw blinding white light, but knew Da Silva was dealing with the same. And although Da Silva's strength was otherworldly, there are simple rules regarding the human brain that apply equally to all. You can be tough, brutal, solid as a rock, but the three pounds of soft tissue between your ears are unavoidably delicate. For better or worse, King had a ream of experience dealing with all the symptoms of sudden brain trauma. Dizziness, disassociation, a sense of surreality: these things terrify even the most seasoned combatant if they're unused to them.

So the supposedly "even" playing field of a double-concussion wasn't so even after all.

Da Silva released his grip on King's wrist and stumbled back through the shallows, eyes wide and uncomprehending. It opened a couple of feet of space between them. King loosened his hips, brought a boot up out of the water, and cracked it forward like a whip. A simple Muay Thai teep kick, but it felt like he'd been charging it up for three weeks.

When he dug it into the soft flesh below the sternum, ribs cracked.

More than one clean break.

Which finished it.

Da Silva fell back, taken off his feet by the force, and slumped down on his rear in the mud. He sat there at the edge of the swamp, feet in the water. Face like a golem, he refused to let the pain show out of sheer stubbornness. But he was hurting. Hurting *bad*. He couldn't move.

King was wobbly on his feet, but had the wherewithal to crouch in the filthy water and run his fingers through the swamp floor. He made sharp, concentric circles until he touched something solid and metal. Snatched up the gun and pulled it free.

His SIG.

He hoped "water resistant" was good enough.

He strode forward, bent down, and snatched Da Silva by the throat. Again he marvelled at the hardness of the man's skin. It felt like gripping a coarse bag of bricks. But two hundred pounds is two hundred pounds, so he had no trouble using adrenaline to drag the man up the bank toward the jungle. When they were between the cover of two giant trees, King forced him down by the throat so he was lying on his back, then pressed the SIG barrel to his forehead.

Da Silva wore a pained grimace that could be interpreted as a wry smile.

Panting for breath, King said, 'What?'

'One man?' Da Silva said in English, his accent heavy. 'I shouldn't have bothered with any of this.'

'Shouldn't have *bothered*?'

King's blood ran cold.

He looked all around.

Da Silva wheezed, brown teeth stained crimson. 'A trap just for you.'

The silence didn't seem isolating anymore.

It was tense.

The calm before the storm...

King had no time to think.

He dragged Da Silva deeper into the rainforest.

64

Dark under a canopy of fronds.

The air impenetrable, a solid, humid wall.

A twisted maze of branches formed a natural shelter on the jungle floor, and King hauled Da Silva's unresisting mass inside. He squatted down beside the man and squashed the barrel harder into the side of his head.

'You'd better start talking,' King said, 'or whatever this is, it'll backfire.'

Da Silva chuckled, shook his head. 'You need me.'

'Oh?'

'To get to Rémi.'

Silence.

Bugs hummed. An exotic bird cawed.

King said, 'Do I?'

'Of course. Or you wouldn't have bothered wasting your life in that prison.'

'Your English is good.'

On his back, the man leered. 'Necessity. I'm self-taught. I deal with *yanquis* every day.'

'*Yanquis* like Noah Dubois?'

A knowing glare. 'Oh, you're good.'

'The best.'

'Not quite. You'd have done better if you were.'

'So I gave it away?'

'Of course you did, boy. But if I'd known you were on your own...'

'You were expecting an armed force?'

'Four men. You can't fit more in our subs.'

Uncertainty rippled in the air. King fought for calm. 'Yet you came alone.'

'Of course. You wouldn't kill me. And I was right. Here I am, still talking...'

'What gave me away?'

Da Silva laughed, a sharp *ha* that cut through the air. King smashed him in the forehead with the SIG's stock. '*Shut up,*' he hissed.

It rattled the man's already compromised brain, killing the laugh before it could grow louder. But Da Silva was tough as nails. He kept his composure. 'One little mistake.'

'Which was?'

'That wasn't my number you were texting.'

A chill ran down King's spine, fighting against the heat. 'Shit.'

'Yeah. Shit.'

King applied pressure with the SIG barrel, twisting it left and right into the soft flesh above his ear.

Da Silva got the message to elaborate. 'The captains of my boats don't talk to me. I can't get bogged down in logistics. You called one of my underlings by my name, and he came straight to me with the phone. Told me something was up. I took over from there.'

'That doesn't make any sense.'

'No?'

'You came here. You approached with your gun holstered. You got yourself taken when you could have put an RPG into—'

He cut himself off, dots connecting.

Destroy the sub, destroy the cash.

Da Silva saw the understanding in King's eyes. 'I work very hard for my money.'

'Not smart.'

'No?'

'You have more subs.'

'Many more.'

'How often does two hundred million dollars roll in?'

'Every few weeks.'

'Then you're an idiot.'

'You were only four men, I thought.'

'Well, it's your lucky day. It's just me.'

'Maybe you're the only one with balls. They won't find three more hiding in the sub?'

'"They"?'

'Yes. They.'

King crouched over the man, peering over both shoulders. The jungle was alive, but still. Insects swarmed in clouds, but there was no sign of human life.

Da Silva said, 'You're not making it out of this jungle alive.'

'And if I do?'

'Then I will take you to Rémi.'

'You'll take me to Rémi regardless,' King said as he sensed movement behind a distant group of trees. 'And you should have sunk your money.'

The certainty with which he spoke must have tickled

some primeval instinct in Da Silva, because the expression on the man's face changed. Hesitancy appeared where there was none before.

King carefully placed the SIG against the side of the man's knee, lined up the bullet trajectory, and fired.

An unsuppressed round.

Like an explosion in the quiet.

The path of the bullet shredded all four major ligaments in Da Silva's leg: ACL, PCL, MCL, LCL. A shocking, irreversible injury. He'd never walk on the leg again properly. And the pain...

Sometimes toughness doesn't matter.

Sometimes it's so bad there's no other option but to scream.

Da Silva squeezed his eyes shut and roared uncontrollably. He rolled to his side, curled into a ball, and clutched his leg. He knew the error of his ways, but by the time he gained control of his mind and tapered the yelling down to a manic, wheezing hiss, it was too late. His eyes still closed, he didn't realise King was nowhere to be seen.

When he heard footsteps stomping through the undergrowth, he rolled to the noise and opened his eyes. He was in too much pain to realise they were multiple pairs of boots.

Four paramilitary soldiers bore down on him. He saw their dark green faces, smeared with camouflage, and the adrenaline in their bloodshot eyes, hopped up on combat drugs. They wore head-to-toe khakis and wielded heavy-duty firepower, sleek black submachine guns and big Kalashnikov AK-47s with curved magazines.

'No!' Da Silva roared, holding his blood-soaked knee. 'No, you fucking morons! Get away from me!'

Their eyes widened in understanding.

They saw the reverse trap.

Da Silva waved them frantically away, but they weren't sure where to go.

The man on the left was the first to turn around.

Jason King fell on him.

65

In these situations, King had learned it's best not to care whether you live or die.

It frees you from anxiety, eliminates hesitation, brings you to your fullest potential.

He acted as such.

Charged out of the hiding hole he'd slunk off to and fired a bullet into the first man's face paint, the entry wound mixing dark red with the dark green. He fell, a neat hole in the centre of his forehead, and King crashed into his limp body on the way down. It flung the body into the second man, knocking them both off their feet, and King shot the second one as he sprawled to the jungle floor.

The third raised his Kalashnikov, but the rifle was big, cumbersome, hard to manoeuvre in close quarters. King swatted the barrel aside before it drifted to his centre mass and shot the man through the throat. He hurled him aside and simply ripped the submachine gun — a modern MP7 with a red dot sight — out of the fourth man's hands. He turned it on the guy and, in haste, put three rounds in his chest. The man splayed back, seriously wounded but still alive. He wore Kevlar under the jungle warfare gear, but a weapon as powerful as the MP7 was designed to penetrate bulletproof vests. As he went down, King finished him off with a headshot.

Da Silva stared wide-eyed.

King turned to him. 'How many more?'

'Many.'

King smiled. 'Don't go anywhere.'

He turned and disappeared into the rainforest, made himself vanish.

Left a grievously wounded Da Silva alone, staring at the bodies of his fallen men, contemplating the choices he'd made.

Contemplating everything.

66

King knew what they'd do.

Knew the men stalking him as intimately as if he were them.

They might be young and desperate, with strength in numbers, and, sure, King was pushing forty, but again it rang true, just as it had in Maine: *Beware of an old man in a profession where men usually die young.*

The commotion near Da Silva — nine gunshots all up — would make them allergic to the area. They'd employ basic jungle warfare tactics, covering a hundred-and-eighty degree arc between trees to protect the man beside them, and they'd move carefully, patiently, tactically, toward the hotspot. If there were many of them, and it devolved into taking potshots at one another through the jungle, King might lose. But the real magic — his golden ticket — was his inhuman reaction speed.

So he used it.

Threw himself into the fray.

Caution fell by the wayside as he charged silently through the shadows, using the denser stretches of canopy to his advantage. He came up ghost-like on the first silhouette he spotted. Materialised like an apparition and laced the man's right arm with a spray of the MP7. Bullets roared and the man screamed, the limb going dead as multiple beads of lead pierced the skin.

It snatched the attention of everyone in the vicinity, which is what King wanted.

He vanished again.

The wounded man turned and fired his AK-47 one-handed into the jungle, shooting vaguely in the direction he'd been struck from. No one was there. He took bark off trees and sent fronds and leaves flying, small green pieces scattering everywhere. One of his comrades shouted a warning in French, likely urging him not to panic.

Easy to say; harder to do.

King used the second shout to identify the pattern, figure out where the line stretched through the rainforest. He dropped prone and slithered on his belly through dense foliage. He couldn't see, but he could travel by feel, and he knew they wouldn't have a clue where he was.

Timing it to the millisecond, he reared up behind the second man and used the crook of his elbow to sink in a vicious blood choke.

Dragged his prey down into the undergrowth.

The guy choked and spluttered, but that was about all he could manage. King pictured his target shooting Violetta and Junior, which gave him the strength to choke him out in a handful of seconds. A little more savage pressure, a few more seconds to break his neck and squeeze the life out of him, and he was left holding a corpse. He rolled to his side and lowered the body quietly to the dirt, then stretched out on his stomach, huge jungle leaves folding over him.

He took stock.

Five down, and one out of action, the man's shredded right arm and screams being used as an effective distraction. Based on the shape of the formation he'd glimpsed, King guessed there were three more in this wave. He, on the other hand, was uninjured, untouched, but already exhausted. Lactic acid swelled in his left arm after the squeeze he'd put on the man he'd choked, serious enough that it was hard to feel his fingers. Sweat fell off him in waves, showering off his face and chin each time he moved. His filthy clothes were soaked. Much more exertion and he'd max out, render himself useless, a panting, shaking target to be picked off at will.

So he conserved energy.

Lay in the shrubs and counted out a full two minutes while pandemonium reigned around him. Men shouted, roared, spat and swore at each other in the chaos. Far away, he heard Da Silva desperately ordering his men around, trying to achieve calm.

Fat chance of that.

King breathed as silently and deeply as he could, shaking his hand out until feeling returned to the limb. He could feel his heart thumping as fast as it could, pushing blood to the fatigued muscles.

He wasn't recovered, but he didn't need to be.

He only needed to stay functional.

For a hundred and twenty seconds, no one had dared come to the aid of the man with bullets in his arm. The guy lay on the ground a couple of dozen feet to King's left, pleading for help.

Finally someone caved.

Hasty footsteps came bumbling in, a man rushing to either help or silence the moaning soldier. King burst up, revealing himself, and got a glimpse of wide and uncomprehending eyes before he put two bullets into the guy's face. Then he turned on the injured one and silenced him himself with a three-round cluster: *tap-tap-tap*.

He slammed his back to the trunk he knew was behind him, turned ninety degrees, and whipped his aim up to the motionless jungle.

He waited.

I know what you'll do.

He knew because he could put himself in the mindset of a paramilitary trooper inexperienced in real combat. Sure, there were drills and simulations and techniques to prepare yourself for the field, but much in the same way as a boxer who's sparred hundreds of rounds can panic in their very first professional fight, training often goes completely out the window.

We're human, after all.

And that's what they did. The five remaining men clustered together in what they didn't realise was fear. With spacing and formation abandoned, they savoured strength in numbers, that instinct of having a friendly shoulder touching yours. That's how they approached. They came through the jungle toward the gunshots in a tight pack, weapons raised, a moving blob of limbs and torsos.

A few had AKs. King spied another MP7 in there somewhere. Serious firepower. If he started potshotting them, he might not get them all.

He took a deep breath.

Sucked all the oxygen down he could find, let it fill his lungs, charge up...

He let it out in a guttural roar.

The equivalent of an ancient battle-cry, loud and deep and full enough to rip through the forest and drown out any of Da Silva's weak encouragements that spurred them forward.

He didn't need them all to panic.

Only one or two.

One man stiffened like something had touched his core. King knew what it was: an amygdala hijack. The pinnacle of fight-or-flight. Sudden and uncontrollable terror from somewhere deep within, followed by—

Run.

He turned and took off sprinting.

Which started a wave.

A second followed, then a third.

Two held their ground, but the disruption distracted them, threw their aim off, meant they didn't see King until they advanced right into his range.

He put a headshot into one, then the other. Back to back. Easy work.

He took off sprinting after the last three.

Predator and prey.

67

The timing was perfect.

King closed the gap on them just as they reached Da Silva, the trio sprinting toward the patch of forest floor on which he lay. They noticed their boss lying in their path, but nothing could stop them. Nothing mattered anymore. The fear mechanism had seized complete control of their brains, and they made to run past him like he was no one, like there were no consequences to their insubordination.

He screamed at them to turn around. Spittle flew from the corners of his mouth. It was clear each shout delivered him agony; with multiple broken ribs, each syllable would cut into him. Even a whisper would hurt. But he was relentless, brutal, able to ignore his instincts and focus on the mission. There was a reason he was top dog and they weren't.

They didn't care.

King gunned the three soldiers down in a wide spray with all the bullets left in the MP7. The rounds stitched through the jungle at head height, ripping through the tops of their spines, obliterating the backs of their necks. They fell forward. A couple thumped into the shrubs and disappeared, but one man tripped over Da Silva as he pitched forward, his body snagging on twisted branches.

The corpse hung there, overshadowing Da Silva.

A dark omen.

A message from King: *If you lay a trap, make sure it works.*

King tossed the empty MP7 away and stomped through the detritus coating the rainforest floor. He found the fallen soldier with the other MP7, snatched it up and ejected the magazine to check its capacity. The clip was full; it hadn't been fired. He loaded it back into the weapon and took the time to catch his breath. His lungs burned. His chest heaved. Another few minutes of a pace like that and he'd have been done. It doesn't matter how fit you are, or how tough. The body has limits.

He was scarily close to his own.

When he'd brought himself down from the brink of vomiting, he turned to Da Silva. For effect, he brandished the MP7. 'More?'

Da Silva shook his head.

Just from the little details of the gesture, King knew it was true. Da Silva swung his head side to side with a mixture of disappointment and begrudging respect. It was clear he had no room for games. Not anymore. The fight was done, he'd played his cards, and he'd lost. There'd be no begging, no pleading his case, no further negotiations. The head shake alone revealed that he was accepting of his death.

Which would be convenient.

But King wasn't through with him.

He yanked the last militant down from the branches, dumping him in an unceremonious heap in the dirt. It allowed him to duck into the natural alcove and haul Da Silva to his feet with his free hand. King held the MP7 at arm's length in the other, refusing to allow it to drift anywhere near the man. Da Silva was grievously wounded, incapacitated, incapable of resistance, but sometimes that doesn't mean anything. Sometimes you can find reserves deep within yourself, and a man as savage as him could do it in a heartbeat.

King stepped back, out of reach. Da Silva wobbled a step, but pulled himself together. His teeth were clenched so tight that King braced to hear the *snap* of a crushed molar. The man was so tough it defied belief. He should be immobile, yet he stepped tentatively over his dead subordinate and limped toward King, putting only the slightest weight on his destroyed knee.

King darted back again.

Made sure to always keep six feet between them.

Da Silva smiled sadly. 'I won't try anything.'

'Uh-huh.'

'You don't believe me.'

'Should I?'

'No.'

'You'll take me to Rémi Poirier.'

'And then you'll let me go?' He phrased the question rhetorically; he knew the answer.

King said, 'Neither of us are stupid.'

Da Silva wagged a finger weakly. His strength was sapping by the moment. 'I respect honesty like that. You're not a pretender. Not like...' He trailed off as he looked all around the scene of slaughter. He scoffed uncomprehendingly. 'One man,' he said, glancing at King. '*One* man.'

'You thought four would be light work.'

'Of course.' He gazed at King, a glint in his eye. 'You're not some *yanqui*. Your skin is, but *you* aren't.'

'I'm sure you have all sorts of opinions.' King jabbed him in the stomach with the barrel of the MP7, eliciting a moan. 'Talk on the move.'

'I won't make it a kilometre.'

No ploy. No scheme. Only the truth. Da Silva could barely stand, his leathery skin paling by the second, blood streaming from the bullet hole in his kneecap. The fact he even thought he could make it that far was testament to his inner strength. He knew King would kill him as soon as he was no longer useful, which made any sort of effort entirely pointless. He should lie down in the leaves and refuse to move until King put a bullet in his head.

He didn't.

He could put one foot in front of the other. Slowly, painfully, tentatively, but he could do it. So that's what he'd do until he dropped. It spoke to some larger purpose, a certain warrior spirit, above material things like drugs and money. It made King wonder why someone of his fortitude was in this business in the first place.

'You only have to make it back to the jeep,' King said.

Hunched forward, Da Silva raised an eyebrow. 'And then?'

'A pit stop at one of your jungle encampments to switch rides. We need something a little more protective for Cayenne. A roof would be nice, at least.'

'We go anywhere near one of my camps and you'll get yourself killed.'

King circled behind him and jabbed the small of his back with the barrel. Da Silva stumbled forward, using all his inner strength not to groan. Eyes wide, mouth a hard line, he set off laboriously back the way they'd come.

King followed close behind like an ominous shadow, and only when Da Silva had no strength to respond did he ask, 'You sure about that?'

68

It took forever to get back to the swamp.

A long, slow trudge through a dark world laced with columns of light. The sunbeams sliced at all angles through gaps in the canopy overhead, lending the jungle a cathedral-like atmosphere.

King kept the MP7 at waist height, but made sure not to take his aim off Da Silva's lower back. All athletic movement initiates from that region; if someone's about to explode into motion, they'll tense their glutes and hamstrings, sending a ripple up their posterior chain. It's unavoidable, and more obvious if you have sharp muscle definition. Da Silva was built like a bull. King would know milliseconds before he was about to make a break for it. He could turn and try to lunge on one leg for King's weapon, but King would shred his spine with bullets before he made it a step.

Da Silva seemed to know this, and made no attempt to try anything. He couldn't, anyway. He'd slowed right down to a wounded hop to regain the energy to speak.

In the newfound quiet, King said, 'You knew this whole time...'

Da Silva shrugged. 'Not really. I couldn't see how an impostor would know my name, or Rémi's. I thought the captain was screwing with me, planning some fucking rebellion. I didn't take it as seriously as I should have.' He gestured to the state of his internal organs. 'Obviously...'

'And why would the captain do that?'

'He was a last-minute replacement. The first guy got cold feet. Took one look at the sub and it put the fear of God in him. But it's not like I can let witnesses walk.'

'You killed him?'

'And showed the next captain his body. Just to make the stakes clear.'

'Maybe if I'd never got involved, you'd have had a mutiny on your hands regardless.'

'Are you trying to spin this into something positive?'

'No. If I've learned anything, it's that nothing's good or bad. It just is.'

Da Silva glanced over his shoulder with a pained grimace. It hurt to twist his core, but he seemed unable to resist the urge to get another look at King. 'Who are you?'

'Keep walking.'

Da Silva complied, in too much agony to protest. But as they covered another few dozen feet, the silence dragged, and talk became irresistible.

'You know,' he mused, his gravelly voice quieter than usual, 'probably a third of my crew bail.'

King didn't speak.

'It's too much for them. And they have no other options. I mean, they fucking *know* what I'll do to them if they say no. I make no secret of it. Fear is ... an important tool. Getting in one of those subs takes courage that, I have to say, is inhuman. I'm guessing when I say "a third," but that's close enough. Think about that. Thirty-three percent of men with nowhere else to turn, so riddled by poverty they're barely able to scrape enough together for the next meal. They see the vessel and their imaginations run wild. They choose death at my hands over a journey so dangerous. I think about this more than you know. I dream about it at night. It fascinates me.'

'Good for you.'

Da Silva sensed the disinterest. His voice grew colder. 'You want to know why I came alone to lay a trap. That is why.'

'Because a third of your men get cold feet?'

'Because these are the most desperate men in the world. And *they* say no. So when I wonder if someone like you, an American with a good life, would make that journey, I cannot help but think, "*No. No fucking chance.*" I underestimate you, it seems.'

'You know nothing about me.'

'That's right.' A pause. 'I wish I could learn before I die.'

'Buy yourself a little more time?'

Da Silva waved a hand. 'You think so poorly of me.'

'Maybe I'd think more of you if you weren't a murderous distributor of poison.'

'The free world distributes more poison than I ever could.'

King hesitated. 'What's that mean?'

Da Silva waved to the jungle around them, dense and claustrophobic. 'You grow up here, life is simple. It's just what's in front of you. You do whatever you can to survive. You realise what you're capable of. You realise you can kill to keep yourself alive. It ... puts you in touch with yourself. But the First World? No one knows themselves. They've never been pushed. They have food, water, shelter, entertainment. *Options.* That's the dream, right? Only they become a soft shell of a human and they hate themselves and they need to take all that guilt and self-pity away so they look for something to numb themselves. It's not my fault I found a way to supply them with it. They'll find it, with or without me. Or they won't, and they'll kill themselves when their hatred grows too strong. Makes no difference to me, and you're kidding yourself if you pretend it makes a difference to you.'

King said nothing.

Charged with passion, Da Silva said, 'You're not active duty. No one recruited you for this. You know how I can tell? Because you're doing more than anyone would ask of you, and you left all the money in the sub, so you've got enough of that. You're some ex-military project, sitting around with nothing to do, figuring you'll keep yourself busy.'

King kept silent, but an unnerving chill materialised despite the heat, sinking into the back of his neck, spreading goosebumps down his arms.

Da Silva said, 'You're surprised I know this. But it's because I'm the same. I fought my way up out of the muck, as I'm sure you did. I conquered what was in front of me, and I took no fucking prisoners. And now I skim five million cash off the top of each sub haul. I've been doing this every three weeks for a couple of years now. I couldn't even count the money I have. I could live in luxury for the rest of my life. You could, too. Could've taken the two hundred million and run. But you came here.'

Silence.

'We're martyrs by choice,' Da Silva said, 'because the alternative scares us to death. Because if you stop, you soften to putty. If you give up, you lose what makes you human.'

'Like Rémi Poirier?'

Da Silva leered. The swamp stretched out ahead, the narco-sub submerged in the brown water, the jeep parked at a slight diagonal lean, as if at any moment it might pitch forward and barrel-roll down the muddy bank.

'If you let me watch you kill him,' Da Silva said, 'it would make my life complete. I would be happy to die after that.'

King shepherded him into the driver's seat, stomach knotted. Da Silva had exhausted himself completely with his spiel, and he slumped over the wheel as King rounded to the passenger side and got in, coating the burning leather seat with sweat.

He rested the MP7 on the centre console and let the barrel hang an inch from Da Silva's broken ribs. 'Just drive.'

'Will you do that for me?'

'We'll see.'

69

S later pulled into his driveway an hour after leaving Bangor.

All sense of urgency had dissipated. He'd kept well under the speed limit the whole way back. Uncertainty plagued him for the length of the drive. If he'd stayed back to hide Timothée and his buddies' corpses, it would've done little good. Even with a professional clean-up, one sweep with a UV light would reveal what happened there. It all came down to the chain of command. If Rémi knew, how fast would he tell Dubois, or was their relationship severed entirely? Would he bother the governor with his own failings, with the fact his hired guns had got themselves killed in some fuzzy triple-cross?

Only time would tell.

He'd taken all three of their phones from the shack, two of which were open, one black-screened and password-protected. As soon as Slater had snatched them up from the crime scene, he'd thanked his lucky stars that two of the three hadn't been dropped on their power buttons to lock their screens. He'd already changed their settings, turning power-saving mode off so the screens never went dark, no matter the length of inactivity.

Now he snatched up Timothée's phone and slowly, carefully, began scrolling through it.

He found the call log and scrolled down for weeks. There was nothing that rang a bell. Certainly no logs with important politicians, and very few anonymous numbers. So maybe it was true. Maybe the governor stayed well away from Rémi's operations.

The phone lit up with an incoming call, and Slater's heart lurched in his chest.

Noah Dubois.

Timothée had him saved as a contact after all.

Endless intrusive thoughts tore through him. *Is it over? Is King's fate sealed?*

Have I botched this completely?

One way to find out.

Slater exhaled air sharply, pulled himself together, and answered on speakerphone. He put on the accent, on the tiny chance it was salvageable. 'Hello?'

'Timothée.' The governor's stern, composed voice.

Slater thought, *Shit.*

It's over.

His words dripping with a French purr despite the walls crashing down on all sides, he said, 'I'm here. Strange speaking to you without ... what is word? ... an intermediary.'

Slater heard Dubois smile, the governor exhaling as he did so. 'Look at you with the big words. You'll be writing poetry in English before you know it.'

Relief blasted through Slater, so visceral and sudden that he had trouble keeping it internalised. He stayed quiet, clenching a fist in silent gratitude.

Dubois said, 'I've been thinking about our chat in the hotel room. Maybe more than I care to admit.'

His voice was soft, quieter now. Perhaps a little intimate.

Slater thought, *No way.*

From rock-bottom to tremendous good luck. The reversal of fate astonished him.

Dubois continued, unprompted. 'Listen, it's Saturday. I hoped maybe you might have remembered, might have delayed making any plans. I'll be at the Astor Platinum Lounge tonight, as promised. I was wondering if you'd like to join me.'

'I'm free.'

'Excellent,' Dubois said. 'Very glad to hear it. Let me take care of everything. I can show you how to truly enjoy a night in Augusta.'

'I'd like that.'

'We can get up to all sorts of ... mischief.'

'I'm looking forward to it.'

A long pause, riddled with all the things that Dubois wanted to say but couldn't, not over the phone. 'Best we leave it there.'

'I think so. But you talk a big game. So it better be the VIP experience tonight, no?'

'*Bien sûr.*' Of course.

'What should I do when I arrive?'

'Say my name at the door. They'll let you straight through.'

Slater feigned hesitation. 'Just one more thing...'

'Anything.'

'What we spoke about in that hotel room ... about Rémi...'

'Rémi hasn't the slightest clue what's going on here.'

'*Merci beaucoup.* I hope we can keep it that way. He is ... a bitter man.' He paused. 'I hope you don't mind me saying...'

'You know we used to be close friends, he and I. Allies on opposite sides of the world.'

Slater's heart squirmed. *Too far?*

'But, yes,' Dubois went on, 'you are correct. He is a lazy, ineffectual slob, drunk on his own power. It's the worst kind of nepotism. Mommy and daddy weren't rich, so he thinks that means he achieved everything through his own merit. He's blind to the fact that he got lucky, that he just sat in the right seat in the right classroom next to the right man who went on to become President. He sees others pour out blood, sweat, and tears and thinks he's a genius because he doesn't have to. He thinks he's outsmarted the system, outmanoeuvred the whole world.'

Slater thought, *Thank God.*

Dubois said, 'So don't worry about what you call him. I've heard worse, and I've thought worse. He's the scummiest of all us scumbags. At least we work hard for what we reap, *oui*?'

'*Oui.* Okay. I trust you.'

'*À bientôt.*' *See you soon.*

Slater said, 'See you then, handsome.'

If he'd misinterpreted the governor's prior comments, the flirting would ruin everything, but after a beat of silence Dubois chuckled, then hung up.

Slater breathed out, and only then did he notice Alexis and Tyrell on the front porch, side-by-side, staring down at the Range Rover. The concern in their eyes was impossible to miss. He made sure not to take it for granted. It was the grandest of all life's prizes to have people care deeply for you, and he knew not to forget that. He had in the past, shunning social norms and close relationships for most of his career to minimise the hurt if he perished in the line of duty.

He wouldn't let himself miss out on any more of his life. He'd thrown much of it away selflessly. He would never take it back — he'd helped more people than he could remember — but going forward, balance was necessary.

Before he could so much as reach for the door, his phone rang again.

King.

He snatched it up in a panic. 'You made it?'

'I've got Da Silva. I cleaned up the trap he tried to lay. We're going after Rémi.'

'*Trap*?'

'He knew it was coming. I was texting an underling until I called the guy by his boss's name.'

'Shit.' Slater hesitated. 'How are you alive?'

'Greed outweighed fear.'

Slater digested the words. 'Da Silva didn't want to sink the money?'

'Not if he could help it.'

Slater blinked, processing all the moving pieces. 'You're in good shape?'

'I'm okay. Just exhausted.'

'When you say "cleaned up"?'

'Twelve men.'

Slater shook his head slowly. 'Just when I was beginning to think you might have lost a step...'

'Three weeks in a box wasn't ideal prep. The fatigue's hitting me.'

'Have some coffee.'

A sly chuckle. 'Yeah, that'll do the trick.'

'I'm putting the governor's head on a stick tonight,' Slater said. 'Does that timing work?'

'I don't think you could have timed it better.'

Slater leaned back against the headrest, closed his eyes. 'We can really pull this off, can't we?'

'Let's not get ahead of ourselves.'

'Where are you?'

'Forty miles south-east of Cayenne. It'll take a good couple of hours to get there, though. I'm in the middle of the jungle. Hoping to reach the Prefecture Building by early evening.'

'And then?'

'I didn't think I'd make it to this point. Gonna be a whole lot of improvising ahead.'

'Good,' Slater said. 'That suits me.'

'I'll let you know when I'm close. We can line up the timing so neither of them catch wind and flee.'

'Talk then.'

Slater finally shoved his door open and stepped out into the chill. He strode right up to the porch, disbelief on his face, and looked up at his family as he said, 'It ends tonight.'

70

K ing put his satphone down and focused on the trail.

Which was critical, as each rocky mound threatened to overturn the jeep.

The suspension jolted as the fat tyres ate up another sharp rise in the track. The chassis bounced and they thumped down on the other side. In the passenger seat, Da Silva clutched his ribs and groaned, face ghost-white. The man had started the drive behind the wheel, but the pain in his ribs had risen to a crescendo, finally rendering him incapable of doing anything other than curling up in a ball and moaning. King had taken over the driving ten minutes earlier.

Invigorated by his call with Slater, he felt a surge of energy, but he knew it was temporary. He needed more food and water immediately, and Slater hadn't been far off the mark with his recommendation of coffee. Anything to get him through to the finish line; if there were combat stimulants at Da Silva's nearest jungle encampment, he'd probably take them. At this point, they were a necessary evil.

He was near-delirious with fatigue. Another vicious pothole threw the jeep's frame down, and Da Silva suppressed a shout by gritting his brown teeth.

King fought for control of the wheel. 'You drive these roads regularly?'

'Have to.'

There was so much King wanted to say, but he wouldn't get satisfactory answers, so he refrained. He held back a spiel. *You don't have to do any of this. You have more money than you know what to do with. You talk about inaction leading to the death of the soul, but somehow that doesn't entail doing anything good or noble with your life.*

If he vocalised it, it'd go in one ear, out the other.

Much like any conversation he'd ever had with an enemy.

Talk means nothing, King realised. Opinions and perspectives on the nuances of the world come from a lifetime of experiences unique to the individual, so trying to make them see the light is largely useless. Best to go about your life, do the right thing, and if evil crosses your path, stamp it out.

Da Silva said, 'It's up here,' motioning into a darker patch of jungle.

'What should I expect?'

'Men working hard to provide for their families.'

King didn't have time for it. He was dehydrated, exhausted, sapped of energy in a hostile realm. 'They should've picked another profession.'

'*Picked,*' Da Silva mocked. 'Ah, the privilege. There aren't choices out here.'

'There's always choices.'

'You sure about that?'

'You could stop.'

'Not a hope in hell, my friend.'

'Which is why I'm here,' King muttered, 'to do what you should have done yourself.'

'Did you not hear me before? Stopping is as good as death.'

There it is.

King said, 'Then you should have killed yourself. Given the rest of the world a chance at a clean life.'

Da Silva shook his head, smiling coldly. 'You're a naïve fool.'

King shrugged. 'Yeah, maybe. But that's better than the fucking demon you ended up becoming.'

'Becoming?' A scoff. 'I was this way from the moment I was born. Out here, it's called necessity.'

King stamped the brakes, snatched up the MP7, and heaved the door open. Ahead lay the outskirts of a shoddy encampment, tent flaps and the remnants of last night's fire sandwiched between tree trunks. He turned to Da Silva. 'Then this is necessity.'

He melted into the gloom.

Da Silva slumped back in his seat, closed his eyes, and waited for his men to inevitably get themselves killed.

The quartet came up on the idle jeep with impressive stealthiness.

They weren't as prepared as the men Da Silva recruited for the ambush, the twelve who lay dead amidst the detritus several miles south. These four wore no face paint, but their paramilitary khakis camouflaged naturally into the jungle, and they kept their wide-eyed gazes locked on their boss, who seemed to be the vehicle's sole occupant, slumped motionless in the passenger seat.

They'd never seen Alain Da Silva stationary in their lives.

Just wasn't in his DNA.

One of them circled to the passenger door and used the barrel of his AK-47 to prod Da Silva in the chest. The man's eyes burst open, pain slicing through him like a hot knife.

'What are you doing?' he barked. 'Run, you morons.'

They hesitated.

Da Silva screamed, '*Run!*'

King hovered in the shadows, invisible.

Gave them their chance.

But steady brainwashing makes people so subversive that they'll defy the one who did the brainwashing in the first place. The men ignored their boss, instead fanning out to protect Da Silva, guns up, eyes wide. They surrounded the jeep on all sides. Ready for war.

Da Silva stared into the undergrowth.

King met his gaze.

Only King's eyes were visible amidst the heavy leaves.

He gave a slow nod.

Da Silva offered one last plea to his men in French. 'Please go.'

'You're not thinking straight,' one soldier said. 'We're here for you. Don't worry.'

'You're not listening to me.'

'We are.' The soldier's voice was stern, uncompromising.

Da Silva recognised they were only digging in deeper. He let out a soft sigh. Couldn't help himself. 'Then give me a gun.'

Without a moment's hesitation, the man handed his AK-47 over the passenger door. Da Silva rotated it in his hands, slipped a finger inside the trigger guard, lined up his aim and fired. He worked the barrel left to right, turning in his seat as the Kalashnikov roared, despite the searing pain in his ribs. Muzzle flashes popped like fireworks beneath the jungle canopy.

King watched quietly, burrowed deep in cover. He kept a close eye on the arc of the barrel. He was tense like a coiled spring, ready to retreat at the slightest cue. It would be simple enough to drift the Kalashnikov over, take a few potshots at King from the jeep. It would solve all Da Silva's problems, but the man no longer seemed to be interested in that.

He killed all four of his men without batting an eyelid,

riddling their corpses with the rest of the bullets in the curved magazine long after they were dead.

Then he tossed the empty weapon out of the vehicle.

He called out into the rainforest. 'There's a truck on the other side of the tents for you. A modified Toyota RAV4. That's what you wanted, right?'

King rose from the foliage without a sound. He noticed the way it affected Da Silva, how it made the man realise he'd only ever been the biggest fish in a small pool.

King said, 'You could have tried your luck at getting rid of me.'

'After seeing the way you react?' Da Silva shook his head, sinew in his neck straining. 'No. Absolutely not.'

'So you've given up?'

'You killed me when you broke my ribs. Before that, I had a chance.'

'That's not a common mindset.'

'I lived with the urge to survive for so long that I became numb to it.'

King got back behind the wheel, threw the jeep into gear, and rolled over the two corpses in front of them. 'If you think this is buying you your life, you're mistaken.'

'I wouldn't respect you if you let me go.'

'You can't respect me if you're dead.'

'It doesn't matter.'

They rumbled to the edge of the encampment, and King spotted the dark green RAV4 sitting between two larger trees, propped up on its customised off-road tyres and suspension. It had a roof, and tinted windows. Much preferable to the jeep and its barebones frame.

Da Silva said, 'It's all about what you do while you're alive.'

King gestured to the camp, with its heavy weapons and

empty 200 litre black plastic storage containers, presumably for the incoming cash. 'Are you proud of this?'

'Yes.' Da Silva groaned as he reached out and eased the passenger door open, anticipating the change-over. 'I don't expect you to understand.'

'Of course I understand. I'm human.'

'I see how you fight. How you talk. You could make anyone do anything. I've already killed the men I trust most for you. You could do terrible things.'

'Of course I could.'

'What stops you?'

King got out and rounded to the passenger side to help Da Silva out, take the weight off his dead leg. 'There's an idea in my head of the man I should be. We all have one. I just stick to it.'

'It's not that simple.'

King said, 'It's always that simple.'

He helped Da Silva hop over to the Toyota.

72

He had Da Silva in the palm of his hand, and he knew it.

Multiple broken ribs and a shredded knee in a tourniquet rendered him incapable of mounting any sort of resistance, and the fact he'd killed his own men rather than allowing King to do it spoke volumes. It proved that Da Silva would feed him Rémi Poirier on a silver platter. If he killed men he respected, he'd happily eradicate a prefect whom even organised criminals despised.

King weaved the Toyota out of the jungle, found a rural road, and gunned it north towards Cayenne. The sky drenched them in gold, a low sun fanning heat over the rainforest. The air sweltered. King had little left to sweat, not even after he'd downed three full bottles of sterilised water back at the camp. He'd given Da Silva a bottle, if only to keep him alive until Rémi was out of the picture.

His view of Alain Da Silva was complicated, to say the least. He left it at that. Didn't pry too deep. He feared the man was a can of worms who'd psychologically manipulate him as soon as he got the chance.

But eventually, talk became inevitable. It was a long, silent drive, and they were two men who'd lived lives that were as different as you could imagine and yet, in some overarching way, the same.

Da Silva said, 'I can't believe you made that trip.'

King bit his tongue. Didn't take the bait. He wasn't here for an ego trip, especially not from some psychopathic drug smuggler.

He knew to ignore it.

But he'd spent three weeks in solitary confinement. No matter the nature of the face across from him, interaction appealed to him.

He couldn't ignore it.

He said, 'It wasn't so bad.'

'That's bullshit.'

'You sure?'

'I've tried sending subs out with only two crew members. There and back is a six-week journey, and the pairs came back different.'

'Different?'

'Like they'd done too much ayahuasca, you know? Passed the point of no return. It broke something in their brains, I'm sure of it. None of them lasted much longer in the business. They all wound up in early graves.'

'You killed them?'

'Sometimes I was the one who had to pull the trigger. But their own actions were what killed them. Their own decisions and failures. I'm no idiot; the subs are hell. The stress and the constant fear of sudden death, for weeks on end. To do it alone...'

'Yeah.'

'I wouldn't wish it on my worst enemy.'

'Which I guess is me.'

Da Silva shook his head. 'I'm glad you're the one to do it.'

'You don't even know me.'

'I don't need to.'

King glanced at him, and noticed again the seriousness of his condition. He didn't have long left. King could let him out on the side of the road and he'd only last a couple of hours, even with medical attention. He'd lost a lot of blood, and he was past the point of agony, now slipping steadily into delirium. Hovering above the pain. The faraway look in his eyes was permanent, and soon he'd fall into the long, dark sleep.

Soon.

Not yet.

Da Silva asked, 'Can I know a little more about the man who brought me down?'

King hesitated, but the long and winding road soothed him into a trance. As they drew closer to civilisation, the potholes stopped jolting the suspension, and the asphalt smoothed out. The sun touched the horizon and, piece by piece, the light began to fade. It didn't feel real, which helped put him at ease, enchant him into talking.

So he did.

'I'm a project,' he said. 'A military project.'

'I figured.'

'They invested in me because I'm a genetic anomaly. I process visual information faster than nearly anyone on earth. I *react* faster.'

'Yeah,' Da Silva said, remembering the jungle and the twelve bodies scattered around the swamp. 'I figured.'

'I'm big and I'm healthy, and that was enough for them. They threw unlimited resources at me to eradicate anything that might be considered a weakness. I didn't cut a single corner because I knew what was on the line, and what was resting on my shoulders.'

Da Silva was silent, and when King looked over, he noticed a glint of nostalgia in the man's eyes. 'You were a one-man operation?'

King stiffened. 'I was.'

'You have many run-ins with the cartels?'

'A handful.'

Da Silva closed his eyes, rested his head back, and scoffed. 'I hear stories about men like you.'

'You're kidding.'

'What reason would I have to joke?'

'Enlighten me.'

'There were more of you, no?'

'Correct.'

'How many more?'

'I don't know.'

Da Silva eyed him, suspicious.

King said, 'It's the truth. There were deniability concerns. It was all kept vague: who I was working for, what their broader intentions were.'

Da Silva chuckled softly. 'This is why you are here. To scrub away your guilty conscience.'

'I wouldn't put it like that.'

'Of course you wouldn't.'

'I never took a job I didn't believe in. I'm fine with my conscience.'

'I don't have one.' Da Silva tapped a grubby finger to the side of his head. 'Makes things a lot easier.'

'Sometimes I wish it were that simple.'

'Ah,' Da Silva said. 'The burden of responsibility.'

The words seemed strange coming from the mouth of a cartel jungle lord.

King said, 'How've you learned English?'

'I told you. Self-taught.'

'You're smart, then.'

'No. I'm a fucking idiot. But I knew how to work to make myself less of one. That's all there is to it.'

'That got you out of the muck, huh?'

'Got me everything in my life.'

'Got you killed, too.'

'Oh, well,' Da Silva said with a shrug. Then, thinking back, he added, 'And don't start thinking I ever left the muck.'

'You could have. Anytime you wanted.'

Da Silva made a weak gesture from King's head to his feet, like, *You're here.*

King shrugged. 'We're both as messed up as each other. Guess the only thing that separates us is a moral compass.'

Da Silva stiffened, as if his initial gut reaction was hostile. After a few beats of silence, he settled back into the chair, folding his arms gently over his ruined ribcage. 'I agree.'

Nothing left to say.

Mutual understanding. Sealed, signed, delivered.

All Da Silva had left was to die.

But first...

The jeep bore down on bustling Cayenne.

73

The debate Rémi was having with himself came to a shattering halt when the office door thundered open.

His new head of security, Jean-Philippe, burst into the room with heavy sweat patches in the pits of his white dress shirt. A vein throbbed on his forehead, and his cheeks burned hot, flushed crimson. '*Monsieur*—'

'*C'est quoi, ce bordel?!*' Rémi shouted. 'Are you fucking serious?!'

Sure, anyone who used a little intimidation on Rémi might turn him into a wet noodle, but he was still powerful enough to take his anger out on his guards. Unlike Alain Da Silva, they would never talk back to him, making them excellent sponges for his insecurities. He'd explicitly told them not to interrupt him, not even for major news.

He had too much thinking to do.

Had to figure out what to tell Noah Dubois, if there was any chance he could save face.

'It's urgent,' Jean-Philippe said. Another vein materialised on his temple. 'We believe there's an immediate threat to your safety.'

Rémi's adrenaline lurched into gear, a sudden, horrible shift. 'Wait, what?'

'This building,' Jean-Philippe said, looking around, 'is … inadequate. You need to come with us right now.'

'What the fuck are you talking about, a threat to my safety?' Rémi wasn't consciously aware that he was standing, moving across the room, obeying instructions even as he verbally shunned them.

'We'll bring you up to speed in the car.'

Far out of his depth, Rémi reached inside himself and found the strength to finally, after all this time, make a power move. He stopped in his tracks, reached out, and put a hand on Jean-Philippe's shoulder. 'Son, I'm not going anywhere until I know what's happening.'

Jean-Philippe gave him the look you'd give a child throwing a temper tantrum. No matter. Not like Rémi's confidence could sink any lower.

But at the end of the day, the prefect was the one in charge, so Jean-Philippe relented. 'F.A.G. troops spotted a vehicle belonging to Alain Da Silva on the outskirts of Cayenne. He's inside. A passenger.'

'So? Okay, sure, he never comes to the city. Does that call for all this?'

'An unknown white male's driving. And Alain's coated in blood.'

Rémi paled. It was like hearing someone had kidnapped the boogeyman. 'He's … what … a hostage?'

'We believe so, yes.'

Rémi looked all around. Outside the open windows, the grounds of the Prefecture Building were quiet, humming with a subdued bustle. Engines whined in the distance, far beyond the perimeter fence, but none were discernible from the rest. He knew it was a figment of his own paranoia, but the air was suddenly tense, hard with uncertainty.

'Okay,' he said, trying not to tremble. 'Let's go.'

Don't forget.

The reminder seared through him.

Noah.

'Wait,' he said, 'one second.'

Jean-Philippe touched one ear, activating the earpiece within. He listened intently, then said, 'No time.'

Rémi was already hustling back to the desk. 'Just wait.'

'Rémi, *now.*'

He snatched up the right phone and, before he could dwell on it any longer, punched in the number he still knew off by heart. He didn't need to pull the contact information up; they used to dial each other from memory alone. They were that close.

Jean-Philippe surged across the room and snatched Rémi by the arm, started hauling him toward the door.

As they moved, Rémi pressed the phone to his ear and listened to it ring.

No answer.

Voicemail.

No matter.

'Noah,' Rémi said, switching to perfect English as Jean-Philippe dragged him out into an open-air hallway over-looking an interior courtyard. 'I apologise for not doing this sooner. I let everything get to my head, the pressure of it all. I'm sure you will understand. Now, listen. I know you've spoken to one of my men: Timothée. I'm sorry to let you know that he can't be trusted. I'm still in the process of getting all the details, but keep clear of him. If you see him, kill him. I made a terrible judgment call hiring him without doing my due diligence, and I take full responsibility. I will fix this. I promise you.'

Rémi went to elaborate, but noticed Jean-Philippe shooting him a dark look. It threw him off, and he hesitated for too long, psyching himself out. With a gasp of irritation, he killed the line.

'What?' he snapped.

The head of security grabbed Rémi by both shoulders and threw him against the wall. It shocked Rémi so deeply that he let out a small yelp. From this position, he could see diplomats down in the Prefecture Building's interior court-yard, hustling along with their heads down. They'd heard the impact, and knew precisely what predicament he was in, but it wasn't any of their business.

It would only get them killed.

'Look,' Jean-Philippe said, staring Rémi in the face. 'You screw my colleagues around every time they report to you. There's no need to sugar-coat it. That's just the way it is. But you're not going to do that today. You're going to listen to me. I'm going to be truly fucking honest with you now, Rémi. I've watched you stumble your way into deals you have no business being involved in. It's a true goddamn miracle you're alive, and that's only the case because there's been no significant attempt on your life. The people you're in bed with ... if they really want to come after you, I mean *nothing*. My men mean nothing. You really think we're going to protect you?'

Rémi's world imploded.

He'd considered Jean-Philippe and his security invinci-ble, had never put enough conscious thought into it to see what was obvious. He was alive because Da Silva allowed him to be alive. Nothing more, nothing less.

He gulped. 'I understand.'

'So when I say we need to get out of here,' Jean-Philippe hissed, spittle flying from his mouth, 'I mean it. When I say it's not safe, I mean it. And whatever *that* was' — he jabbed a finger at the phone — 'you better pray your apology is accepted, because all I'm hearing is that you're way out of your depth in multiple different pools. Someone is eventually going to drown you, and there's nothing I can do about that, but for now my job is to keep you alive.'

Rémi nodded, pale as a sheet.

'Now,' Jean-Philippe said, stepping back and gesturing down the corridor, 'let's move, please.'

Rémi took off running.

Now a servant to all.

74

D ubois put on his costume.

Whoever invented suits deserved all the riches in the world.

They show exactly how wealthy and important you are, and you're not ridiculed for wearing them.

Tonight's costume in question was a Shelton wool suit from Tom Ford, jet-black and single-breasted. The smoothness of its texture was a full-body stimulation. He got a genuine dopamine hit slipping the pants on and throwing the jacket over his dress shirt, both cut to a slim fit. The cuffs were tailored, and he slotted steel cufflinks on so they circled his wrists just right.

He sized himself up in the mirror and nodded once. Before he left for Astor, he'd have his PR team snap a couple of shots, maybe throw one of the good ones up on Instagram. Make it look natural, like it was taken without him realising, at the apex of a smile. Like someone off to the side of the shot had said the funniest thing in the world. All that nonsense that helps a post go viral.

He'd set an all-time record for Instagram engagement

with his last post in a dressy suit: 98,000 likes, 2,000+ comments.

The ladies love a well-dressed Frenchman.

It's less important governing well and more important presenting yourself well on social media.

Just the natural progression of the world.

It only sunk in a few weeks back, late one night as he sat up stressing over whether his illicit empire might come to light. There were too many moving parts now, between the Coast Guard overseeing deliveries and the shipyards in French Guiana and the useless lazy sack-of-shit Rémi Poirier in charge of it all. "In charge" was certainly a loose definition, but at the end of the day it was Rémi who could bring this whole house of cards crashing down. What Dubois realised, though, that night as he cradled an Old-Fashioned, was that this was the new world. It could end up all coming to light, and it might not even matter.

Deny, deny, deny.

The playbook was out there, on display for every dictator and warlord to see. Label anything that hits the news cycle as false accusations, pivot into blaming someone else for the state of the world, press on with whatever you were doing before the mob tried to bring you down unjustly. It didn't matter who you blamed, but it was better suited if they were defenceless, incapable of fighting back, and it helped *immensely* if you were famous, if you had fans regardless of how many people hated you.

If it hit the headlines that he was involved in this submarine mess, he'd target immigrants. He could already see the speech in his head: *Unfortunately, I cannot help it if these illegals reach out to try to drag me onto their shipwreck as it goes down. I have no involvement with these savages.*

Probably too extreme. His PR team could shape it into

something a little more appealing. Or, if the backlash was too strong, he could go left-wing with it. That's what people didn't understand: all politics (left and right) is a tool to control the narrative, shape a story out of some real-life mess, make it all neat and pretty.

He'd get out from under this, and he'd find that control he yearned for.

His phone buzzed on the dresser. The contact name glared on the screen.

RÉMI POIRIER.

Dubois' first thought was, *Fuck you.*

Rémi had silent-called him only a couple of hours ago, the ultimate petty move. Dubois despised childish games, and a call made only to waste his time frustrated him more than he could put into words. But he had to consider the fact he was in dirty business with the prefect, that there was every chance this new call was regarding a serious development. He couldn't let his lesser emotions get in the way.

He had to answer.

But he spent too long thinking about it, and it went to voicemail.

No matter.

He tried to forget it happened. Downstairs they were all waiting for him: PR, bodyguards, an assistant to brief him on any pressing matters for the next morning. He couldn't take drugs to the point of losing his mind anymore; he had responsibilities. He'd have to behave himself a little during this rendezvous with Timothée. Every part of him wanted not to.

A notification flashed on his phone screen.

He had a voicemail.

Surprising. Rémi must have left it by accident. Dubois picked up the phone, dialled his voicemail, and listened.

He anticipated a couple of seconds of silence, followed by a hasty hang-up.

Instead he listened to Rémi's flustered confession.

His brow furrowed as the prefect pressed on. Each sentence churned his guts, but he listened carefully to the words contained within.

'I'm sorry to let you know he can't be trusted. I'm still in the process of getting all the details—'

Dubois listened to the rest, but it was inconsequential. Those couple of sentences mattered most. He considered what Rémi had told him, and maybe what he'd left out.

From the hall outside his bedroom, a guard called, 'Sir, the car's here.'

Dubois took a breath.

Not to be trusted, Rémi? he thought. Out loud, he whispered, 'You're not to be trusted either, old sport.'

As far as he was concerned, they cancelled each other out.

Back to square one.

It helped that Timothée was one of the most beautiful men he'd ever laid eyes on. Rich dark skin, gorgeous green eyes, and that musculature...

Beyond belief.

He told his guard, 'Coming,' and swept out of the room.

75

King stamped the brakes, rolling to a halt in a picture postcard setting.

The dead-straight avenue sported sandstone walls and decorative palm trees, an affluent stretch of Cayenne leading ultimately to the Prefecture Building and a host of other diplomatic offices. The sun beat down on the Toyota, but King had the AC blasting, banking as much energy as possible before he burst from the car and the sweat started flowing again.

Da Silva clung to life beside him.

Stopped in the middle of the deserted street, King turned to the man. 'We should talk.'

Da Silva blinked, barely conscious. He slumped a little further down in his seat. The upholstery had changed colour over the course of the drive, shifting from beige to a deep, dark red. 'We've been talking.'

'We've been jousting. Let's get down to the real fucking core of it.'

Music to Da Silva's ears. 'I thought you'd never ask.'

King chose his words carefully. 'Do you have any respect for me?'

A pause. 'A little.'

'Do you have any respect for Rémi Poirier?'

'Not an ounce.'

King let that hang there.

Da Silva said, 'Okay.'

'Okay?'

'I'll do it.'

'You don't know what I'm going to ask.'

Da Silva lifted a hand with what strength he had left, used it to wag a finger. 'Of course I do. You know why?'

King said nothing.

Da Silva said, 'We're warriors, you and I.'

King shrugged. 'I wouldn't say—'

'Of course you wouldn't. Because you think what you're doing is right, and I think "right" doesn't exist.'

King said, 'Alright. I'll accept that.'

'I don't care what you accept. But I'll kill Rémi Poirier for you.'

'That's not what I was going to ask.'

'No?'

'No.'

'Spit it out, then.'

'I was only going to ask you to try.'

'You don't think I'll make it?'

'You're on death's door.'

Da Silva spat blood in the passenger footwell. 'That'd only stop someone like Rémi.'

King could manage a smile, despite it all. He pointed down the avenue. 'You see it?'

Da Silva said, *'Préfecture de Cayenne.'*

King threw the driver's door open. 'Raise hell.'

'You'll leave me all alone in here?'

'Yeah.'

'I could drive away.'

King stared at him. 'You wouldn't make it to a hospital in time.'

'No?'

'No.'

King levered out of the driver's seat, rested his hands on the door frame. 'Do something that matters with your last couple minutes.'

'You think so little of me. "Couple minutes."' Da Silva snorted derisively.

King took a huge risk and stepped back from the car. 'Have at it.'

Da Silva said, 'Take a gun.'

King threw one of the rear doors open and fetched an AK-47 off the seat, along with a couple of spare magazines. He tucked the mags into his belt and ushered Da Silva forward.

The man crawled over the centre console with a muted groan, dragging his dead leg behind him, and flopped into the driver's seat. His face was ghost-white as he levered himself into a seated position. The agony overwhelmed him, and he let out a wheeze. He looked ready to pass out.

'One day,' he said, 'maybe you'll realise I'm not the enemy.'

King said, 'Whatever you say.'

Da Silva pointed down the road to where the Prefecture Building sat under bright sun. 'The men who sit in there and get into bed with criminals ... *they're* the enemy. Sure, I do the groundwork. But that's a whole lot more noble than whatever the fuck Rémi does. Sits behind a desk and makes the choice to sell out. He's *got* the choice. This' — he gestured to the blood coating him head to toe — 'is all I ever know.'

King went against his conditioning. He reached out with an open hand.

Da Silva shook it.

Bracing himself against his shattered ribs, he said, 'Any respect for me?'

The way he asked it, he didn't expect an answer.

King held his gaze. Thought briefly about the moral conundrum. Was it this man's fault, who did all the brutal groundwork, actually *carried out* the killings, but had himself only ever known blood and sweat and suffering? Or was it the fault of the man who handed down the orders, who had the distance and the birds-eye-view to know better, who sat behind a desk and decided to be evil?

It wasn't black and white, but King answered, 'Some. More than Rémi.'

Da Silva nodded.

The man gripped the wheel and stamped the accelerator and took off down the avenue.

Faintly, King thought he heard a guttural war cry rip out the open driver's window.

76

It was something from his worst nightmares.

Rémi and Jean-Philippe were halfway out the Prefecture Building's front doors, having thrown aside the barred metal gates protecting the portico, when they heard the engine screaming.

Rising to a crescendo.

Approaching...

Wasn't hard to see where the noise came from. The building overshadowed a large square centring on a three-tier fountain that had once been grand, but was now rotting away, its decorations caked in grime and the water at the bottom festering in a dark shade of green. Past the fountain, on the other side of the grounds, a Toyota RAV4 with tinted windows barrelled down Rue Héder, a long road leading straight to the building.

Jean-Philippe whipped to the sound like a beady-eyed hawk and said, '*Merde.*'

He yanked Rémi back inside and ushered out the three security guards bringing up the rear. They hustled out without hesitation, all brave and competent men. Rémi felt a flicker of disbelief, like: *People actually run toward danger?*

He'd heard of heroism. Never seen it in the flesh.

Never so much as been in a fight.

Jean-Philippe slammed the gates shut, putting bars between him and Rémi and the outside world. Which seemed like the right call, but claustrophobia pressed in on Rémi, gave him the uncontrollable urge to run out the back. He imagined himself racing through the wooded Pointe Saint-François, diving into the water and just swimming.

Swimming for his life in the open ocean.

It'd work, probably, but he wasn't brave enough.

Jean-Philippe pulled Rémi behind the cover of one of the big double doors, but the prefect couldn't resist taking a peek. Some morbid fascination.

The guards had drawn their weapons, and now they fired them into the Toyota as it burst off the road and into the square, wheels thumping on grass, churning dirt everywhere. It veered wildly around the fountain as the windshield exploded, bullets shattering the glass. He caught a glimpse of Alain Da Silva behind the wheel, face bloodied and swollen, teeth bared, hands gripping the wheel.

Da Silva's chest jerked, shoulders lurching upwards.

Hit by a round.

Didn't matter.

One guard had the wherewithal to abandon the firing position and leap aside, but the other two kept firing, emptying their pistols into the old SUV.

Da Silva crushed them, squashed them like oversized bugs on the hood.

Blood sprayed, and the meaty *smack* was like nothing Rémi had ever heard before.

He recoiled from the sound, stepping into the line of fire.

Jean-Philippe shouted, '*No!*' and pushed him hard, sending him stumbling down the hallway deeper into the old building. He was barely able to keep his feet. He ran, arms pumping. He'd never experienced adrenaline in all its power. He couldn't think or see or hear. There was only a roaring in his head, a desperation to get away.

A bomb went off behind him.

The impact was all-encompassing, and for a moment he truly thought the building had been hit by a missile. Shoes slipping on the slick tiles, he threw a look over his shoulder as he sprinted.

The gates were warped and bent, smashed open by the RAV4's nose. Jean-Philippe was on the floor, dragging himself along on his stomach, blood pouring from *somewhere*. One leg twisted grotesquely behind him, foot facing the wrong way. He'd been caught by the vehicle, a victim of Da Silva's berserk charge.

The driver's door flew open, and Da Silva lurched out, unsteady on his feet, bleeding all over. He screamed, '*Rémi!*' at the top of his lungs.

There was no sound on earth more terrifying.

He kept running as Da Silva limped over to Jean-Philippe. Despite his better judgment, Rémi looked over his shoulder again. Couldn't help it. He had to see.

Da Silva fired a round almost casually through the back of Jean-Philippe's head.

Rémi's heart dropped.

He faced forward again.

Caught a forearm clean across the throat.

He was travelling at such speed that it threw him off his feet, twisted him almost a full hundred-and-eighty degrees in the air. He experienced none of this, only saw the walls and floor and ceiling spinning and a blur of motion before he landed on his shoulder on the tiles, rupturing something. He had little experience with physical pain. He screamed.

When he came to his senses, one of the men from his office was dragging him up to his knees, some intern or administrative assistant whose name he didn't know. Through a bleeding split lip, he mumbled, 'W-what are you doing?'

The guy — young, white, baby-faced — held Rémi out at arm's length like a prize. The man shouted to Da Silva, 'You want him, right?! Take him!'

Da Silva hopped on one leg down the corridor toward them, dragging one leg behind him. He moved painfully slow. It was a fever dream.

Rémi tried to resist, started squirming.

The young guy clubbed him across the back of his neck with a closed fist. 'Go on!' the man shouted at the approaching monster. 'He's all yours! The rat's been nothing but trouble. Everyone knows. We all hate him. Please, do what you want. Just leave us alone. *Please!*'

Da Silva grinned, blood dripping from his mouth.

Rémi burst up from his knees, finding some strength finally, and circled behind the man. He shoved the guy forward as hard as he could.

Da Silva fired.

Hit the guy in the face, killing him, but the assistant's body fell into him. If Da Silva was fully functional, he could have swatted the corpse away like a fly, but he had to step back on his bad leg to brace against the sudden weight, and the knee gave out completely. There were no ligaments left to keep him upright.

He went down hard.

Cracked his skull against the tiles.

Dropped the gun.

Rémi scrambled over to it, possessed by overwhelming survival instinct, and snatched it up. He didn't know the make or model or where the safety was. This wasn't his world.

But he could aim it from three feet away and slide his finger into the trigger guard.

Da Silva looked up from his back, barely conscious, all the corpse's weight on his chest.

He smiled at the ceiling. 'Life's a bitch.'

Rémi pulled the trigger.

The first time he had ever shot a gun.

Hands shaking, he dropped the pistol like it was white-hot and took off. Deep down, he knew he'd never be able to explain this, to protect himself from incrimination. But he had resources; after years of illegal profits, his personal fortune was unlimited.

Wouldn't be hard to start a new life.

He ran for it.

He didn't trust the roads anymore, feared all of the cartel descending on him.

He'd have to swim.

77

Rémi surged out the back of the building, throwing aside flustered government employees who shouted things at him.

Questions like, '*What's going on?!*' and '*Are we under attack?!*' along with the odd accusation: '*This is your fucking fault!*'

As he ran across the rear grounds, someone shouted down from the second floor. 'If it isn't the consequences of your own actions, *faux cul!*'

Faux cul: hypocrite, two-faced, phoney.

It would have hurt him to know how universally hated he was, if he could hear over his pulse thudding in his ears.

He sprinted through the Poudrière de Cayenne, an old building that used to store gunpowder, now an historic monument. He paid his surroundings no attention. The woods beyond beckoned, dark and inviting. He knew they narrowed to a tip upon reaching the ocean, and from there he'd simply have to make it up as he went along.

Not exactly his forte.

He could only make decisions like, '*Yes, you can build your submarines and sail them to America.*'

He plunged into the tree line, soaked in sweat. He savoured the shadows as he sprinted, taking in great heaving lungfuls of hot air. The trunks flashed by, and the commotion at the Prefecture Building fell away, insulated by the woods. He whooped and hollered as he ran. He'd just killed a man who'd terrorised him for years, and adrenaline was keeping the shock at bay. He was invincible.

A shape flashed between the trees.

Somewhere to his right.

He ignored it, kept running. Ahead he caught his first glimpse of the Cayenne River. A limitless body of water, brimming with infinite possibilities. He figured, feeling like this, he could swim for miles. As soon as he was somewhere safe, somewhere he could access his vast illegal wealth, he was home free...

He pushed himself faster. He'd never run this fast or hard in his life. Despite the avalanche of stress chemicals, his body started growing heavy, at the limits of exertion.

Just a hundred feet more.

He had to stop himself from reaching out toward the water, grasping for it as he sprinted.

His footsteps thudded on the dirt: *boom, boom, boom.*

Then, horrifying in its suddenness, footsteps came in between, sounding right behind him. *Boom(boom)boom.*

Footsteps that weren't his own.

He looked back and his jaw went slack.

A man was on his tail, running no more than six feet behind him, looming like some nightmarish shadow. The huge man kept pace effortlessly, gracefully matching Rémi's all-out sprint.

The shadow said, 'Hello, Rémi.'

Rémi couldn't reply. He was exhausted to the bone, at the very end of his reserves, face flushed crimson and chest spasming as he gasped for breath.

Without so much as a break in stride, the figure leapt forward and tackled him just as he burst from the tree line.

Drove him down into the mud of the deserted coastal swamp.

78

All King's years of self-discipline and suffering paid off in times like these.

Without so much as losing his breath, he stayed behind the oblivious prefect, having intercepted Rémi right before he plunged into the trees. He kept pace for a minute or so, able to use his dexterity to keep quiet, and only when Rémi drained himself to exhaustion did he close the gap, making his presence known.

Rémi turned as he ran.

The prefect's face fell, horror spreading.

That tiny moment made the whole journey worth it.

Rémi Poirier was a soggy tub of skinny-fat, just as King expected. Men like him always were. Noodle limbs, a sagging gut, a shocking mop of curly black hair. He had beady little eyes, a thin mouth, and a double chin. More importantly, he didn't have a gun.

The fool.

King had the AK-47 slung by its strap over his back, but he wouldn't need it. He surged forward and crash-tackled Rémi into the mud, making sure to put a little extra force into it than necessary. The prefect's soft body drove through the top layer and hit the hard dirt beneath, and the wind went out of him with a muted cry. Mud splashed in his mouth, and he snapped it shut. The thick muck blinded him.

This swamp, King mused as he got to his knees, was a little nicer than the last. A few dozen feet ahead it morphed into the Cayenne River, vast and sparkling blue. Rémi was lucky, really. Most had a far worse view at their time of death.

King dragged Rémi into a seated position, where the prefect sat gasping, searching for air to refuel muscles deadened by the rush of lactic acid. Insects hummed, and far away a commercial boat whined into the mouth of the river, too far away to spot them unless they knew where to look.

Between ragged breaths, Rémi said, 'They're looking for me back there.'

His accent was slight; his English impeccable.

'You know,' King said, 'I'm not so sure they're interested in coming to your aid.'

Rémi bowed his head. The truth cut him deep. This was six years of bad decisions catching up to him all at once. His mind would be in pieces, almost unable to comprehend. Get away with it for so long and you start thinking you're invincible, no matter how hard you try not to. Maybe Rémi had always feared cartel retribution, but he must have feared it for so long that it became unreal, something that would never actually happen.

The prefect stared at his feet, still panting. 'I don't understand...'

'What?'

'I set it up so—' A heaving, uncontrollable sob forced its way out, cutting him off mid-sentence. He squeezed his eyes shut and spluttered the cry out of drooling lips, like an over-sized toddler in a high chair. To give him a little credit, he pulled himself together fast. Probably recognised his only chance was to talk his way out of it, so he wiped the terror off his face and started again. 'I set it up so something like this would be impossible.'

'That's just not true, Rémi.'

The prefect said nothing.

King said, 'I made it possible, so you clearly didn't set it up that way. But I'm sure you tried.'

'I have the airports.' Rémi waved a hand, a vague gesture. None of this meant anything now, but he was thinking out loud. 'I have the coast. And I mean *all* of it. The 9th Marine Infantry Regiment reports to me here, and the 3rd infantry keep a close eye on Kourou. There's a lot going on over there with the Space Centre. I was always wary of it. They're bringing in new employees all the time; if Alain wanted to hit me, that's how he could have got them in.'

'Got who in?'

'Outside help. I always knew that's how he'd do it. He's got the power of the cartel, but they're jungle boys, not exactly advanced at urban warfare. We'd have seen them coming miles away.' A pause, and a sigh. 'We saw *you* coming. But it was too late.'

King said, 'That wasn't exactly a genius strategy I carried out there.'

'Not the last part. But getting in-country, and then getting Alain to do your dirty work.' He bowed his head and closed his eyes. 'Both those things are fucking impossible.'

'Wrong word,' King reminded him.

Rémi looked up. He was crying. 'Can you tell me how, at least?'

'You stalling, Rémi?'

A shrug. 'What would that achieve?'

At least he was self-aware now. Finally.

King hadn't planned to talk, but something changed his mind. 'Da Silva was simple enough. He hates you.'

'Everyone hates me.' He scoffed. 'Crazy, isn't it? In a world of killers and drug lords, I'm somehow the worst of the bunch. I've never even got my hands dirty.'

'That's why they hate you, Rémi.'

'Yeah.' A sigh. 'I get it.'

King shook his head, stared out at the river. Talking more to himself, he said, 'They always get it. Always too late.'

'How did you get in?'

King stared at him. 'You still haven't put it together?'

A vacant, empty look. No way he'd figure it out in this state.

King said, 'What you've been sending to Maine. I brought one back.'

Rémi's eyes widened. Under the mud and blood, his flushed skin paled. 'The whole way?'

'The whole way.'

'On your own?'

'Yeah.'

The look in Rémi's eyes was different now, like he no longer thought of King as a mere mortal. 'Alain warned me, you know? He invited me to one of his shipyards the other day, made me trek out there to tell me one of the subs was compromised. I thought nothing of it. He told me it was probably a crew mutiny, and that he'd clear it up. Then he laughed at me. We both knew he could have called me, but he made me come to humiliate me. To show me who the real boss was.'

'You didn't bunker down when you knew there might be trouble?'

'I fired my old crew.' Rémi gazed into space, like he couldn't believe the words coming out of his own mouth. 'My head guy, Thibault, was a stone-cold killer. He and his men. They'd have held you off for long enough for me to escape. I know it. And I got rid of them. Threw a tantrum because they feared Alain and didn't fear me. I thought, "*I'll show you.*" Sent them packing and swapped them for Jean-Philippe, an old boy who I knew wouldn't cut it. My ego. My fucking ego...'

King nodded slowly. 'I *thought* it was too easy.'

'I, uh ... I think I was born disadvantaged ... or something. I'm so fucking scared all the time. I can't operate like you, like Alain. I don't know why.'

King stood up, swung the strap on his shoulder so the AK-47 landed in his hands.

'We're all as scared as each other,' he said. 'I'm scared. It's just choices.'

Rémi squeezed his teary eyes shut, nodded his understanding.

King said, 'You had all the advantage in the world.'

He riddled the prefect with bullets.

Made it quick.

What was the point of prolonging it?

What's done is done.

He slung the Kalashnikov over his shoulder and walked away.

79

The Astor Platinum Lounge was invisible.

Which told Slater it was more exclusive than the showy establishments, for the same reason that supercar brands don't bother advertising. If you need a billboard to sway you, you're searching for something else.

Augusta was dark and frozen, the air like ice at the peak of winter. He wore the cheapest overcoat he owned, which still cost a pretty penny. He could have dressed to the nines, but he still had a role to play. Timothée had obviously done some good work for Rémi, but based on his living conditions he wasn't made of money, and he didn't seem the type to hoard cash for a rainy day. What came in, he probably spent, and there clearly hadn't been much to spend.

Slater crossed the bustling street and walked up to the bouncer in front of the metal door. There was no branding, not so much as a small sign identifying the club. Again, if you needed it spelled out for you, they didn't want you.

Slater said, 'Here to see Noah.' He kept his voice down for sensitivity reasons. The governor wasn't someone to be seen around these parts.

The doorman was six-foot-six, closer to three hundred pounds than two, all muscle and artificial testosterone. Slater could have wiped the floor with him.

The guy took a good long look at him, then stepped aside. 'In you go.'

Slater made to move past. The guy reached out and grabbed his ribs with hands the size of dinner plates. It took all the willpower Slater could muster not to break his nose.

The man patted him down roughly, turning out all the coat pockets, running his hands intrusively across Slater's glutes and inner thighs. His behaviour suggested an air of *"you must like this."* Dubois must have briefed him on Slater's supposed sexual orientation.

Slater stood completely still and emptied his mind.

Finally, the doorman stepped back, wearing a smug look. 'Had to be sure. Important clientele, you know.'

Slater nodded and pushed on the door. It weighed a ton and the entranceway within was close to pitch-black. He descended a short flight of stairs, and the door *boom*ed overhead as the bouncer swung it shut behind him. Soft green light behind wall-mounted mirrors elongated shadows. Muffled conversation flowed under closed doors. This wasn't the main space, but a long corridor of private suites.

Dubois' right-hand-man, Winston, stood guard outside one of the closed doors. He faced the opposite wall, unrelenting in his composure. Didn't so much as give Slater a side-eyed glance. Only when Slater walked right up to him did Winston pretend to notice him.

Winston reached out with probing hands.

Making sure to lay the accent on thick, Slater said, 'Guy upstairs already did that.'

'Protocol.'

'Right.'

Winston was a little less violating, but still made sure every inch of Slater's body was devoid of concealed weapons or wires. You couldn't be too careful. When he stepped back, he lowered his voice. 'You know what you're in for?'

Slater furrowed a brow.

Winston whispered, 'Be careful.'

He reached back and pushed the door open.

Slater stepped through into a suite made to resemble a sixteenth-century library, both in aesthetic and spirit. All the walls were bookshelves, lined with weighty tomes. A walnut desk rested under a coffered ceiling. Pilasters gave the impression of supporting columns, adding a certain weight to the atmosphere. A log fire blazed in front of a tasteful assortment of armchairs which all seemed priceless, like they could be on display in a museum.

Noah Dubois sat in one of the chairs, wearing an expensive wool suit.

He rose as Slater entered. Winston pulled the door shut behind him.

Slater jerked a thumb over his shoulder. 'Is he going to wait out there the whole time?'

Dubois said, 'I've asked for privacy.'

Slater crossed the room. 'Good.'

80

Dubois offered a drink, poured in anticipation of Slater's arrival.

Slater took the tumbler of top-shelf French vodka. As his fingers enclosed the glass, his heart skipped a beat.

He hadn't thought this part through.

He hadn't touched a drink or drug in well over a year.

As he grappled internally, Dubois said, 'Rémi told me something very interesting about you.'

The skipping in Slater's chest turned to full-blown palpitations, uncontrollable despite his self-mastery. If he had to go to war in this labyrinth of dungeons, unarmed against unknown forces, he didn't like his chances. He'd taken a colossal risk coming here, and the walls came crashing down as he stood there, fighting to save face.

A log crackled in the fireplace.

The sputter frayed his nerves.

Slater said, 'Oh?'

Dubois looked deep into his eyes, standing only a few

feet away. 'He said you weren't to be trusted. That you're a traitor.'

Slater didn't blink.

Dubois sipped his vodka on the rocks. Probably a hundred dollars snaking its way down his throat. 'He said I should kill you on sight.'

'Really?'

'Any reason you can think of that you aren't to be trusted?'

Slater twirled the tumbler gently through the air, tracing a pattern. 'You want to know something, Noah?'

Dubois was composed, but beneath the surface something bristled. Slater saw the man could flick a switch, turn to ice in a moment.

Slater said, 'I haven't touched a drop of alcohol in a long, long time.'

Dubois raised his hackles. It was almost imperceptible, but Slater could detect imperceptible things. Then the governor let the tension out, switched to an air of disappointment. 'That's a shame. I was very much looking forward to a good time.'

'As was I,' Slater said. 'So, in that case...'

He raised the tumbler to his lips and downed the vodka.

Dubois smiled.

Inwardly, Slater reset. As soon as he stepped foot in the suite he'd known what he needed to do, but it wasn't the end of the world. Taking a drink was only a big deal if he let it become one, if he beat himself up over his own failures. That's what triggers relapses: the frustration with yourself that makes one drink turn to two, then three, then ten. He had no anger, no irritation with himself, no ego. Internally, there was only peace. Only acceptance. So as the spirit burned its way down his throat, the taste smooth as butter, he let it go. He would move on and forget it, and all would be well.

And he'd won Dubois over. That was clear as day.

Slater used the governor's surprise to his advantage and pressed on. 'I've broken my sobriety. You understand what a big deal that is, Noah?'

Dubois was transfixed, out of practice in playing defence against charisma. Slater could tell that was usually the governor's trick, winning people over with relentless confidence and smooth-talk, but now he was on the receiving end he didn't know what to do besides listen and obey.

Dubois nodded. 'I do.'

Slater tilted the empty glass toward the man in a mock salute. 'We'd better make this a night to remember, then. Better make it worth it.'

Dubois nodded again.

Slater said, 'Are you in?'

'I'm in.'

'That's good. Now what have you got for me?'

Dubois hesitated. 'A top-up?'

Slater shook his head. 'What *else* have you got for me?'

A pause. 'I was saving all that for later. You've only been here a couple of minutes. Come on, relax. Sit down. Savour another couple of drinks.' He didn't sound convincing; no weight in his words. He'd lost control of the conversational ebb-and-flow. He wasn't sure how to come back from the momentum shifting in Slater's direction.

Verbally, emotionally, it was war, and Slater treated it with such seriousness. He turned on the charm. 'You like wasting time, Noah?'

'No. I don't.'

'Excellent. Nor do I.' Slater clapped his hands together, waited a beat, then raised an eyebrow.

'I have a little ketamine.'

Slater smiled. 'I thought you'd never ask.'

Outside the room, the sound of Winston's heavy footfalls on carpet floated under the sealed door.

Walking away.

Giving them privacy.

Game time.

81

S later pictured moving fast, and extrapolated the consequences of doing so.

He could choke Dubois to death this instant, and maybe Winston wouldn't hear. Getting out was another story. The way he'd come in was a write-off; he was ninety-nine percent sure the door would be locked from the inside. The backrooms of a club like this were for meetings and practices that society shunned, and you wouldn't be able to just waltz out as you pleased. There'd be security screenings, endless guards, and a maze of locked doors.

Slater's best shot had been the Riverside Inn, where he doubted there were any of the measures in place that Dubois would usually take. But that hadn't been an option, or he would have blown King's cover. Now Alain and Rémi were dead, and it was fresh enough that the news hadn't spread, hadn't left French Guiana yet. So it had to be here before Dubois found out his operation had imploded. Had to be the Astor, which must be one of the most inconvenient locations in Maine to kill someone and get away with it.

He couldn't move fast.

Couldn't rush it.

Some way, somehow, this had to look natural, and had to happen before Dubois got the text that the Prefecture Building had been breached and his business partner was dead, that his illicit empire would soon come to light and destroy the reputation he'd so carefully cultivated.

Dubois sat in an armchair by the fire and opened a small wooden box, its design ornate. Within were two plastic baggies, both labelled "K" and filled with fine white powder. He took one out, shook it, and flicked the bottom of the bag. The universal ritual before indulging.

Slater sat in the opposite chair. Dubois dragged a small table between them. He tapped the full contents of the baggie out onto the polished oak, easily seven or eight lines worth. With a heavy silver credit card, he funnelled them instead into only four rows, each line fat and heavy with powder. He withdrew a pristine hundred-dollar note from a money clip, rolled it up with a deftness that suggested this was common procedure, and offered it to Slater.

Slater said, 'You first.'

Dubois shrugged, unbothered. 'I much prefer this to coke. I don't know if you're the same. The way I see it, I don't need to be any more alert. With work and ... extracurricular activities, let's call them ... I'm juggling more than I can handle. My mind's racing twenty-four-seven, just as it should be. My father taught me that. If you're sitting back and contemplating what you've done, you're not moving forward as fast as you could be, and that's a greater sin than any of the crap they spout in news or books. Isn't all that shit hilarious? "Greed is a sin." What a fucking joke. A "sin" is sitting back and letting your life waste away, while criticising anyone who's actually out there getting something done...' He trailed off, a faraway look in his eyes, then snapped back to reality. 'Sorry. I'm rambling. Point is, ket over coke. If I'm having some naughty fun, I'd rather feel tranquillised than even more frenzied. You know?'

'I'm the same.'

'It's funny,' Dubois scoffed, waving the bag. 'I need to place an order for this stuff. Get it shipped to me. Actually *pay* for it. Isn't that wild? I bring ten tons of coke into Maine every few weeks. I've got mountains of the stuff. If only blow was for me...'

Slater pointed to the lines. '*These* are for us. And I can't wait.'

That was all Dubois needed to hear. He hunched over the fattest line, pushed one end of the bill into his nostril, and snorted as he dragged the Benjamin along the table. He threw his head back, his eyes squeezed shut, and continued sniffing, pinching each nostril closed in turn. When he opened them, they were alive in wonder. 'Oh, *God,* that hits hard. I can't feel my face.'

He passed the note to Slater.

Outside, there was commotion. Hushed murmurings, lots of footsteps, the sounds of many men moving up and down the corridor. No one beelining specifically for Dubois' suite, but Slater's imagination ran wild. Simply to get in here, he'd needed to leave his weapons behind, which changed everything. Charging out there without knowing the terrain was tantamount to suicide.

Slater hunched over the line of ketamine closest to him.

It stared up at him, almost twinkling in the firelight, one end beckoning. He'd lived this life. He knew what instant gratification led to. He didn't mind compromising his own integrity in the name of some greater good — like killing the piece-of-shit across from him — but that amount of drugs might render him incapable of doing anything other than rocking back in the armchair and sinking into a black hole.

Especially with where his tolerance was currently at.

A couple of years ago, this would have been a breeze.

Dubois said, '*Whattt* are *youuu* waiting for?' His words were already slurred.

Slater bent forward, hunching over the K.

He exhaled the air left in his lungs, preparing to snort.

His heart pounded.

You're not ready.

He stuck one end of the banknote in his nostril and made a noise like he was inhaling as hard as he could. In reality, he sucked the ketamine up as gently as possible, holding the bulk of the line within the walls of the rolled bill itself. The trick would only last a second or two before the stuff fell out, aided by gravity, so Slater exaggerated the end of the gesture, dragging the bill off the tabletop as he snorted the last of it. When he took the bill out of his nose, he whooped a cry of joy to draw Dubois' attention upwards as he lowered the tube beneath the tabletop, out of the governor's line of sight.

Most of the ketamine fell in a neat pile to the carpet.

A little had gone up Slater's nose, numbing his nostril walls, but he wasn't some rookie. Keeping his wits about him was all that was necessary. He could handle much more than that, but it was vital to keep Dubois well ahead.

Slater smiled across at Dubois. 'Let's go again.'

Dubois' head lolled on his shoulders. His eyes glassy, unfocused, but he had the wherewithal to voice his true intentions. Drugs are great for lowering inhibitions. He said, 'Don't you *wanttt* to get *undresseddd* a little?'

'You've got to earn it.'

Dubois smacked his lips as he gazed vacantly all around the room.

Then he shrugged, bent forward, and snorted the entire second line.

He fell back in a heap.

The door flew open, making Slater's heart leap. He looked over his shoulder.

Winston stepped inside with a pistol in his hand.

82

Everything on the line.

Winston swept across the room silently and invisibly, evoking the aura of a big cat stalking unsuspecting prey. The way he held the gun at his side but kept his eyes transfixed on Dubois and Slater spoke volumes. He was here to assess, to make sure his boss wasn't in a position to be taken advantage of. The milky whites in his wide eyes shone in the darkness, the flicker of fire bouncing off them.

Slater had a role to play, and survival meant pulling it off without the slightest suspicion. If he let on that he had his wits about him, Winston would pull the plug.

Which, in this case, meant the discreet use of that Glock in his hand.

Slater pushed all conscious awareness behind his eyes and strained, tensing every muscle in his neck and face that Winston wouldn't notice. This forced tears out, wetting his vision, and he used the lack of focus to intentionally drift his gaze all over the place.

Through the sheen of blurriness, he looked up at the vague shape looming over the armchair.

Studying him.

'H-hey,' Slater mumbled, slurring his speech. He rocked his head back and blinked hard a few times. Worked his jaw side to side.

Winston hung over him.

Slater couldn't see his expression. Couldn't see his face at all.

Didn't know if this would be his final moment.

Winston raised the gun.

Slater tensed his whole body, prepared to explode upward, to toss the armchair he was sitting on into Winston's chest and throat.

But Winston used the Glock as a pointer, gesturing with the barrel toward Dubois. 'Take care of him, huh?'

Slater mumbled something indiscernible and raised both his hands in a shrugging motion. 'He ... he ... he's the one who ... wanted to do this m-much.'

Winston lowered himself into Slater's ear and hissed, 'I told you to be careful.'

'Yeah,' Slater muttered. 'You-you-you got it.'

Winston shook his head and headed for the door. He lifted his voice again. 'You two play nice now.'

Dubois shrieked a guttural sound to capture his bodyguard's attention. Winston looked back.

Dubois slurred, but his elevated voice was laced with anger. '*Leave. Us. Alone.*'

Winston nodded. 'Yes, sir.'

Slater cleared his own gaze long enough to catch a glimpse of disobedience in Winston's eyes, of frustration and scorn. He noted that for future reference.

Winston stepped out and shut the door behind him.

Slater shot to his feet, quiet as a mouse. Dubois' eyes were closed again, and nothing would pull him from his trance. Slater flipped the box of drugs back open and took out the second baggie. He popped the seal, pinched it between his fingers to keep the mouth open, and walked over by the governor's armchair.

Dubois opened his eyes.

Slater held the bag low, out of eyesight.

The governor smiled, flashed those alluring eyes that had granted him all the power in the world. Governor hadn't been enough. He had to overreach, had to take all that charm and charisma and use it to create a world of gross excess at the cost of the vulnerable working class.

Dubois reached out for Slater, made to touch his chest. Slater wondered whether the governor was gay or bisexual. If it was the former, then his wife was a cover, the mother of all PR moves. It would certainly point to an initial lie, the first big deception of his life. If, in his reluctance to come out of the closet, he'd realised how easy it was to pull the wool over the public's eyes, it might have sparked the fire that the cartel poured fuel on.

Slater wondered all this, then realised he was stalling.

Gently, so as not to leave any marks that might arouse suspicion, he pulled the governor's lower lip forward with two fingers. The gap revealed his lower gums, exposing them to firelight. In his total inebriation, Dubois couldn't see much of anything, but he smiled at the prospect of Slater starting the foreplay.

Slater tipped all the powder in the second bag into his gums, and let go of his lip to snap his mouth shut.

Dubois didn't react.

No panic, no attempt to pry out the fatal dose packed against his teeth. His face was already numb from the first two lines, so he couldn't feel how much was in his mouth. He worked his lower jaw side-to-side absent-mindedly. His thoughts were faraway, his mind detached from reality.

Slater waited for Dubois to spit all the powder out.

It didn't happen.

Five minutes went by, the heroic dose kicked in, and Noah Dubois turned catatonic.

He slumped back, frothing at the mouth, and Slater sat there waiting patiently until his breathing stopped.

Dubois took one final, ugly breath and went still.

Slater had prepared the rough shape of a speech on the drive from Millinocket to Augusta. Unable to help himself, he'd thought of everything he might say to the governor before he killed him. Upon arriving, though, he'd realised it wouldn't change a goddamn thing, and decided to just get on with it. The words weren't worth the hassle.

He stood up, crossed the suite, and slipped out the door.

Walked straight into Winston.

83

The bodyguard had materialised from the darkness like he was moulded to it.

Just like that, Slater knew Winston was a serious player with a serious past. Definitely ex-military, maybe even ex-SF. They were equally sized, and maybe Slater had an edge in reaction speed, but Winston was armed. When that's the case, it renders all other comparisons obsolete.

They faced off, less than six feet apart in the shadows.

As soon as Slater noted Winston's presence, he let the cloudiness come back to his eyes, but there'd been a brief moment where they'd been sharp and clear, untarnished by ketamine. Had the man seen?

Did he know?

Winston said, 'S'goin' on?'

Slater was keenly aware of the Glock in the man's hand. Against someone with combat experience, there was no use diving for their weapon. It'd work on an amateur, but all Winston had to do was dart back out of range and fire the kill shot if it looked like Slater might make a lunge.

If Winston wanted him dead, he was dead.

Slater mumbled, '*Youuu* needa check on him.' He jerked a thumb over his shoulder.

Winston didn't look past Slater. Didn't rip his gaze away for a moment. Just stared into Slater's eyes. 'What am I going to find?'

Slater brought a hand to his mouth, some vague gesture. 'He's ... *frothing.*'

Winston raised an eyebrow, his face all hard, cold lines. 'Is he?'

Slater noted the total lack of concern.

Winston said, 'He's very good with his drugs, the governor. He never goes overboard.'

Slater shrugged.

Winston said, 'You don't look or sound as high as when I checked in on you.'

Slater lifted his gaze up, down, left, right. '*Mmm...?*'

'Are you acting, Timothée?'

Slater wiped the cloudiness out of his expression, turned his eyes clear as ice in a split second. He dropped the accent and said, 'Let's talk about how this is going to play out.'

Winston jolted, the shift making his heart leap.

Slater didn't look away. 'I'm not Timothée and I think that's very fucking obvious to you now. I had a goal coming here. I didn't achieve it. The question is: where do we go from here?'

Winston was statuesque. 'What didn't you achieve?'

'I wanted information. I planned to coax it out of him when he was at his most ... exposed.'

'Are you gay?'

'No.'

'You're certainly committed, then.'

Slater said nothing.

Winston said, 'Who are you?'

'I say we leave it at this. The moron overdosed, I didn't get what I wanted, I was never here.'

Winston snorted. 'Yeah, 'cause I'll cover for you…'

'You could shoot me. I see you thinking about it. What's stopping you is that chill down your spine. You can get a read on me the same way I can get one on you, the same way I know you're ex-military. You think you might be signing your own death warrant if you raise that gun in my direction. And you might be right. But, really, it's simpler than that.'

'It is?'

'I didn't kill him. You'll have to take my word for that. I gain nothing from his death, and I had everything to gain from his life. So it's a damn shame. But let's say you don't believe me. Let's say you manage to put a bullet in me without me ripping you apart first, then what? Then you've got two bodies on your hands and no explanation. You have to face your superiors and say, "This was an assassination and I didn't stop it when I had the chance."'

Winston's expression was stone.

Slater said, 'But you can't control his vices. You can protect him from a direct threat on his life, but you can't stop him putting his own life at risk, can you? You're not a babysitter. You're a bodyguard. You look for outward threats, not sabotage from inside the inner circle. An overdose absolves you. It's not your fault.'

Silence.

'You got an assassin's body,' Slater said, 'then it's your fault. You kill me or try to keep me here, you only create a mess for yourself. And trying to kill me might not go the way you hope.'

All quiet in the corridor.

Not so much as a footstep.

Winston said, 'That all?'

'You need more?'

Winston's gun hand jerked.

Slater's adrenaline skyrocketed.

But the bodyguard only returned the Glock to its holster. 'No. I don't.'

He stepped aside.

Slater moved to slide past, but Winston reached out and gripped his wrist with a thick-fingered hand. Held him in place. 'You tell me one thing, though.'

'Uh-huh?'

'You tell me the truth.'

They hovered there, neither wanting to give an inch, the air humming with tension. Slater could tear his hand free with relative ease, probably beat Winston to death without making so much as a sound to alert the guests in the other suites. It didn't matter if the guy was ex-SF. Slater was levels above; always had been.

But something compelled Slater. He looked into Winston's eyes and said, 'He had to go.'

Winston nodded. 'Thank you.'

He let go of Slater's wrist and walked into the suite. As he went in, he called over his shoulder, 'Tell Ron I cleared it. Say, "Arrow."'

The door slammed shut.

Slater took the stairs two at a time and rapped on the back of the metal door he'd entered through. It swung open, revealing the single doorman had become a trio. They were three heavyset bodybuilders, a veritable wall of muscle, but neither of the new pair were as tall as the first guy. He was the one in charge.

Slater said, 'You Ron?'

The huge man nodded.

'I'm leaving.'

Ron smiled smugly, shook his head. 'Doesn't work like that.'

'Winston says, "Arrow."'

Ron's face paled. 'Christ.'

One of the other guys said, 'What's that—?'

Ron beckoned Slater out, then hurried through the doorway, ushering his two colleagues inside. They offered feeble protests, but they did as instructed. Right before the door swung shut, Slater overheard Ron saying, 'Well, now you've seen something you shouldn't have.'

Bang.

Sealed off.

Slater turned and strode away. It probably wouldn't go well for them — extra muscle turned to extra witnesses — but there was nothing he could do about that. Only when he was across the street did it sink in, that he'd walked voluntarily into a minefield and come out the other side.

The prefect of French Guiana, and the governor of Maine.

Slain in unison, along with Da Silva.

Three titans felled.

Their operation in tatters.

And tomorrow the sun would rise and life would go on.

At times like these, Slater often grew dejected, turned melancholic as he ruminated on the pointlessness of it all. At least, that's how it used to be. He would put everything on the line for an op, leave a small piece of himself in the ruins he left behind, and then curse his handlers for sending him right back into the fray, like the work he'd done meant nothing. Eventually he came to learn it all means nothing, but there's beauty in that. Noah and Rémi were dead and a couple of scumbags would probably take their place, but the point was that Slater had tried.

Tried and, this time, succeeded.

Tomorrow, he'd go again.

Find some new problem, some new injustice.

It's never over.

As far as he was concerned, there was no better way to live a life.

EPILOGUE

Another Saturday afternoon.

Another crowd in the tavern.

As he pushed the door open and stepped inside, King appreciated the warmth a little more than usual. He'd only been back from South America for three days, and still hadn't fully re-adjusted to Maine's arctic air. His limbs felt a touch heavier than usual as he crossed the floor, weaving around tables packed with unruly beer-drinkers. For some reason, the fatigue of this last op lingered. The stress had worn him to the bone, three weeks in a floating can stripping away any trace of the physical condition he'd started the journey in. He hadn't exercised since returning to Maine, couldn't seem to muster the energy. Which was practically heresy, considering he used to work out with broken bones, a relentless freight train with a single-minded purpose.

Life was about adaptation, though.

Pushing forty now, he had to manage his gas tank. Simple as that. He had the experience to pull off greater feats than when he was younger, but he couldn't recover the way he used to. The time in the narco-sub and the war in the jungle had taken a piece of him, and he needed time to let his system fill up the gaps, replenish what was lost. He'd brought himself to total exhaustion, and if he needed a couple of weeks of downtime afterward, so be it.

He had all the time in the world.

She was on the same stool, drinking the same brand of cider. It was her weekend ritual, a couple of pints at the tavern and a smattering of small talk with the locals who stopped by the bar to send her their well-wishes. She was respected in the community, a staple of Millinocket.

He walked over and took the stool next to her without a word.

When she glanced his way, he said, 'Thought I might find you here.'

Dawn Cates smiled. 'You look thinner, dear.'

'Nothing beer won't fix.' He ordered a pint of Bissell Brothers Swish from the bartender.

She sipped daintily from her cider.

They sat in silence for a little while, appreciating the atmosphere. As King grew older, he started to realise you didn't need to be in any hurry to fill the gaps in a conversation with frivolous talk. Given Dawn's age, he was sure she was far more familiar with that revelation. Eventually, the quiet was disrupted by a young man in a red flannel shirt passing behind them, a blue-collar worker with a huge bushy beard. He placed a hand gently on Dawn's shoulder and said, 'Mrs. Cates.'

Dawn smiled before she turned, recognising the voice. 'Hello, Dwayne.'

'Keeping well?'

'You bet. Gosh, you're bigger each time I see you. What're they feeding you out there?'

'They keep me busy. Work me hard. But I put them onto Cormac McCarthy, just like I said I would. Even gave Jase my copy of *Blood Meridian*. Ain't that something?'

Dawn made sure to look at him, and make sure he was looking at her. 'That really is something. I'm proud of you.'

'Thank you, ma'am. I'm in a hurry, but—'

She shooed him away. 'Off you go. Dismissed.'

He nodded to her, then turned and nodded to King out of some implicit respect. If he was in Dawn's presence, he must be trustworthy: something like that.

King nodded back, and Dwayne swept away.

Dawn turned on her stool to face King. 'An old student.'

'What'd you teach?'

'English. Thirty-two years right here in town.'

King said, 'They all love you. I haven't been here long, but I know that much.'

She turned inward, shutting down the conversation in as pleasant a fashion as she could manage, the sign of someone truly humble. She wanted to pivot to any other topic than her own accolades, but couldn't seem to think of anywhere else to go other than: 'So where have you been?'

'Around.'

'You certainly haven't.' A pause. 'Your friend approached me a week after you went away. Outside the grocer's. He implied all sorts of things.'

'Oh?'

'He said I might hear things about Lubec Body Works. In the news, and whatnot. But I've been checking. There hasn't been a peep about Lubec. Every headline is about the governor...'

'Shame about that.'

She shook her head. 'Kids who don't know any better:

that's who you hear are overdosing. Not politicians. It's a mess out there...'

'Addictions don't discriminate.'

'I suppose not.' She looked him in the eyes. 'You wouldn't have had anything to do with that, would you?'

'You kidding?'

'Mostly.' She took a drink. 'Couldn't have been you. You were away.'

'And now I'm back.'

'Did you have a nice trip?'

'Not really.'

'What a shame.'

King gave a shrug, his huge shoulders rolling up like boulders. 'Sometimes these things are necessary.'

'Your friend said one other thing.'

'Mmm?'

'He told me Louie would be happy ... if he was looking down...'

King ruminated as he sipped the froth off the top of his pint. 'I don't know about that. I'm not sure Louie could comprehend vengeance.'

She stared openly at him.

Facing his beer, he said, 'But if he could, well...'

'This can't be traced back to me, can it?'

He glanced sideways. 'I've got no idea what you could be referring to.'

She shrugged. 'I'm just an old girl making up all sorts of stories.'

'There you go.'

'But if I was curious...?'

'It'll come out eventually. Look for Noah Dubois in the headlines. It's only going to get worse ... how he's remembered.'

She stiffened.

He scooted his stool back. 'I best be off.'

'And where will you be as the story … unfolds?'

'Laying low. Hoping I don't end up in the headlines, too.'

'I'm sorry,' she said, 'if it was my fault you ended up in that mess.'

He drained the pint and waved a hand dismissively. 'You only pointed me in the right direction, Dawn. The rest was up to me.'

She looked solemn. 'So this is it, then?'

'What do you mean?'

'I imagine you and Will are off now. Too much heat?'

'We're not going anywhere.'

Her frown became a small smile. 'You like Millinocket?'

'The town, sure,' King said, 'but more so the people.'

Her kind old eyes bored into him, making sure he knew she meant it when she mouthed, 'Thank you.'

'For what?' he said with a wink, and swept out into the cold.

KING AND SLATER WILL RETURN...

Visit amazon.com/author/mattrogers23 and press **"Follow"** to be automatically notified of my future releases.

If you enjoyed the hard-hitting adventure, make sure to leave a review! Your feedback means everything to me, and encourages me to deliver more books as soon as I can.

And don't forget to follow me on Facebook for regular updates, cover reveals, giveaways, and more!
https://www.facebook.com/mattrogersbooks

Stay tuned.

BOOKS BY MATT ROGERS

THE JASON KING SERIES

Isolated (Book 1)

Imprisoned (Book 2)

Reloaded (Book 3)

Betrayed (Book 4)

Corrupted (Book 5)

Hunted (Book 6)

THE JASON KING FILES

Cartel (Book 1)

Warrior (Book 2)

Savages (Book 3)

THE WILL SLATER SERIES

Wolf (Book 1)

Lion (Book 2)

Bear (Book 3)

Lynx (Book 4)

Bull (Book 5)

Hawk (Book 6)

THE KING & SLATER SERIES

Weapons (Book 1)

Contracts (Book 2)

Join the Reader's Group and get a free 200-page book by Matt Rogers!

Sign up for a free copy of '**BLOOD MONEY**'.

Meet Ruby Nazarian, a government operative for a clandestine initiative known only as Lynx. She's in Monaco to infiltrate the entourage of Aaron Wayne, a real estate tycoon on the precipice of dipping his hands into blood money. She charms her way aboard the magnate's superyacht, but everyone seems suspicious of her, and as the party ebbs onward she prepares for war...

Maybe she's paranoid.

Maybe not.

Just click here.

ABOUT THE AUTHOR

Matt Rogers grew up in Melbourne, Australia as a voracious reader, relentlessly devouring thrillers and mysteries in his spare time. Now, he writes full-time. His novels are action-packed and fast-paced. Dive into the Jason King Series to get started with his collection.

Visit his website:

www.mattrogersbooks.com

Visit his Amazon page:

amazon.com/author/mattrogers23

Made in the USA
Monee, IL
24 January 2022